DEATH AT EDEN'S END

Also by Jo Allen
Death by Dark Waters

DEATH AT EDEN'S END

Jo Allen

An Aria Book

First published in the United Kingdom in 2019 by Aria,
an imprint of Head of Zeus Ltd

Copyright © Jo Allen, 2019

The moral right of Jo Allen to be identified as the author of
this work has been asserted in accordance with the Copyright,
Designs and Patents Act of 1988.

All rights reserved. No part of this publication may be reproduced,
stored in a retrieval system, or transmitted, in any form or by any
means, electronic, mechanical, photocopying, recording, or otherwise,
without the prior permission of both the copyright owner and the above
publisher of this book.

This is a work of fiction. All characters, organizations, and events
portrayed in this novel are either products of the author's imagination
or are used fictitiously.

A CIP catalogue record for this book is available from the
British Library.

ISBN 9781035903603

Typeset by Silicon Chips

Cover design: Charlotte Abrams-Simpson

Printed and bound by CPI Group (UK) Ltd, Croydon, CR0 4YY

Aria
c/o Head of Zeus
First Floor East
5–8 Hardwick Street
London EC1R 4RG

www.ariafiction.com

To Alan, Ian and Elen.

Author's note

All of the characters in this book are figments of my imagination and bear no resemblance to anyone alive or dead.

The same can't be said for the locations. Many are real but others are not. I've taken several liberties with geography, sometimes where the plot required it, and sometimes because I have a superstitious dread of setting a murder in a real building without the express permission of the homeowner. So, for example, you won't find Jude's home village of Wasby on the map; you will find the village of Langwathby, but none of the cottages in Eden Strait matches the description of Monica's; and Eden's End nursing home is not only entirely a figment of my imagination but can't be accurately placed on a map.

I hope fans of the Lake District and Eden Valley can forgive me.

Prologue

Life flashed before her eyes like a drunk's story, a random sequence of unconnected events without form or theme.

She was a fighter, determined each breath wouldn't be her last, but even as she clung with frail fingers to the strong wrists that held her down she was troubled by how swiftly her dreams and her dramas sped away. Image by image, she clawed them back and forced them to make sense. Monica, swathed in white lace and screaming at her christening as the priest poured holy water over her and the devil fled. Two uniforms, in confusion on the floor. Monica again – a joyless, spiritless adult now – telling her off over some triviality as if she were Violet's mother rather than her niece. A lover leaning in to kiss her, his hand unyielding in the small of her back as he triggered the affair that would play out against a backdrop of searchlights and flame, its soundtrack the sirens of the Blitz and the textured harmonies of big bands.

His passion had so nearly been the death of her.

Memories attacked her like a stream of angry wasps as she pushed against the hands holding her down and compressing a soft mass over her face. The irredeemable, unrewarded pain of childbirth. The cold white walls of the prison cell where she'd dwelt in the aftermath of her personal apocalypse. Lungs burning from the effort of resistance, she wrung the concession of another breath to add to her long life, then one more, until her assailant's grip weakened.

She would live.

It was a momentary lapse. Whoever it was came back at her, harder than before. Bright lights danced across her vision until the newsreel of her life stuttered like an old cine film, spotted by time. Love featured yet again, smiling at her, the narrow French cigarette dangling from his lips as he undressed her with his eyes. The closer she came to death, the stronger the images became, the more vivid the memory of how much she'd loved him.

She remembered, too, something she'd spent seventy years fighting to forget – the look on his face when he realised she'd betrayed him and he was too late to save himself. *Forgive me*, she pleaded with his ghost. *It was because I loved you.*

Her struggles grew weaker as she reaped what she'd sown and a killer's hands dragged her to her death. In heaven or in hell, she would have to account for her misdeeds. *I have no regrets*, she told herself, as even his image, the last thing she ever saw, faded into the darkness of eternity and death eclipsed her. *No regrets.*

But that wasn't quite true. She would have liked to die like her lover, staring into the face of her killer.

I

Detective Sergeant Ashleigh O'Halloran took a moment to rearrange the papers on her desk and enjoy the Friday afternoon luxury of choosing what to do next. There was no shortage of options, all jostling for primacy within the shortest possible timescale, but it was refreshingly unusual not to have a meeting scheduled, a queue of messages or a long list of demands from her colleagues, from lawyers, from prosecutors, social workers or probation officers, all demanding to be done yesterday. Casting an eye over her to-do list, she scanned the options. A report on an assault case – suspect arrested, remorseful confession forthcoming and only the paperwork to complete – at least meant she'd have something ticked off the list by the end of Friday afternoon. That would do. She turned back to her laptop, just as Jude Satterthwaite opened the door to the open-plan office and paused on the threshold.

Jude was a mighty presence in the office, one you couldn't ignore, a man whose attraction stemmed from inside rather than out. Ashleigh, who appreciated any kind of beauty – male or female, natural or man-made – couldn't rank his looks in the same bracket as her estranged husband, Scott, but nevertheless allowed herself a moment to look at him out of the corner of her eye. Not that he wouldn't notice, because as a senior detective he had an eye for detail and automatically kept track of everything around him. He must be used to the attention by now because she wasn't the only person, in the office or out of it, who couldn't seem to stop watching him. Dark hair, close-cropped to the point of severity; smoke-grey eyes that saw everything with suspicion and cynicism and hid, she was sure, an angry heart; sharp cheekbones in too thin a face. All detracted from what should have been a handsome whole, but on the rare occasions he chose to employ it, his smile engaged and included the coolest opponent.

'Doddsy.' Jude swooped across the room, long strides taking him past her in a breeze of masculinity to where DI Christopher Dodd, known to all as Doddsy, was deep in conversation with another of their colleagues. 'Spare me a minute, if you have one.'

So it wasn't her he was after, though her turn would come. Jude made a point of going round all those he worked with to keep up with what was going on, even when he wasn't involved at anything other than a supervisory level in any of their ongoing investigations. Fridays were a favoured time, if he wasn't otherwise occupied. Realising she'd stared too long and someone other than Jude was bound to notice, she turned back to her computer.

It was five minutes before her phone rang. Glancing down at it, she recognised the number with a sinking heart. She'd cleared out her contacts list in a symbolic purging of her old life when she'd moved up to Cumbria a couple of months before and Scott's had been the first number to go, but she should still have known. She'd thought of the devil and he'd put out his horns. You didn't shed a man as persistent as Scott just by leaving him and starting a new life elsewhere.

She stared at the phone for a moment while it rang out, resisting him but lacking the resolve to cut him off unanswered. In the end it was the barely suppressed annoyance of the constable at the next desk that drove her to answer it, in as businesslike a manner as possible. 'Ashleigh O'Halloran speaking.' Formality was her friend, the best way to keep trouble at a distance.

'Ash. What the hell is this?'

'Scott.' She lowered her voice. 'I'm at work just now. This isn't a good time.'

'It'll never be a good time, will it? We need to talk. I've handed in my notice to try and make things work with you and what do I find when I get home? A letter from a solicitor? Have you gone mad? You don't really want a divorce.'

She picked up her pen and tapped it on the desk in some annoyance. When she'd married him, she hadn't understood that he was so insanely self-serving he didn't seem to care whether or not she knew the truth. 'Let's keep to the facts, shall we? You didn't hand in your notice. It was a fixed-term contract. Let's not pretend you made any sacrifices for me.'

'That's not the point. Come on, Ash. You know you don't really want this.'

It wasn't as if they hadn't had the conversation before. The only thing that had changed was that he'd called her bluff once too often and she'd carried out her threats, but it seemed even the cold print of a solicitor's letter hadn't got the message through. 'I can't take personal calls at work.

Call me this evening.' It would be easier to deal with him when she had the moral support of her housemate. Lisa knew the whole story, knew Scott and was unconditionally behind her, shoring her up against the eternal siren call of her dead romance.

'You can't hang up on me. I'll keep ringing back.'

Scott's a bully, Lisa had said. *You have to stand up to bullies*. Empowered, Ashleigh drew upon her friend's sound common sense. 'I'll turn my phone off.'

'No you won't. You need it for your work. So let's just talk this through now and be done.'

'I've told you a dozen times why it isn't working. Read the solicitor's letter. It explains it again.' She had a separate phone for work and she could have cut him off, but somehow he'd forced her into the discussion on his terms. The detective constable seated to her right, Chris Marshall, was trying his best to pretend he wasn't listening and, though she could hardly blame him for hoovering up the office gossip when information was the currency in which they all dealt, his sympathetic smile pushed her to act. She didn't want his pity.

Clasping the phone to her ear, she got up and stepped out of the office and into the corridor, pausing immediately outside the door. It wasn't private but at least the number of people who could listen in was limited. 'You know it wasn't working.' If it had been, he'd have placed a higher value on fidelity.

'We just need to work harder at it. Our relationship is important to me. You can't just let it go.'

It was a divorce, not a miscarriage of justice. Her lip curled with what was almost genuine amusement. Maybe he really believed their marriage was for ever, though it had never been sufficiently important for him to curb his serial womanising to save it. Either way it was characteristic of him to reconfigure history to fit his requirements, to believe what he wanted rather than acknowledge the facts as they stood. Scott would never have cut the mustard as a detective. He lacked objectivity.

Her solicitor had advised her against getting caught in the crossfire of the accusations and recriminations divorce was bound to entail. 'I'm not going over it now. It's neither the time nor the place.'

Someone appeared at the end of the corridor and Ashleigh's heart sank further. The last thing she needed was to display her weakness to a man even more senior and even less sympathetic than Jude, and Detective Superintendent Groves not only ticked those unwelcome boxes, but he also had a habit of running his eyes over her like a farmer deciding how much to bid for a prize heifer. Word in the office was that Groves was counting the days to his retirement, but he wasn't counting them nearly as enthusiastically as his junior, female colleagues. She turned away from him to confront the blank white wall of the corridor.

'Ash! Why aren't you talking to me?'

She shuffled back towards the door. One judgemental, sexist man was as much as she could deal with at one time. 'I can't. I'm busy.'

'Ash.' Scott was pleading, now. 'You're still my wife. Don't I have a right to some say in what goes on in your life?'

'No, you've no right to that at all. Sorry, Scott. Not any more.' Groves came closer, tilting his head with an expression of interest. The devil or the deep blue sea? She took the easy option, ducking back into the office where the stares and sniggers of her workmates at least had the value of kindness.

'What you do impacts on me.'

Groves passed the glass door, paused, smiled inwards towards both Ashleigh and her younger colleague Aditi Desai, who was seated immediately inside the door, and, to her relief, moved on. 'Oh, Scott. I know you're angry. I know you don't want this. But I've told you why it won't work. So let's just let it go.'

'Don't you dare cut me off!'

She snapped. 'And don't you dare speak to me like that! We'll keep it to official channels from now on. Everything I have to say to you is in the letter. All the things you wouldn't listen to when I said I wanted to talk. Read it and think about it. Get your solicitor to write to mine, if you must. But don't ever contact me directly about it again!' She ended the call and turned towards her desk, almost colliding with Jude's tall figure as she did so.

'Is there a problem, Ashleigh?'

The room went quiet. Acknowledging that, he stepped past her to the door and out into the now-empty corridor, nodding at her to follow him. She went pink under his thoughtful gaze, a flush of humiliation pricking her skin. Sometimes Jude was so cool as to be cold. Ashleigh prided herself on her emotional intelligence, her great strength being in divining other people's motives and persuading them to talk about them, and you didn't have to be a genius to see Jude had learned early that he could only trust himself. Somewhere in his past there must be some kind of betrayal as great as that which Scott had inflicted on her.

'No problem at all.' The phone rang again, and she snapped it off again without answering it. 'Nothing I can't handle.'

'I don't need to tell you you don't have to take hassle from the public. If someone's harassing you, make sure you log it. And if it keeps happening, let me know.'

'I can handle it perfectly well, thank you.' It rang again. This time she answered it. 'Scott. Don't call me again. I've told you already. I'm busy. This isn't the right moment. Goodbye.' In the absence of a pocket in which to bury it, she held the phone behind her back like a guilty schoolgirl with an illicit cigarette, cursing herself. She should never have allowed Scott to get to her, but somehow she always ceded him the advantage. It was because, after everything that had happened, she still cared. 'Sorry about that, Jude. I hope it didn't bother anyone.'

His lifted eyebrow confirmed it had. 'You created quite a stir.'

'Yes, I'm sorry. It was a personal call.'

'Do you usually share your private business with half the office?'

'I didn't make the call.' Thank heavens; the phone remained silent. Scott must have got the message that he wouldn't get anything more from her that afternoon, though it wouldn't stop him trying in the future. 'It won't happen again.' She'd block his number, if she had to.

'You caused a few ripples. I shouldn't need to tell you. I can't have this kind of thing going on in the office.'

Jude was strict but usually fair, and his standards, though high, were those he adhered to more closely than he expected anyone else to. Everyone took the odd personal call at work, but she didn't think she'd been aware of him doing so during the couple of months she'd been with Cumbria's police. 'I'm sorry. Next time my husband calls, I'll hand him over to you and you can explain the rules. He doesn't seem to want to listen when I do it.' Though she could think of no better way of sending Scott's jealousy to stratospheric levels than by asking another man to deal with it, she was the type of woman who could handle her own affairs. They were difficult – undeniably so – but she could handle them.

Under Jude's stare, her self-confidence wilted a little. Generally speaking, she'd noticed men didn't respond well when she mentioned a husband. She guessed Jude was as interested in her as she was in him, intrigued and attracted in equal measure but not yet ready to test the waters to any degree.

'Fine. Then if you're not too busy, perhaps you'd like to come and brief me on what you've been up to. On the professional front, of course.' He turned and headed back in to the office and Ashleigh, mightily relieved at the continued silence of her phone, followed him in.

2

Standing in the plushly carpeted reception area of the Eden's End nursing home, Becca Reid paused, patted her various pockets in a vain search for her car key, patted them again just in case, and turned to the desk with a sigh. 'Karen. I must have dropped my car key down in Mrs Hodgson's room. Do you mind if I leave my bags here while I run down and get it?'

Karen Grant, the manager at Eden's End, had her phone clasped to her ear and was giving every indication of being bored to tears by whatever the person at the other end of the line was saying to her. Raising a hand in acknowledgement, she nodded, sighed, spread her bulk over the chair in front of her computer, still listening, and began typing with one hand.

Taking that as agreement, Becca dropped her bags by the desk and, as quickly as she could without running, made her way back down through the dining area, along a wide carpeted corridor and into a lobby at the side of the building. There, she stood aside to allow one of the care assistants to squeeze past, manoeuvring a trolley laden with a vast metal teapot, cups and saucers and a plate of ginger biscuits on a paper doily, before she tapped on a door. 'Sorry to bother you, Mrs Hodgson. It's Becca again.'

'Becca?' The old lady, settled in her chair with a knitted blanket over her knees, peered uncertainly at her. 'Already? Didn't I just see you?'

'Yes. I think I must have dropped my car key.' Yes, there it was, on the floor under the bed where it must have fallen, skidding away from her pocket while she'd knelt to dress Mrs Hodgson's leg. She swooped on it. 'I'll be back in a few days as usual, to change the dressing.'

'Oh, good. Very good. Well, it's been nice to see you, Becca, my dear. If you see Klemmie, could you tell her I wouldn't mind my cup of tea? I called her a while ago and she said she'd be with me straight away.'

Marjorie Hodgson was usually sharp as the proverbial tack, but today she seemed to have lost track of time. 'She's bringing the teas now. I saw her out in the corridor. But I'll tell her. The biscuits look as if they might be homemade.' Karen, who baked as therapy for the dual curses of boredom and loneliness, must have struggled the previous day, because there had been a plate of ginger biscuits waiting on the front desk, free to all comers, when Becca arrived for her weekly visit.

She closed the door behind her, pausing for a moment in the square space at the centre of the annexe where Klemmie had parked the trolley while she did the afternoon tea round, darting from room to room. The care worker gave Becca a cheerful grin as she opened the door to Violet Ross's room with her elbow.

'Mrs Hodgson wondered—' Becca tossed an apologetic nod towards the room she'd just left. Klemmie was always cheerful, no matter how unreasonable the request, but everyone was busy and no-one needed any more hassle.

'I'll do her next. Tea and biccies, Violet!' The colloquialism sounded strange in Klemmie's perfect but heavily accented English as she disappeared into the room.

Becca waited a moment longer, checking her pockets one last time. Where the car key went, house keys could all too easily follow, and the last thing she needed was to come trailing back to Eden's End in search of them at the end of a long day, to find Karen had gone off duty and locked them in the safe; but the keys were safely there. She checked her watch. It was four o'clock on Friday afternoon and for once she was ahead of schedule. She turned to head back along the corridor.

'Violet, wake up.' There was a clatter of crockery from inside the room as Klemmie set tea and biscuits down, presumably on the bedside table. 'Violet!'

In the ensuing pause, Becca tensed and listened, her attention caught by the note of panic in Klemmie's tone. She moved to the door. 'Klemmie? Is everything okay?'

'Violet? Violet!' Klemmie had been shaking the old lady, far too vigorously, and turned as Becca appeared at the doorway. 'Becca. I think she's dead!'

Violet Ross was a hundred years old and lived in a nursing home, so Klemmie really shouldn't have been surprised. That said, the old woman had always given the impression of someone who would, if it were possible, live for ever because she couldn't bear to miss a tiny piece of someone else's business by dying. If for no other reason, Becca herself was astonished to find it was this particularly durable old lady rather than any one of half a dozen more fragile candidates who had passed so quietly away in her chair.

She crossed the room in a few swift steps and lifted Violet's thin wrist. The delicate skin under her fingers had acquired a strange, translucent quality and there wasn't so much as a flutter of movement in the veins. To judge by the faint flush of warmth that lingered about her, Violet's lifeblood had only recently stilled. 'Run and fetch one of the nurses. I think Ellie's in the canteen.'

The woman bolted past her, barging into the tea trolley so the crockery rattled like an alarm.

'Klemmie!' Mrs Hodgson's plaintive voice drifted out into the corridor. 'Klemmie, what about my tea?'

Becca laid Violet's hand down where she'd found it, resting on the arm of the wing-backed chair in the window bay. In her experience the dead so often looked peaceful, but Violet managed to look outraged, as if she'd fought death all the way and he'd only defeated her by foul means. Her perfectly set white hair was slightly disarranged, as if she'd woken before dying, knowing what was happening to her but powerless to prevent it, and her finely featured face bore an expression of resistance, mouth slack and open, a faint shadow lingering beneath her open, staring eyes.

A hundred, Becca said to herself, with a measure of awe. Violet had been a force of nature. Not many people at Eden's End had warmed to her, though Becca had and her affection had been repaid. She, along with Klemmie and a few honoured others, had been instructed to address the old lady by her Christian name whereas so many others had been kept at a distance by the rigorous formality of 'Dr Ross'. Violet had lived to a venerable age and been blessed by good health and spirit with which to bear her increasing frailty, remaining in complete control of all her senses until the day of her painless departure. Passing away in her chair as she stared out towards the damp softness of the Eden Valley, grey and green and brown, was surely the way she would have chosen to die. Quite what she had to look so disgusted about was something of a mystery.

'What's going on?' Ellie, the head nurse at Eden's End, bustled in, her thin frame bristling with indignation, Klemmie trailing behind her. Ellie hated being disturbed on her break. 'What's Klemmie talking about? I can't make sense of her when she rattles on like that. Sometimes I think she forgets how to speak English. Is Violet ill?'

Used to being patronised by Ellie, Becca stepped back. The head nurse was younger than she was and considerably less experienced, but seemed to think a mere district nurse was in her job because she wasn't good enough to do any other, rather than through choice. 'Not ill. I'm afraid she's passed away. Klemmie found her just now.'

'She should have come to find me straight away, not called you. This really isn't your job, Becca. Haven't you got something else to be doing? You district nurses always claim to be so busy.'

'I was just coming out of Mrs Hodgson's room.' Turning to Klemmie with an encouraging smile, Becca was surprised to see a round tear sliding down the woman's cheek as she drew her hands across her broad bosom in the shape of a cross. 'It's okay, Klemmie. Don't look so upset.'

'She's dead.' Repeating Becca's actions, Ellie laid the corpse's hand down. 'That's all I need. More paperwork. Death certificate and all that. Klemmie, run and get Karen.

Someone will have to tell the old woman's niece. It is her niece who comes in, isn't it? That's nothing to do with me, at least.'

'Will there be a post-mortem?' Becca had dated a policeman for years, and it was exactly the kind of question he would have asked. She thought of him, high-minded and always looking out for a breach of the law, without so much as a flicker of regret.

'There's absolutely no need for that.' Bristling, Ellie flicked a strand of dyed black hair back behind her ear. 'Let's not make our lives any more complicated than they already are.'

'But surely in a case of unexplained death—'

'Unexplained? The woman was a hundred, for heaven's sake. I can't think of anything more easily explained than dying of old age. Let's just get the body eased out of this place as smoothly as the spirit was, shall we? It's in everyone's interests.' She stepped away from the chair as if to declare the matter closed. 'For heaven's sake, Klemmie, stop whining. It's a normal, peaceful process. Think of it as beautiful. There's no need to get tearful about it.'

Tiring of Ellie's irritability, Becca remembered she had other things to do. 'I'll tell Karen on my way out. Come on, Klemmie. Mrs Hodgson will catch one of us and eat us alive if you don't get her a biscuit soon.' She put her hand under the woman's elbow and guided her out into the corridor. 'Are you all right?' she asked, in a low voice in case the news spread more quickly than anyone wanted. 'If you'd rather, you can go and get Karen and I'll do the tea round.' Which wasn't what she'd meant to say, and was an act of kindness she really didn't have time for, so she was mightily relieved when Klemmie shook her head.

'I'm all right.' Klemmie dashed the tear away. 'I'm sorry. But she's not kind.' She tossed her head in the general direction of Ellie. 'You think I'm silly, but I don't like seeing dead people.' She gave herself a little shake. 'Coming, Mrs Hodgson! I'm sorry. I'm late.'

More slowly this time, Becca made her way up to reception where Karen was just ending the call. 'Oh, God! Some people can talk. I'm not even sure what that was all about and I definitely didn't need any of that information.' She heaved herself to her feet and came over to the counter, stretching out a hand to the plate of ginger biscuits. 'I shouldn't, but it's Friday. Are you all right, Becca? You're looking thoughtful. Didn't you find your key?'

Becca touched it, safely in her pocket, as a reminder of how easily she could escape the place. 'Yes. But there's a bit of bad news. Poor Dr Ross has passed away.'

'Violet? That's not where I'd have put my money.' Karen looked round, guilty at her slip of the tongue, her inadvertent lack of respect. 'Goodness, how terrible. Still, she'd had a good innings. I'd better call the doctor, I suppose. And her niece. Is anyone with her? Who found her?'

'Ellie's with her. Klemmie found her when she went to take the tea.' Thoughtfully, Becca picked up her bags. 'Klemmie's a bit upset.' Which was code for a warning: *don't let Ellie hassle her*. Not that Karen would heed the warning because no-one liked to be told how to do their job, but she owed it to Klemmie to try.

'Oh, is she? She really shouldn't be. It's a fact of life and she did choose to work in a care home. Are you quite sure Violet is actually dead?'

'Yes. I checked and there was no pulse. And Ellie confirmed it.' Once more, Becca contemplated Violet's face, outraged at the indignity of death. She didn't quite understand why it troubled her so much. 'I wondered if there should be a post-mortem, but Ellie said not.'

'She's right. Why put ourselves through it if it isn't entirely necessary? We'll just get the doctor to do the death certificate. That'll do. Thanks for what you did, Becca. I suppose the show must go on.' Brushing crumbs from a laminated sheet of paper on the desk, Karen paused for a second like a diver frozen with nerves on the highest board, then ran a polished fingernail down a list of numbers, stopped beneath one of them and dialled.

'I don't suppose you'll need me for anything else?'

'No, I don't suppose so. You'll be in again soon?'

'Probably. I think I'm on the rota for Monday. Next Friday, too.'

'I'll see you then. I'd better warn you. Monica might want to talk to you. She was very close to her aunt, and sometimes people want to talk to anyone who was with their relatives when they died. But I won't offer, and if she asks, don't feel obliged. Hello… yes, Karen Grant here, at Eden's End…'

Becca, sighing, took her leave and headed off to the next patient. When she got to her car and loaded her bags into the boot, she sat in the driver's seat in stillness for a moment, looking at the skeletons of the oak and chestnut trees in the grounds and the birds fluttering through them, complaining about the approach of winter. And then, driven by some impulse she didn't understand, she called Jude Satterthwaite.

Ashleigh had been working with him for two months and Jude, his attention caught from the moment she walked in, still couldn't rationalise his response to her. A strong — very strong — physical attraction undoubtedly dominated, but the irritation that came with it nagged at his better nature. Maybe, he thought as he watched her pick up her handbag and head out of the office at the end of the day, it was because he wasn't comfortable with the challenge she presented. The problem wasn't her — sexy, smart, and confident — but him, too damaged to cope with what she dared him to think. That was why he was always so short-tempered with her and why Doddsy, his close friend and colleague, had more than once had to badger him into apologising for his brusqueness.

Jude prided himself on being a good man-manager, and he thought most of his junior officers would have agreed with his assessment. That made his inability to treat Ashleigh with the same equanimity as the rest of them all the more galling, until he became angrier with himself and with everyone else on top of it. Taking a private phone call in work hours wasn't so grievous a sin, yet he'd allowed himself to behave like the possessive husband who seemed to be giving her so much trouble.

And then there was Becca. He looked down at his phone, in further irritation. He'd have kept it switched off at work if he hadn't been burdened with the responsibility of a trouble-prone younger brother, an emergency-in-waiting who was the one caller he daren't ignore. Becca knew he never answered personal calls when he was on duty, and if he'd been tempted to break the rule just that one time – as far as he could recall, the only time she'd phoned him in the three years since they'd split – he couldn't have done it after taking Ashleigh to task so publicly for the very same transgression. Yet Becca hadn't just called him once, but twice, implying that it was important and so putting pressure on him to respond.

'Are you ready to head home?' Doddsy stopped at his desk on the way out, shrugging his dark woollen coat round him against the chill of early November. 'I was going to suggest a pint.'

Jude considered. On another night he'd have been tempted, because when he was in this kind of mood Doddsy's equable good humour and sense of proportion were the best balm for his irritable soul, but Becca's messages proved a formidable obstacle. One would have been difficult enough to ignore, but two suggested there was something wrong. 'I've got a couple of calls to make before I leave.'

'Another time.' Tucking the ends of his scarf into the collar of his overcoat, Doddsy moved to the door, looking every inch the traditional detective.

'I'm free tomorrow night.'

'Tomorrow, then.' Doddsy closed the office door and Jude was left alone with the phone. He stared at it for a while, then looked out of the window into the darkness of the autumn evening, at the orange glow where the lights from the town of Penrith reflected back off the low cloud, and at the lights of traffic static on the rain-drenched purgatory of the A66 in the Friday night rush hour. Eventually, his circumspection gave way to briskness and he picked up the phone and flicked through the call log. Becca had made two calls, left one voicemail. *Jude. Sorry to bother you. I know you're busy. Perhaps you could call me when you have a minute.*

That was the trouble with working in a business where the tiniest detail might be important. He couldn't leave anything unresolved. He called her number, taking a moment to compose himself and think of the right form of words, sufficiently neutral, in case he forgot himself and slipped into the endearments of years before. 'Becca. I just picked up your message. Is everything okay?' Impressed with how businesslike he sounded, he smiled at his own reflection in the window.

'Oh, Jude. Yes.' She sounded tired. 'I'm just back home. It's been a busy day.'

'Nothing wrong?' he pressed her, though quite what could be wrong that would be made right by calling him was a puzzle.

'I wondered if you were at home this evening. If you are, can I pop round? I need some advice.'

He allowed himself two deep breaths before his sour temper reasserted itself. He was a reasonable man, but Becca had been the one who ended their relationship and he couldn't let it go. Nor would he let her forget it, because as long as he was still hurting, as long as her rejection of him kept him from starting again with someone better, he couldn't allow her to think he might forgive her for it. 'I'm still at work.'

'I can't think of anyone else to ask. And I don't want to talk about it over the phone.'

It was a plea, and he answered it for old times' sake. 'I could meet you for a quick drink.'

'That would be fine. Where would suit you? I could come into Penrith if you want.'

Becca lived out of town, inconveniently opposite his mother. If they met somewhere local to her, he risked someone seeing the two of them together and then the Chinese whispers would assume unmanageable proportions by the time they reached the people he didn't want to hear about it. Even his mother, who'd sided with him scrupulously over the split, somehow contrived to remain very close to Becca and would be on the phone to him within minutes of hearing they'd been seen together. 'Sure, why not?' He named a pub within walking distance of his house. He'd probably need a drink to deal with her, and he wasn't on call. 'I can be there in half an hour.'

'Give me a bit longer.'

'Seven, then. I'll see you.'

'Thanks, Jude. I appreciate it.'

'No bother,' he said, too briskly, and even as he rang off he was cursing himself, both for agreeing to see her and for being so grudging about it.

3

'I'll get you a drink.' Becca bounced to her feet as Jude approached the table where she was sitting, backing away from him as if she was afraid he might try and kiss her, her hands held up in front of her partly in apology and partly in self-defence.

She needn't have worried. He saw her often enough to be used to the bitterness that ambushed him whenever they met and he'd learned to keep control, but he should have been over those feelings by now. Clearly, even in his midthirties, he wasn't as mature a man as he liked to think. 'I'll have my usual.'

Settling himself as always in the corner where he could exercise his policeman's prerogative and keep an eye on everyone in the room, he watched as she bustled across to the bar, trying too obviously to act as if they were two old friends getting together for a drink. In the three years since they'd split he'd learned at least to seem dispassionate in her company, but she was more transparent and every glance she tossed over her shoulder towards him, every self-conscious laugh as she chatted to the barman, betrayed her unease. All shy smiles and muted colours, always striving to please, she lacked the extra oomph, the subtle but insidious sex appeal, that imbued Ashleigh O'Halloran's every movement with equal measures of promise and threat.

At the thought of Ashleigh, his lips curled into an involuntary smile. At last it was time for him to move on to someone else and whatever Becca wanted from him, this meeting was one he could treat as the first meaningful step in the transition from spurned lover to friend.

'Eden Gold.' Almost tripping over the obligatory wet Labrador sprawled on the floor, Becca set his pint on the table in front of him then slid into the chair opposite, anxious brown eyes focussed on the floor, on the table, on her hands, on anything but him. On the other side of the bar an open fire cast leaping shadows into their dark corner as he raised his glass, clinking it against the tumbler of J2O she lifted in salute. 'Cheers.'

'Cheers.' He drank, deeply. He'd wasted time worrying about this meeting. There was no longer anything Becca could do that could hurt him. 'What's your chat? You must have a hell of a problem if you need my help.'

He thought she stiffened at that response, even though he'd made a point of laughing as he said it. 'I don't know if you'd call it a problem. I need your advice.'

'Go on.'

'I was up at Eden's End this afternoon. You know it?'

'The nursing home up at Edenhall?' East Cumbrian by birth and upbringing, rooted in the place and its culture and privy to many of its secrets, Jude knew his patch as no-one else did. In his line of work he didn't have a lot of cause to visit nursing homes, but he knew Eden's End. Formerly a private home that had crumbled into dereliction and been rescued two decades before, it sat on the ridge between the village and the main road from Penrith to Alston, small but spectacularly expensive, a final retreat for the wealthy who wanted to see out their last days looking towards the otherworldly beauty of the Pennine Hills.

'Yes. I go there on my rounds, a couple of times a week. They don't have anyone with the specialist skills in vascular care and there's one patient... well, I don't suppose you need to know the details. It's enough I go there.'

Jude waited while she unclipped a black hairgrip from her shoulder-length brown hair and replaced it, anchoring a long strand to her scalp with a frown.

'Anyway. One of the residents died this afternoon.'

'Unexpectedly?'

'I don't know. The thing is, she was a hundred and she was frail. I don't know any details about her state of health, but she had all her faculties and she always seemed very robust. She wasn't my patient, but I chatted to her when I could. I got on well with her. She'd sit in the lounge and speak to everybody who came through. She was the sort of person who needed to know everyone and everyone's business.' She flicked a mischievous look across the table. *Just like you, Sherlock*, she might have teased in the days before their relationship had soured.

He pretended not to see the look. 'It's hardly surprising a resident of a nursing home died. Did you find her?'

'No. It was one of the care staff, a Polish girl – I say girl...' Becca shook her head, laughing at her inexactness. 'She must be in her mid-forties. She's been at the home a year. Longer, maybe. She got on very well with Violet, too.'

'Violet's the lady who died?'

'Yes. Violet Ross. This afternoon I was just outside her

room on my way out, and Klemmie went in to take her some tea. I heard her calling that Violet was dead so I went in.' She stopped and stirred the ice in her glass, a frown of concentration on her face. Jude recognised the look, that of a witness desperately trying to recall and refine every detail of a scene they hadn't thought important as it played out in front of them. 'I checked for a pulse and there wasn't one. She was still warm. I'm not a doctor, of course, but I'd say she'd died fairly recently. Within minutes.'

'Where was she?'

'Sitting in her chair by the window, as if she'd fallen asleep looking out at the hills. I sent Klemmie to get Ellie, who's the head nurse and she came down and confirmed Violet was dead. Then I left.' She frowned again.

'And?'

'There won't be a post-mortem.'

'Would you expect there to be?'

'No, because she was so old. And maybe there was some underlying health issue I didn't know anything about.'

'But you think not.'

She shifted her glass around the table, chasing a puddle of condensation that had run down the outside and pooled on the polished wood. 'Other than old age, I'd be surprised. If there was, it wasn't obvious. That's why it's so difficult. I asked Ellie about a PM. I said I thought there should be one, but she said there was no point.'

Jude drank deeply. It would be easy to switch into inquisitor mode, treat Becca like any other witness, but he didn't want to do that. 'Any reason why?'

'I think she thought it would be a nuisance. Just another chore.'

'So what made you think there should be one? The woman was a hundred. It's hardly unusual.'

She met his eyes at last, an agonised expression. 'I know you like facts, Jude.' At least she was kind enough not to accuse him of being obsessed with them. 'I know instinct isn't admissible in court. But I just can't help feeling there's something not right about it.'

Ashleigh, easily the most talented of the interviewers on his team, relied heavily on instinct, though her job meant she had to be ruthless in hunting down the evidence to back it up. For that reason alone – even if he hadn't known Becca so well he could understand how difficult it was for her to seek his help – he was inclined to listen to what she had to say, absence of facts notwithstanding. 'Okay, I'll buy it. What makes you say that?'

'Don't laugh. It was the look on her face. That was all. She just looked… well, furious. She looked as if she was disgusted with the way everything had ended. It wasn't like Violet. I didn't talk to her a lot, but she struck me as someone who would be happy enough to die quietly when the time came, but she looked as if she'd been cheated of the rest of her life.' She curled her ringless hands around the glass. 'I knew you'd laugh.'

'I'm not laughing.' Jude banished the smile that had sprung, without reason, from nowhere.

'There's something else. When I'd gone, I remembered. Her glasses were on the arm of the chair and they were broken.'

'Were they broken before?'

'I'd be astonished. Everything around her had to be just perfect, or someone would know about it.'

'Then it sounds to me as if you're right and there should be a post-mortem.'

'That's what I think. If I'm wrong, I'm wrong. There'll be no harm done. But if I'm right and there's something unusual about it, it doesn't matter that she's old, does it? It doesn't matter that she'd have died soon anyway. Because it isn't about that, or about convenience, or rocking the boat. It's all about justice.'

You're speaking my language, at last, he wanted to mock her. It had been his determination to pursue justice, to upset the status quo and with it the delicate balance of their friendship groups, that had led to their break-up three years before. When Jude had delivered his younger brother Mikey into the hands of the law after discovering him with drugs, Becca had deemed his reaction disproportionate and the fallout had gone on to cost him life-long friendships. One of those friends, Adam Fleetwood, had been convicted of drugs offences and was serving a prison sentence because of it.

I don't feel guilty, Jude admonished himself, though sometimes when he remembered how close he'd been to Adam he experienced a qualm. 'Yes. Justice is the most important thing.'

'And there's no-one to fight for Violet.'

'Isn't there a care home manager?'

'Yes.' A turning-up of Becca's freckled nose gave a clue as to what she thought. 'I mentioned it to her but she said Ellie was right. I thought she would. She always does the easiest thing.'

'There must be someone else you can tell. If the head nurse and the manager aren't doing their jobs—'

She stiffened slightly, as if he'd insulted her. 'Ellie's a professional. I can't rat on my colleagues.'

'Yes. She's a colleague. It's not as if she's your friend.' He fought to keep the hard edge from his tone and failed. If he'd thought about it before, he might have expected to feel some sense of satisfaction at seeing Becca in the same trap in which he'd been caught, knowing the right thing to do and yet accepting the unhappy implications of doing it. When the moment came all that intrigued him was seeing which way she'd jump and – if she chose the right way; the difficult way – whether she'd look back and judge him any differently for what he'd had to do.

'It probably is natural death.' Her fight with her conscience played out in front of him. 'On the other hand, if someone did do it—'

'Who'd want to?'

'I don't know. That's why there really should be a PM. Because sometimes – I know it hardly ever happens – but you do hear of people with a God complex. Not that I'm suggesting Ellie – not anyone, really – I'm sure no-one had any reason to hurt Violet. But what if someone did do it? What if it's someone else next? And what if there's been someone else before, and nobody noticed? If they get away with it this time, who's next?'

Her thought processes were tracking his, years too late to save what had been so good between them. 'I don't think you need me to tell you what you have to do.'

'But I don't know how—'

'Don't tell me there isn't a mechanism for whistle-blowers in the NHS.'

She tilted her chin towards him. 'You know there is.'

'Then you don't need my advice. It's easy for you. You have an anonymous helpline and no-one but me need ever know it was you who called. Your friends aren't going to drop you for doing the right thing.' He couldn't stop himself adding a barbed comment. 'Like mine did.'

When her back was up and her mind set, Becca wasn't afraid to challenge him, but today there was no fight in her, at least on that. 'You're very unforgiving.'

'If I was unforgiving I wouldn't be here.' But he hadn't forgotten what it was like, and going through what Becca was going through was beyond difficult. He sat back and looked at her, coolly. 'You want my advice?'

'You'll tell me to report it.'

'Yes. You couldn't have saved Violet, but you're right. If someone else does die and it turns out to be criminal, you'll have that person on your conscience.' She wouldn't be able to handle that. Becca was born caring, destined to look after others. If she hadn't chosen nursing it would have been teaching or charity work. She ran the Brownies and the Rainbows in the village, looked after people's pets when they were away on holiday, picked up small children when they skinned their knees in the street, offered tissues to crying strangers. No-one in need of even the slightest dash of human kindness had ever slipped past Becca Reid. Except him.

'I'll do it tomorrow.'

He tilted his head at her, trying to gauge her determination. Would she? Or would things seem too difficult in the distant morning? 'Do it now. Use my phone, if you want to be sure no-one will find out it's you.' He'd been flicking his fingers over the phone screen even as he spoke to her, knowing how the conversation would go, preparing the way to its inevitable end, and pushed it across the table to her. 'Here. I googled the number.'

She looked at it, there on the table before them, and with the greatest show of reluctance, she picked it up and dialled.

He refused her offer of a lift, just as she'd refused his offer of a second drink (both offers born out of politeness alone) but his heart lifted as he walked the short distance from the centre of Penrith to his house in Wordsworth Street. He was free of her presence at last. Eventually, time would release him from the last of his feelings for her.

As he strode up the hill to the safety of his front door, he couldn't help asking himself what had made her call him when there was only one course open to her, but he knew the answer. She'd wanted someone to tell her to do the right thing, and he was the only person she could trust to do it.

A sense of optimism blossomed within him. So, after all that had happened, she needed him for something. And he was smiling as he turned into his front gate.

The wedding ring, tucked into the corner of Ashleigh's jewellery box, winked in the lamplight, the golden last link in the chain that had once bound her to Scott. She closed the box as soon as she'd opened it, the second she'd taken that glimpse she didn't want and didn't need. It had taken a long time for her to let her marriage go, long after she realised philandering was ingrained in Scott's soul and would last as long as the cheeky smile, that even when he was old and fading, he'd be parked in the corner of some care home making eyes at the nurses, the carers and the visitors. It would be a joke for everyone, and his charm and enthusiasm would harm no-one and lighten everyone's day, but as he'd burst into his prime, the last stages of his youth seasoned by experience, his eye for the girls – and their eyes for him – had caused nothing but distress to Ashleigh, the one woman he'd tried, and failed, to commit to.

It was a shame. She'd loved him and perhaps, in the darkest, most shameful shadows of her soul, she still did, despite the way he'd treated her, but in the end her sense of self-preservation had won out. In the long term, loving Scott would have destroyed her and she was too strong to let it.

'I gave you every chance,' she muttered, opening the box again as if it contained a snake and folding the ring away in the bottom layer where she wouldn't see it unless she chose to look. Relationships came and went and marriage, her one flirtation with optimism, had proved yet again that it was better to be cynical. She didn't want to be angry with him but if he couldn't accept the marriage was over and his infidelity was the cause of it, then anger was inevitable. She needn't feel guilty because he couldn't cope.

'Ash! What are you doing up there? Are you hiding a man in the wardrobe?'

Ashleigh grinned, shoved the box into a drawer and locked it into darkness, then headed down the stairs. 'I wish.'

'You need to find one.' Lisa, her housemate, was standing in the kitchen with a bottle in her hand, tilting it recklessly over the second of two glasses on the worktop. Rich red wine splashed over the top and ran down the stem. 'What took you so long? I was getting tired of waiting. If I didn't have a phobia about drinking alone, I'd have started without you.'

'I was looking at my wedding ring.' Ashleigh got crisps out of the kitchen cupboard and filled a couple of bowls. She'd known Lisa for twenty years, since they'd come together on their first day at an exclusive, expensive private school on the outskirts of Manchester, and they'd grown up together. Lisa knew every detail of everyone Ashleigh had ever dated, and Ashleigh was probably the only person who truly understood that Lisa, in her turn, had no romantic interest whatsoever in men, or women, or anyone else. That made their relationship the only risk-free one she'd ever shared.

'You've no regrets?'

'Not one.'

'So what drove you back into that trap? A bad day?' Lisa's gap-toothed, freckled grin was that of a tomboyish teenager. 'Or a new man?'

Ashleigh thought of Jude. She kept no secrets from Lisa, but how could he be a secret when there was nothing between them to hide? 'No. It's a bit more brutal than that. Scott phoned.'

'Jeez.' Leading the way into the living room, Lisa sprawled on the sofa, her wine splashing recklessly in its glass. 'What did he want? Promising to embark on a life of monogamy again?'

'We didn't get that far.'

'I hope you'd have more sense than to believe it if he did.'

'It's a bit late for that.' Less judgemental of the man she used to love than Lisa, Ashleigh set her glass down on the side table and crossed the room to close the curtains. Outside, a jogger ran past, head down against the wind. For a moment she thought it was Jude, but it wasn't. Anyway, he'd stayed late in the office, scowling at her over that personal phone call – another stick to beat Scott with, another reason to break the chain and cast it off for ever. 'But he seems to think I'm being unreasonable about the divorce.'

'He doesn't learn, does he?' Lisa inspected her archaeologist's fingers, digging the dirt from beneath her thumbnail with the nail of her forefinger, then looked up with a grin. 'Persistent beggar. Don't fall for it.'

'I knew it would happen.' Ashleigh's lips twitched into an affectionate smile, but it was for Lisa's unconditional support rather than for Scott. 'He wants us to try again. Work harder at it.' As if she hadn't already done all the work, given all the ground, as if they didn't both know that when she tried and he failed he'd be harping on at her again for yet another last chance.

'He won't change.'

'I know. So does he. But he thinks because he loves me and I used to love him I should put up with him and it'll all be all right. Because it's just the way he is. He can't help himself and he regrets it every time.' Ashleigh sat down and took a larger slug of wine than she'd intended. Ever since she'd instructed her solicitor to instigate divorce proceedings she'd expected Scott to call. It was only now she was home and relaxed that she realised how much his distress had shaken her. 'He phoned me at work. Almost got me into trouble with the boss—'

'Your boss ought to be a bit more sympathetic.'

'He's still getting used to me.' Unable to help herself, she licked her lips, then felt Lisa's judgemental gaze upon her and grinned. 'Don't worry. He'll be fine. It's not him I'm worried about.' She corrected herself, immediately. 'I'm not worried about Scott, either. It's just I thought I'd put all that pain behind me and now it's flared up again. He was genuinely upset, as if I'm the villain. I don't need that.'

'No. I was right. You need another man. By way of distraction. And it won't do any harm to make the point to Scott. Stop him thinking you care.'

'I don't care. And you have a one-track mind.'

'I live in the twenty-first century. You aren't going to fall in love again, are you, or not straight away. You've taken too big a hit to the heart for that. But I know what you're like. Sooooo… touchy-feely.' Lisa's hands fluttered in a display of abstract symbolism as the wine worked its magic. 'You need people. Passion. Pleasure. So get out and have a bit of fun. Nobody's going to hold it against you.'

Sitting back, one arm stretched along the sofa back, the other hand cradling the glass of wine, Ashleigh relaxed. 'I'm sure loads of people would. But yes. I can look elsewhere.' Because Lisa was right. Life was a game, and she was ready to play.

4

'What are you doing in here? The room's empty. There can't possibly be anything for you to do.'

Straightening up, Klemmie Marcowics twitched the cushions back into position on the chair where Violet had died. In her imagination the old woman's expression reproached her, dead eyes turned upwards to the ceiling, a trace of spittle still trickling down the side of her mouth. In silence, she stepped back as unobtrusively as she could as Violet's niece bustled in, keeping her back to her, dipping her head in a gesture of respect to her friend's absent soul.

Through the reflection in Violet's mirror she saw the woman staring at her, dark eyes hard with suspicion. 'I hope you haven't touched any of my aunt's belongings.'

'I'm cleaning,' said Klemmie, by way of the required explanation, though that wasn't why she was there. She was there because she couldn't stay away. Violet Ross, sixty years her senior, had become her only real friend in a thoughtless world and now she was alone. To reinforce her lie, she picked up Violet's glasses from the arm of the chair and folded them closed. One side was askew, so she turned the glasses over and over in her fingers, trying to force it back into place as if by doing so she could turn back time and have a friend again.

'Karen said there wouldn't be anyone here. Wasn't the room cleaned as soon as my aunt was taken to the undertakers? If not, why not?'

It was easier, under this kind of interrogation, to pretend to be stupid. Placing the glasses on the polished teak tabletop, Klemmie composed her expression into one of sullen incomprehension and turned the blankest possible look towards the newcomer. 'Sorry, Miss?'

'Don't you even speak English?' Tall and intimidating, the woman shook her head, placed long thin hands on narrow bony hips and glared.

'A bit, Miss.' Klemmie was fluent, but she wasn't too proud to play stupid if it made her life easier.

'Did Karen tell you to come in here?'

'I don't think so, Miss.'

Monica Roland sighed, far too obviously, as if the sigh itself was part of a foreign language Klemmie wouldn't understand. 'You should not be in here,' she said, loud and slow. 'We do not need you to clean. I've come to take Dr Ross's things away.' She gestured to the dresser and the wardrobe, heavy mahogany pieces that had arrived with Violet and would leave shortly after her.

Playing dumb meant Klemmie didn't have to obey Monica's instructions, or not immediately, so she replaced the glasses, picked up a towel she'd dropped over the arm of the chair and folded it over her arm before she turned back. Violet hadn't liked her niece, not because Monica was ever anything but perfectly dutiful, but because their two characters were fundamentally incompatible, the one a free spirit and the other bound by obligation and social convention. Klemmie, who tended much more to the former than the latter, stood where she was for a moment longer, sharing company with Violet's spirit for a final few seconds and offering her a silent psychic apology as she did so, only hoping the dead woman could understand. She crossed herself with her free hand, deliberately trying to draw Monica's attention from the towel she was holding and towards the crucifix around her neck. Her last moment with Violet was coming to its end. 'Sorry for your loss, Miss.'

'Thank you. Now if you don't mind, I'd like you to leave. I'm going to pack up my aunt's belongings. The furniture will be collected later – if I decide to keep it.' She opened the wardrobe and shook her head, in obvious disapproval. Violet, who cared nothing for anybody's views and a lot for luxury, had kept a thick fur coat there to annoy people, though she never wore it, and Monica looked the sort of person to be torn between disapproval of its origins and proper respect for its value. A half-look back towards Klemmie implied she might choose to unload these damaged goods on a deserving case. *If she dares*, thought Klemmie, insulted, but in the end value seemed to win out in Monica's mind and she closed the wardrobe door without another word.

Despite instructions, Klemmie stayed put. As soon as the room was finally empty, even before the next person moved in – and the waiting list for Eden's End was so long that most people on it died before they set foot in its expensively carpeted lobby – it would be stripped of any sense of Violet's overwhelming personality. 'I could help you.'

'Thank you, but that won't be necessary.' This time,

Monica's gesture of dismissal couldn't be ignored. With reluctance dragging down her every step Klemmie shuffled towards the door, only to be reprieved by Karen clattering along the corridor towards them.

Klemmie gave way to her boss. There wasn't room for the two of them to pass in the doorway – Karen's fondness for home baking extended to eating as well as preparing it, and the quantities of both reflected her struggle to keep on top of her job – and at least standing back in fake respect bought her a few extra seconds in Violet's room. Shrinking away, she hoped to be overlooked.

'Ms Roland.' Something had propelled Karen into uncomfortable haste. Her round face was scarlet with exertion and her speech randomly punctuated by snatched breaths as her lungs struggled to keep pace with her lips. 'I'm really sorry. So awkward. Oh dear. I do hope you haven't started packing Violet's things yet.'

Monica turned away from the wardrobe with an over-obvious sigh, as if the fur coat wasn't the only thing to offend her. 'I was about to start.'

'I'm terribly sorry. I have to ask you to stop.' Karen puffed to a temporary halt. 'I've had a phone call. I think we may be getting a visit from the police.'

'The police?' Monica's jaw dropped, mirroring the expression on Violet's dead face. Equally aghast, Klemmie shrank back into the corner, fighting the coward's reaction to run. The police?

'Well, no. I'm sorry. That sounded sensationalist.' Karen, red in the face and flustered, gave way to her confusion. 'No. I haven't spoken to the police. I'm sorry. I got confused. They aren't involved at this stage. But they might be.'

'Why?'

'I'm sorry. Oh God. Let me start again. It appears someone has reported Dr Ross's death to the Clinical Commissioning Group as potentially suspicious and so the police might be involved at a later stage. But I'm getting ahead of myself. I'm sure everything will be fine, but there's to be a post-mortem.'

'A post-mortem?' Monica Roland moved from offence to outrage with a seamlessness surely born of experience. 'Is that entirely necessary? And even if it is, as her next of kin shouldn't I be asked for my consent?'

'I'm afraid I don't really understand the technicalities of it—'

'You're in charge here. It's your job to understand.'

If anything, Karen's flush deepened, scarlet flooding well into the roots of her short blonde hair. 'Yes. I'm sorry about the confusion. The way they explained it, if there's a suspicion about the death, the coroner can require a PM should take place. And that's what's going to happen.'

Klemmie had worked with Karen long enough to know she was quick to skate over the complexities and quicker still to jump to the Doomsday conclusion. Whether or not it was the law, it didn't matter. She suspected not, because if it was the manager would have come out with it straight away, but having regrouped, she'd come back solidly, too confident to allow any argument. Either way, the prospect of police involvement was surely something no-one would welcome.

'I'm most distressed to hear that.' Monica did, indeed, sound distressed but she backed down.

And so she should. Twisting the edge of her plastic apron between her fingers, Klemmie decided she'd waited long enough not to look guilty and it was time to leave. 'Excuse me, Karen. I'd better get on.'

'What were you doing in here anyway, Klemmie?' Karen, it was obvious, sought distraction, any excuse to get away from the procedures she didn't understand.

'I came down to see if there was anything I could do to help.' With a single, simple sentence, she'd let Monica know how well she could speak English, and the woman was scowling at her now, as if everything was Klemmie's fault and she knew she'd been lied to. She looked like a bad enemy to make, but it was too late to undo the deed.

'No, nothing needs to be done. In fact, there's nothing that can be done, even if we wanted to. I'm afraid the place has to be left untouched until the results of the post-mortem are out. In case the police need to be involved.' Karen drew a long, agonised breath and rushed back in, almost as if she were reassuring herself rather than her listeners. 'Though I'm sure that won't be the case and whoever has reported it was merely being overzealous. And as such, I welcome the post-mortem. Because of course we have nothing to hide, and so there's nothing to fear.'

The police. Karen might welcome external intervention but Klemmie most certainly didn't. Suddenly uncomfortably aware of how long she'd lingered, how close she'd come to being caught out, she edged past Karen and into the corridor. She should never have come into the room and risked drawing attention to herself.

'I for one would be glad if the police were called, even

though I'm sure there will be no sign of foul play. Because they may be able to help me establish the whereabouts of my aunt's gold brooch.'

Holy Mother of God. Klemmie, pausing in the lobby, again suppressed the urge to run. That wasn't the turn she'd expected the story to take.

'I'm sorry, Ms Roland. I really don't understand you.'

'My aunt's gold brooch. It was shaped like an eagle. So big.' Monica held finger and thumb and inch or so apart. 'She was extremely fond of it. It doesn't seem to be here.'

Hands on hips, Karen edged forwards, blocking Klemmie's view. 'Perhaps it's slipped down—'

'I don't see it.'

'Ms Roland. I hope you aren't suggesting—'

'I'm suggesting nothing. I'm stating the facts. The brooch, which was in the drawer of this dressing table when I visited my aunt last week, is no longer there.'

'Ms Roland.' From inside the room, there was the sound of a drawer creaking open. 'I must insist you don't – we've been specifically asked not to touch anything until we hear the results of the post-mortem. Then, I'm sure, we can have a proper look and find your aunt's brooch. It must be in here somewhere. In the meantime, rest assured. I'll make sure the room is locked and the keys placed in the safe.'

A couple of brisk steps took Klemmie round the corner, out of sight and up the back stairs out of the way before the two women could carry their polite disagreement into a public space and, hopefully, before they remembered she was there or thought to ask questions. She'd popped down to Violet's room in her break and she had barely five minutes of it left before Mrs Hodgson began her ritual bemoaning over the lateness of her morning coffee and biscuits, but she had to take the risk.

'Klemmie.' Ellie, emerging from the ladies' loo, surprised her. 'Where are you off to now? I want you to—'

'My break.' Not daring to stop, Klemmie surged on, breaking into a run the second she was round the corner. Karen might be pathologically unobservant and Monica Roland preoccupied with her loss, but Ellie missed nothing and queried everything, dressing her nosiness as banter. *Is that a gun in your pocket or are you just pleased to see me*, she'd have joked in the worst-case scenario. And then what?

Thank God she hadn't noticed the telltale bulge beneath that all-concealing plastic pinny.

After running up the back stairs, Klemmie unlocked the door that led to the two staff flats at the back of the building. Karen occupied the larger one and Klemmie herself stayed in the smaller: bedroom, bathroom, kitchenette and small living area, its tiny window looking out at dense spruce woodlands that masked the silver snake of the River Eden and reminded her of the forests of the Tatras.

Knowing time was valuable, that her best hope lay in keeping her head down and avoiding any kind of attention, she reached into her pocket for the World War Two handgun Monica had so nearly caught her stealing from Violet's room, and tossed it on the bed. Then she turned to the narrow bedside table and pulled out the top drawer. On top of a pile of handkerchiefs, not even concealed, Violet's golden eagle brooch winked at her with the sparkle of two tiny ruby chips that passed for its eyes.

Later, if she had a chance, she'd find somewhere secure

to hide this duo of incriminating objects before someone asked awkward questions, but in the meantime, temporary measures were all she had. She folded gun and brooch inside a handkerchief and slipped the package underneath the mattress.

5

The call, when it came, wasn't unexpected. Jude had learned to treat any summons to his superintendent's office with a large measure of suspicion, if only because the two men were both too similar and yet too different to allow a fully functional working relationship. Over the five years they'd been forced to work together they'd refined it to one of necessary formality, largely based on written or digital communication. Keeping apart worked well enough and they coped when circumstances forced them to meet, as long as Damon Groves could control his irritation with Jude's attitude and Jude could restrain his temper in the face of his superior's patronising approach to his male colleagues and borderline inappropriate behaviour to his female ones.

Groves, on this Monday morning, must have been in too much of a hurry to sit down and draft out an email and so had decided to cut that particular corner and risk the direct approach. 'Satterthwaite. Just the man.' He looked up from his desk when Jude appeared, but kept scowling. 'I've a very interesting case for you.'

'Oh?' Jude hovered in the doorway. Given his boss's sensitivity about rank and precedence, it was always wise to wait for an invitation to sit.

'Yes. It's an unusual case, if you fancy playing Poirot. A nursing home, a suspicious death, a whistle-blower. And as of this morning, we have a very interesting post-mortem result.'

So Becca had been right. Jude stood frozen for a moment, his habit when he was thinking. It was better not to give away what he knew, because she didn't want her name public and he could understand why. It might be the part of the whistle-blower had to become known, and if it did he'd make sure her identity was kept confidential, but her connection with him meant even internal circulation of that particular piece of information could make things difficult, for either or both of them. 'Oh?'

'Yes. On Friday afternoon, a one-hundred-year-old woman, Violet Ross, died at the Eden's End nursing home in Edenhall. You know it?'

'That's the big house between the village and the Langwathby road.' The name of the place always made him smile. Its owners had tried to change it to something more uplifting and village gossip had it the headed notepaper still tried to claim the place as Eden View, but the locals were having none of it and the old name stuck.

'Yes. On Friday evening, an anonymous caller to an NHS whistle-blowing helpline indicated they had suspicions about the circumstances of Violet Ross's death. They gave no reasons, other than they thought she was in good health, and there should have been a post-mortem but that no post-mortem had been arranged. The initial response from the care watchdog was that it was likely to be mismanagement rather than malpractice, but as a formality they arranged for a post-mortem to take place. That was in Carlisle this morning.'

Used to Groves's pauses for dramatic effect, Jude sometimes made the effort to endure them, but today he was keen to get on with things. 'And?'

'It's homicide. The woman was suffocated. We don't yet know what with. The fibres in the lungs are away to the lab for analysis, but the results are enough to fire the starting gun on a murder investigation.'

Jude stifled a smile, not because murder was in any way humorous, but because of the inescapable irony of Becca's choice having proved, inevitably, to be the right one. She was right not to want the story to get out, because if it did she might suffer the same vilification from her colleagues that he had from his friends. 'Are there any suspects? Any indication of motive? Any clues at all?'

'There'll be suspects galore. There always are in these places, with so many people in each other's way and not all of them fully *compos mentis*. They'll have plenty of opportunities.' Something pinged into his inbox and, looking away from Jude, he made a sharp note on his pad. 'As for motive, that's for you to find out, though I don't imagine you'll be short of those, either. You find everything from the family wanting to inherit to the old soldier in the next room who thinks he's back at El Alamein. It shouldn't be a complicated one, but it's enough to keep you out of mischief for a couple of days.'

That was almost certainly meant to be a joke, but Groves had always made it plain he thought the promotion to Chief Inspector had come too soon. Jude took refuge in stiffness. 'Let's hope so. Can you brief me on the details?'

'I've forwarded you all the information I have.' Groves sat back, laying his pen down on the desk in front of him, in a gesture of delegation. 'Let me know how you get on. Pass it off to a junior, if you wish. DI Dodd might manage it. It shouldn't be beyond his competency.'

That dismissiveness put Jude's back up yet further. Doddsy was capable of dealing with far more complex cases than this promised to be but he was busy dealing with a series of assaults at a Keswick holiday park. And in any case, if there was homicide involved, Jude preferred to keep a close eye on it himself, though he'd have no hesitation is enrolling his friend as his deputy. 'I'll certainly get him involved in my team, sir.'

'Keep me updated.' The mention of Jude's team always caused Groves to stiffen very slightly. Like a number of his colleagues, he found Jude's reliance on a close circle of people, with whom he got on and who worked precisely the way he liked, to be exclusive and off-putting, but he couldn't argue with the method. The crime figures showed they got results. 'That's all, Satterthwaite. I'll let you go and hunt down your old soldier. Don't take too long over it. There are plenty of other things for you to do.'

'Thank you.' Shuffling backwards out of the room like a courtier leaving the presence of his monarch, Jude sighed with relief as he escaped into the corridor, and headed down to his desk. This wasn't the way he'd have chosen to get started on seeking justice for Violet Ross. It might be murder or it might, if some twist lay in the investigation, turn out to be manslaughter but he was undoubtedly dealing with a crime scene and the golden hour, the priceless period when there was most to learn from it, had passed. Becca's quick thinking and active conscience had almost certainly prevented Violet Ross's death being processed and passed off as natural, but the wheels hadn't got in motion quickly enough to allow them to take advantage of it.

He checked his watch as he flicked open Groves's email and scanned through it. Almost noon, on Monday. Becca had reported the matter at just after seven on the Friday evening and the post-mortem had been ordered the following morning. He knew how places like Eden's End worked. The room would have been cleaned and turned round within hours of Violet's death, ready for the next person pending only the removal of her belongings. At least the room had been locked since Saturday lunchtime.

It was a matter of hours, but you could lose a lot of evidence in half a day, especially if someone had a vested interest in you doing so.

Tapping his pen on the desk, he formulated his plan of action, already picking the team he'd want to work with. The very first thing was to get down to the scene of the crime – and he would take Ashleigh with him.

'It's obviously far too early to identify any kind of motive.' Jude pulled his Mercedes up on the wide gravel frontage outside Eden's End, where windows opened out onto a long slope, lush green fields speckled with sheep, the silver snake of the River Eden and the undulating spine of the Pennines. 'As always I'm approaching this with an open mind. But I think we can risk a guess about what it might be.'

'Money.' Ashleigh opened the passenger door and swung her legs out of the low-slung seat with the elegance of a duchess. 'It's almost always that. But mercy killing has to be in the mix, too.'

'From what I understand, she wasn't in any pain.'

'Then perhaps you could call it convenience killing, if that isn't too harsh a way of putting it. And we mustn't rule out the mentally unbalanced. Think of Shipman. Doctors and nurses – and people with no medical training at all, I suppose – can get a little drunk on the taste of power.'

'I'd wondered about that.'

'I know it's very unusual, but it does happen.'

'It's unusual for people to get caught, yes.' And if you did have that kind of complex, nursing homes would be a great place to indulge it, with death as the end game.

'We shouldn't tar everyone with the same brush.' Ashleigh swung the strap of her briefcase over her shoulder and stared at the building. Her long shadow reached out across the gravel towards him. 'Far from it. But you know how it is. Sometimes there's a rotten apple.'

'That happens in all walks of life.' Becca had mentioned the head nurse and her lack of tolerance for her charges. That might prove a fruitful hunting ground. He paused for a second, in the act of locking the car. 'What do you make of the place?'

'It's very grand, isn't it?'

'It's very exclusive.' As if drawn by her teasing shadow, he came round and stood next to her. Every day he worked with Ashleigh, he found it harder to be close to her without being conscious of her vitality, her sheer, earthy attractiveness, acutely aware as he was of the abstinence Becca's rejection had forced upon him. With her obvious sexuality and her refreshing approach to life Ashleigh had first struck him as the kind of distraction he needed least. Now he wasn't so sure.

But he was professional. Turning his back, he looked towards the house. Victorian in style, it was resplendent with a double front and matching extensions to the sides. Its doors and window frames were newly painted in environmentally sympathetic pine green, the grounds cared for even in November. Under a huge, almost leafless chestnut tree, comfortable wooden chairs offered views of the hills and promised summer shade, and in the background a ploughed field rolled away down to the grey and green layers that marked the river and the woods. The chack-chack of a jackdaw broke the silence and in the background the sun chased shadows across the fellside.

'You'd need a lot of money to contemplate spending your dying days here.' He could quite understand why an impecunious relative might not appreciate seeing their inheritance evaporate quite so quickly, whittled down by a few thousand more every time they came to visit but, he reminded himself, he had an open mind about motive. The only thing he could be certain of was that someone other than Violet Ross had played a part in her death. 'Let's go on in.'

'Is that Tammy's car?' Ashleigh nodded to a silver four-by-four parked to one side of the forecourt next to a CSI van.

He nodded, in approval. Tammy Garner was the best of the force's crime scene investigators, the one who was closest to his wavelength. If there was anything to be found, which he doubted, she'd find it. 'Yes. Doddsy got her on the case for us.'

'Was that hard?'

'She's always in demand. He had to get her taken off

something else. I take my hat off to him. I didn't think he'd do it.'

'He's some man.' Straying away from the car and treading carefully around the puddles that followed heavy overnight rain, Ashleigh dug out a pocket camera and clicked away as Jude looked, reviewed, evaluated and filed away the information in front of them.

As he did so, he relaxed. Leaving Doddsy in charge of the incident room and bringing Ashleigh with him had been the right choice. Her reliance on instinct might be unorthodox, but in two months, he'd learned it was always good to have her out at the scene. Sometimes she saw thing differently to everyone else. 'That's a positive start. Let's see what else we can find out. I've told you all I know about the case, and it's very little. So let's go in and see what else we can find.'

'The place is like Fort Knox.' Taking the lead with the self-confidence Jude had come to admire but which certain of their colleagues regarded with suspicion, Ashleigh lifted her hand to the buzzer. 'I suppose it has to be. They can't risk losing anyone. When I started on the beat back in Cheshire, I swear I spent half my time rounding up elderly people who'd gone astray. Hello? It's DCI Satterthwaite and DS O'Halloran, in to see Ms Grant.'

They waited in silence for thirty seconds before a large woman, her blonde hair clipped short, opened the door. Dressed in an outfit that defied any kind of continuity and suggested she'd thrown on every black garment in her wardrobe in a panicked attempt to show respect, she would have been a fine-looking woman for her age – fortyish – but for the grey tint to her skin and the excess flesh that dragged her features downwards. Her face was an agony of fear and uncertainty and her gratitude that they weren't in uniform was barely disguised.

'Chief Inspector. Sergeant.' She lowered her voice, not needing to remind them of her desire for discretion. 'Come through into the meeting room.' Hustling them through with a shamed look over her shoulder, she closed the door behind them in some relief. 'So awful you had to come here. Do sit down. Of course when I heard I thought there must be some mistake. Surely there is some mistake. Coffee?'

'No mistake at all, I'm afraid.' Sitting down at the table Jude nodded his thanks to the offer of coffee and reached out long fingers to the plate of chocolate-dipped shortbread. Home-made, by the look of it. There were perks to the job, after all. 'The post-mortem indicates that Dr Ross's death wasn't natural.'

She stared at him in bewilderment. 'But what else could it have been?'

'That's what we're trying to find out.' As she always did, Ashleigh swung into action, cutting across Jude's rebuttal of any misdemeanour, focussing her attention on the interviewee, inviting confidence. For the life of him, Jude couldn't work out how she did that, how she made it so easy for witnesses to confide in her, even when – as everyone always did – they had secrets they were reluctant to share. Already, having placed coffee and cups on the table, Karen Grant was sinking back into her chair, eyes focussed on the junior detective and an expression of immense gratitude on her face. Here, it was evident, was someone she felt she could talk to.

So much less for him to do. Jude settled back to listen,

to observe how Karen would negotiate the traps Ashleigh would lead her into, and to think.

'I can't believe this happened on my watch.' She shook her head, and the string of jet beads around her neck rattled beneath her accumulated chins. 'There must be some mistake. Violet was a hundred, you know, and such an extraordinary character. When Klemmie said—'

'We want to know everything you can tell us about Dr Ross. That's important. But maybe you could start by telling me what happened.'

'Yes. Yes, of course.' The manager composed herself, a fat forefinger barely fitting through the narrow handle of her coffee cup. 'The first I knew? I was in my office on Friday afternoon when Becca Reid came up to fetch me.'

Glad to be unobserved, Jude sucked in his cheeks and maintained an expression brutal in its neutrality.

'Becca's the district nurse. She comes in twice a week to see one of our residents. Sometimes it's one of her colleagues, but usually her. She'd been in seeing Marjorie – that's Marjorie Hodgson, in the room next to Violet – as usual, and she came running in to say Violet had died. Klemmie found her when she went in with the afternoon tea.' Karen reached for a biscuit.

'Klemmie?'

'Klemmie Marcowics. She's one of our carers. She's Polish. You'll want to speak to her, of course. I'll arrange for that.' The biscuit snapped between Karen's fingers. 'And I've asked Becca to come by this afternoon, because you'll need to speak to her, too.'

Forewarned was forearmed. Not that Jude thought he couldn't treat Becca with complete impartiality even when he wasn't expecting to see her, but it reduced the risk of him accidentally giving away her part in this drama. For something to do, he wrote the two names down on his pad. 'And then?'

'I went straight down to Violet's room. Ellie Jack was there – she's our head nurse – and she confirmed that Violet was dead.'

'Were you surprised?'

Karen considered. 'Yes and no. Violet never thought about dying, even though she was so old. She just seemed to assume she'd go on for ever, and I suppose we all believed it because she did. But she was old, so it's all nature, isn't it?' Karen's speech had accelerated and she pulled herself up, getting out a tissue and dabbing at her forehead. 'Ellie said it looked natural to her. And so of course, I called Violet's niece, and she came straight away.'

'Her name?'

'Monica Roland. She arrived after about half an hour. She'd been visiting that afternoon and had only just left, about ten minutes before Klemmie came round with the tea. She lives up the road in Langwathby. I made her a cup of tea and talked her through what to do next. She spent some time alone with her aunt and left not long after five. The doctor arrived shortly afterwards to certify the death. I called the undertakers and they came within the hour.'

'And after they'd gone, you cleared the room?'

'It's standard practice. We stripped the bed and cleared the towels, and the girls came in and deep cleaned first thing in the morning. Obviously, if I'd known… I'm terribly sorry. I had no idea.'

'Of course you didn't. You did exactly the right thing.'

Ashleigh paused for a second, before leaning in a little more closely. 'You must love your job, Ms Grant.'

'Oh, I do love it. I love it very much.' Karen fanned her face with her hand, hiding behind it, the gesture of a liar. 'But it's busy, of course, and very stressful. I'm never off duty. And of course I'm grateful to the owners for… well, for giving me the chance.'

Jude made a note. The chance to what? It would be interesting to see what brought Karen Grant to Eden's End, because whatever she claimed, she wasn't giving the impression of being a woman overwhelmed by personal happiness and job fulfilment.

'And then?' Ashleigh prompted.

'Yes. And then I got a call on Saturday to say there was going to be a post-mortem and the room shouldn't be touched. Ms Roland had just arrived, to clear out her aunt's things, but we were able to lock the room before she could remove anything.'

In places like Eden's End, where time was money, death blew through with unseemly haste. Jude shook his head, the list of people to interview lengthening. Becca. The niece. The head nurse. The carer. 'Who are the other residents on that floor, Ms Grant? Do they stay in their rooms, or do they move around?'

'Normally they wouldn't be in their rooms in the afternoon. Most of them spend their time in the lounge, but it's being decorated at the moment.' She paused and sipped her coffee. 'In that cluster of rooms, we have four residents. There's Marjorie. She doesn't move around unaided, and Becca was with her. She has an issue with her leg. Then there's Pauline, though she's in hospital just now so her room is empty. And on the other side of Violet there's Colin, but he spends a lot of time in his room. He's in his nineties.'

Jude remembered his boss's throwaway remark. 'Is he an old soldier, by any chance?'

'Yes.' Karen shot him a look of astonishment. 'How did you know?'

'It's an educated guess. He's the right age.'

'Of course. Well, ask him about it if you dare. He'll be only too glad to tell you everything.' She flicked her eyes up to the heavens. 'Just make sure you allow plenty of time for it.'

'There was no-one else in the area at the time?' Jude paused a moment, struggling with the terminology. 'Perhaps some of your elderly patients with dementia… might become a bit confused?'

She understood him well enough. 'We have one or two with those issues, but they live in a separate wing of the house. We try to keep our residents together with people of similar capabilities. It's better for everyone. And I have to say, Violet had lost none of her faculties. Not only did she know exactly what she was doing, but she made sure she knew what the rest of us were doing, too.'

'Tell us a bit about yourself, Ms Grant.' For a moment Jude thought Ashleigh was going to entice the home's manager into her confidence with a promise of first names, and implicit offer of friendship, but she held back from that fatal mistake, relying instead in the open honesty of her blue-eyed gaze. 'It must have been a terrible shock for you.'

'Of course. It's always a shock when we lose a friend.' Karen put the cup down, on safe ground. 'Eden's End is termed a care home, and we try to make it as much like a home as possible for our residents. Good food. Local ingredients. An informal atmosphere, all very relaxed. That's why it's such a shock when anyone dies. Violet was very popular.' A flush crept above her stiff collar, the sign not so much of a liar but of someone who was exaggerating, spinning the story to her own advantage. 'I was very fond of her.'

'I'm sure you were. And obviously all the other staff and residents—'

'We were all very fond of her. She was very forceful, but that was her manner. Everyone was used to it. She meant no harm.'

'It's good she wasn't lonely. Did she have many visitors?'

'Not many. She never married, as far as I'm aware, and had no children. I suspect she'd outlived most of her friends. It happens. But her niece was good to her. She came every day. Monica Roland.' Karen's shoulders shifted into a confrontational set at the name, only to relax again when she turned her attention back to Ashleigh. 'She was with her on the day she died. She left about fifteen minutes before Klemmie found her.'

Becca, Jude remembered, had thought there was still warmth in Violet's body. He must go back and check against the time of death in the pathologist's report, and against the nurse's evidence. If Becca was correct, the window for the murder was narrow and the number of potential culprits would surely narrow with it.

'How long had Dr Ross been in Eden's End?'

'Two years all but a month. She arrived just after I did. As new arrivals together, we were naturally close. She came here expecting to see out her days in comfort and security, and that's what we were able to do for her.' A sniff, and Karen mined the pockets of her huge black skirt for a handkerchief. 'Until the end. Or so you say.'

'Thank you so much.' Ashleigh threw Jude an inquiring look and acted upon the nod he gave her in return. 'We won't distress you any longer, Ms Grant. I'm sure you're very busy. But I'd like to go down and see Dr Ross's room, now. And perhaps while we're down there you could draw us up a list of everybody who was, or who could have been, in the room on Friday afternoon.'

6

'Your CSI did say she'd try and get away as soon as possible, so Colin and Marjorie can come back,' Karen appealed to Jude, as she led him and Ashleigh down the stairs. Despite the complication of the decorators in the lounge, she'd managed to relocate the two residents remaining on Eden's End's superior floor to give Tammy a clear run without attracting too much attention. 'Our residents really don't like their routines being upset, but obviously we didn't want them unsettled by what's going on, either. And talk spreads around this place. The less they know about the details, the better for everyone.'

Karen was nervous. It wasn't her words that gave her away but the unintentional mannerisms that shadowed them – the pauses for snatched breaths, the moments when she blinked for too long between phrases like someone praying for unlikely intervention, the incessant fidgeting with her string of heavy jet beads. Jude hurried to reassure her. 'Tammy will be very quick and very thorough. You can be sure of that. She and her colleagues are very discreet.'

'Good. Here you are.' Karen hovered on the edge of the hallway. 'That's Violet's room, there. As you can see.' She gestured to an open door, where two figures in forensic suits were busy placing items of clothing in bags.

Jude nodded, taking in the layout. Violet's door, like the one to the left of it and the two on the adjacent wall to the right, bore a metal nameplate engraved in copperplate. There were other doors, without nameplates. 'Where do these go?'

'These two are cupboards. One's for towels and linen and the other is for cleaning things. The third one is a fire door. It leads to a corridor with access to the side of the building.'

'That door's kept locked?'

'Not locked, as such, because of fire regulations, but it has to be secure. The staff all have fobs they can swipe to let them in and out. Some of our residents' regular visitors have them, too.' She opened the door as she spoke.

Jude took a look down the dark, narrow corridor, a possible route of access and escape for an outside killer. A winter breeze crept under the door, stirring a leaf on the mat. 'Did Dr Ross's niece have one?'

'Yes. Monica had one, though she never used this door. She always came in through the front, like all visitors do. They have to sign in. But one fob works for all the external doors. It's easier for the staff that way.'

'Is the door used much?'

'Quite a lot. It's a quick route out to the bins. And the staff sometimes nip out there for a cigarette break. I don't like them to smoke at the front of the house.'

Tammy would look, of course, but any evidence that had been left on Friday evening would almost certainly be lost. Jude turned back to Violet's room. Hearing their voices,

Tammy had turned and stepped out into the lobby, leaving her companion inside. 'Hey, Jude.' She pulled down her mask and grinned at him, knowing he found the joke tired and old. 'Have you come for a look around?'

'We won't come in. I just wanted to get an idea of the lie of the land.' But Jude advanced as far as the threshold and took a look inside. Violet must have been privileged or rich or both, because she'd occupied what might easily have been the best room in the building. It had one of the bay windows he'd so admired from the front, with heavy satin curtains in a rich shade of red, framing the breathtaking view of distant fells. Apart from the state-of-the-art hospital-style bed, the furniture was old, massive and mismatched, probably Violet's own – a huge wardrobe with warped doors, a chest of drawers beside the bed, a table whose polished top bore the circular stains of many a glass of gin. The big, wing-backed chair that stood near the window must be the one in which Violet had died. Tammy's colleague was busy taping away at its worn arms in search of clues. 'How much longer will you be?'

'We'll be clear in an hour or so. Less, with luck.'

'Brilliant.' He smiled at her, before turning back to Karen. 'Thanks, Ms Grant. We'll get the investigators out of your way as soon as possible, but I'm afraid I won't be releasing the room immediately. I'd like to keep it locked and sealed for the time being.'

'At least you'll be able to get your other residents back to their rooms without any more distress.' Ashleigh, too, was casting an eye over the crime scene and its surroundings.

Karen twisted her fingers together. 'I've had Monica on the phone already this morning, wanting to know when she can collect her aunt's things. She's very keen to get everything cleared out and all the paperwork done. There's the funeral, too. Some people like to get to closure as quickly as possible.' She shook her head, as though Monica Roland's enthusiasm for moving on was too great for human decency to bear. 'I suppose I understand that.'

'I can't promise anything, except that we'll let you know as soon as possible.'

Karen was still staring into Violet's room with a layman's fascination. Keen for a word with Tammy, Jude headed off this unwanted interest with a repeat of his earlier request. 'I wonder if you could do me a favour while we're down here? Could you run up to your office and put together a list of everybody who was in this area, or around this area, on Friday afternoon, and their contact details if you have them?'

She drew her attention from the room. 'Of course. I'll go and do that now. And you can speak to them whenever you want. Most of them are somewhere around just now. I asked Becca to come along this afternoon in case you wanted to speak to her. She's up in the dining room.'

It was Becca's day off. Quite how he knew that, Jude wasn't sure. It was a detail that stuck in his head from something his mother had said, or something he remembered. To fortify himself against the past, he turned and smiled at Ashleigh, allowing his soul to be warmed by those intense blue eyes, and then got himself back to duty. 'Thanks. We can speak to her when we've finished here.'

'I'll go and tell her.' With some reluctance, Karen turned her back on what was going on and disappeared up the stairs.

Jude turned back to business. 'So, Tammy. Found anything?'

Stepping out of the room again, she regarded him, thoughtfully. 'No. I didn't expect anything. Did you?'

'They've cleaned the place?'

'I'll say they have. There's no way anyone's going to catch the management out on their health and hygiene procedures. I've never seen a carpet so clean. There's the odd hair, of course, and the odd fibre from clothing. But even if there was more, I can't help thinking it won't help you. There will be too many people who have good reason to be in and out of here.'

'We'll get a list of them. Maybe what you find will throw up someone who shouldn't have been in here.' But that wouldn't necessarily solve the problem. There was every chance the killer had a perfect right and a very good reason to have been in Violet's room.

Very close beside him, Ashleigh peered over his shoulder and into the room. There was a faint smell of cleaning fluid. 'Do you think someone cleaned it particularly thoroughly to hide the evidence?'

Tammy shrugged. 'You guys are the detectives. I'm just the hired help.' But it was a running joke, and she grinned at them as she spoke. 'I've taken samples from the cushions and the pillows so we'll soon see if the lab can match them up with the fibres in the lungs.'

'What about her personal belongings?' Jude assessed the furniture. 'Was there anything unusual there?'

'Not on first sight. I'll get an inventory. I've taken dabs from the furniture and we might get something from that.

Come down and have a look through it, when we've finished. I won't be that long.'

'Becca.'

Becca was spending half of her precious day off loitering in the Eden's End dining room, sitting in silence with a cup of coffee while the world went on around her and she waited to speak to whichever underling Jude had dispatched to conduct the preliminary interviews. Guilt seared through her as she remembered the conversation she'd overheard between two of the carers, speculating about what had happened and who was to blame. *They must think someone killed her. Nobody here would do that. But someone might have made a mistake.*

When Ellie, the obvious candidate for that mistake, had come past, her expression so ferociously defensive no-one had dared canvass her opinion, Becca had ducked her head, cursing herself for allowing Jude and his irresponsibly inflexible conscience to railroad her into reporting the death as abnormal. The post-mortem must have uncovered something, and of course that should be followed up, but she wished she'd had the strength of mind to leave it to someone else, or at the very least to take the decision for herself without consulting him. Because now he knew, and the last thing you should ever do with Jude was show him a sign of your weakness.

'Becca.'

The voice came again, so quiet the first time that she'd barely heard it but now accompanied by a timid yet firm tug at the sleeve of her jumper. She pushed the coffee away and turned to find Klemmie at her shoulder, peering at her with myopic eyes. 'Sorry, I was miles away. Are you all right?'

'I'm still so upset about Violet. Did you know the police are here? They're looking in her room.'

'Yes. So Karen said.'

'Karen. Pfft.' For a moment Klemmie forgot her concerns and gave way to contempt. 'She's no use. Too busy chasing her heels. What we say in Poland.' Klemmie tapped her head with a finger and rolled her eyes. 'I don't know what you say. She doesn't know what she's doing. But the girls are saying someone must have killed Violet.'

Becca sighed. By reporting the incident, she'd put herself in a position where she must either live as a liar or be known as a telltale. She chose the former. 'I've no idea what it's about. Karen asked me if I could come in and talk to the police about something. I thought there must have been a break-in. Though if there was, I don't know why they'd want to talk to me.'

'They have people in white suits down there.'

'Perhaps someone broke in and stole her things. After she'd died.'

Klemmie slid into the seat beside Becca and regarded her unhappily, eyes wide but this time, Becca thought, brimming with fear rather than grief or surprise. 'I don't know what to do.'

'What about?' There was a plate of cupcakes in the middle of the table, feather-light but sloppily iced. Quite what message that gave about Karen's state of mind, Becca couldn't work out, but it was a safe bet she'd got up early to make them and that therefore she hadn't slept well. She didn't need one, but what the hell? It was her day off and there wasn't much else to cheer her up. 'Here. Have a cupcake and tell me all about it.'

Shaking her head over the cupcake, Klemmie leaned in. 'I can trust you, can't I?'

Oh God, Becca said to herself with a sigh, *not another secret*. Maybe she deserved it, having offloaded a secret of her own onto Jude just days before, but he was so much better equipped to deal with these things than she was. 'Of course you can. What's the matter?'

If possible, Klemmie leaned in even further, so that a wisp of her long hair settled on the shoulder of Becca's jumper. 'I haven't done anything.'

Fear crawled over Becca's skin. Surely she wasn't about to hear a confession? 'What haven't you done?'

'You know I liked Violet. We were friends. But she gave me a present. Last week.'

'What sort of a present?'

'Only a brooch. A small thing. On Saturday her niece was looking for it. I heard her telling Karen it was missing. We aren't really supposed to take gifts, but I didn't think it would matter. It was just a small thing. She said it wasn't worth much, but the niece told Karen it was valuable, and she thought someone here had stolen it. And now the police are here.'

Becca sat back. This, at least, was something she could offer instant advice on. 'You probably shouldn't have taken it, at least without asking Karen if it was okay. But if that's what happened the best thing is for you to tell the police about it when they talk to you.'

'Why will they want to talk to me?' The woman shivered a little. 'I didn't hurt her.'

'No, but you found her. They need to talk to everyone, to find out what happened. You really mustn't be afraid of the police. They're not trying to pin this on anyone who didn't do it.' The one thing she could still say in Jude's favour, assuming he was the investigating officer, was that his conscience was as straight as a Roman road, never deviating from the direction of the truth, no matter how difficult the route. 'I expect that's why they want to talk to me.'

'But they'll think I stole the brooch.'

'Not if you tell them about it straight away. Don't wait for them to ask.' Poor Klemmie. It was astonishing, the kind of pickle some people managed to get themselves into, but she believed the woman had a good heart and an honest one.

Seeing Karen appearing at the door of the canteen, Becca shook her head at Klemmie and raised a finger to her lips, ending the conversation. And – dammit – Karen wasn't on her own. She had Jude with her, and the pair of them had another woman marching purposefully behind them – about Becca's age, with a long blonde ponytail whose end curled into a sensuous ringlet, blue eyes that flicked across the room in a constant assessment of everything, a navy blue designer jacket that matched Jude's own as if they were in uniform but which flaunted a scarlet silk lining. 'These are the detectives now. I think,' she added, so as not to seem too knowing.

Karen homed in on them like a missile, even as Klemmie backed away towards the tea trolley, which she must have been in the process of circulating. 'These are the two ladies who found her. This is Klemmie Marcowics. She's one of our carers. And Becca Reid. Becca doesn't work here. She's a district nurse and she was visiting on Friday. I've asked her to come in because I know you'll need to speak to her and get any details you can from her.'

Becca, reluctantly, got to her feet and presented Jude with her most neutral expression.

'It's all right, Ms Grant.' Jude allowed himself to turn and face her, a smile lurking on his lips. 'I know all about Becca that I need to.'

There were things she'd shared with Jude that not even her mother knew. Under the interested gaze of his colleague, Becca's face flamed in embarrassment at the thought of some of them, and at some of the things he didn't know. She turned away from those grey eyes that saw too much and addressed herself to Karen, who could be trusted to see nothing. 'Jude's teasing me. He and I have known each other for years. We used to live in the same village. I can catch up with him at any time.'

'Oh! Becca, you should have said. Then I wouldn't have dragged you in.'

'It doesn't matter.' Becca turned away. 'If it's okay, Jude, perhaps you could talk to me about this some other time?'

'Of course. I know where to find you.'

She picked up her handbag and turned to leave, seeing his lips twitch as if he knew her thoughts. 'Jude Satterthwaite,' she hissed in his ear, as he drew rather closer to her than was necessary, 'if you dare say what you're thinking, I'll report you to your professional standards department!'

'Then I'll keep my thoughts to myself.' He turned back to Karen, the knowing smile still in place, so Becca's blush flamed even hotter and the blonde detective's expression grew even more interested. 'Thanks very much for being so helpful, Ms Grant. I don't suppose you can find us a space where we can talk to people in private when we're here? I'm conscious you still have a job to do, and we don't want to be too obvious.'

'Yes, of course. The meeting room where we were earlier. Would that suit?' Karen led Jude and his companion onwards and out of the dining room.

Becca, cooling down, turned around to see that Klemmie had fled, no doubt to brood on quite how she was going to get herself out of the mess she might be in. She picked up her coffee cup and returned it to the counter, where two of the staff were preparing for the evening meal.

'Policeman, eh?' one of them said to the other. 'I can't wait to be interviewed. He can take down my particulars any time.'

Affecting disinterest, Becca turned her back on the two of them, on Karen, on Jude and on his female colleague, on Klemmie and on the whole world of Eden's End, and headed away to enjoy what was left of her day off.

7

'Let me talk you through the mystery.' Like a teacher in front of his class, Jude stood poised in front of the whiteboard in the incident room, marker pen in hand, and looked around the table where his key team sat in expectation. For this case, expecting a lot of desk work, he'd drafted in a second DC, Aditi Desai, but the others present were the three on whom he'd come to depend. Doddsy, ever-reliable, had been only too pleased to offload the case he'd been working on to a colleague and step into this one as Jude's deputy. DC Chris Marshall, whose unerring instinct for tracking down information through the depths of the internet was matched only by his patience in approaching hours on end at the computer, sat with his laptop open, ready to field any question that came his way. And Ashleigh, the model of professionalism, sat with her blonde head bent over her notebook.

His gaze lingered on her a moment longer than on the others. 'I assume you've all had time at least to look at the stuff I forwarded to you, so I won't do any more than outline where we are. We can start by looking at who we know could have killed Violet Ross and who, out of those people, had a reason to do it.'

'And the people who could have done it but we don't yet know about.' Aditi was sitting forward with her chin on her hands, paying full attention.

'Those, too.' He turned to the board. Someone – young Chris, probably – had already been hard at work assembling information and the board was adorned with a photograph of Violet, a studio photo dated a couple of years previously. She had, he thought, an impish smile and was posing not unlike Aditi, with her hands clasped under her chin, staring into the camera and beyond into the soul of the viewer. Even in her late nineties she'd been unquestionably glamorous, her white hair perfectly coiffed and the fingers of both hands adorned with ruby and diamond rings that matched the choker around her neck. 'As yet I know very little about Violet, other than her age and that she was in good health. Can anyone add to that?'

'I can't find much. She seems to have lived pretty quietly.' Chris Marshall shook his fair head, apologetically.

Jude nodded, unsurprised. There was every chance Violet's private life would hold the clues to the mystery, but she belonged to a generation that kept their secrets, or at the very least maintained discretion about them. If there was confidential information to be had about her they wouldn't find it on the internet, but buried deep in the long-held memories of the living or the letters of the dead. 'I imagine we'll find out more from her friends and relatives, but this is what we do know. She was born in 1919, at the close of the First World War. She never married, or if she did, no-one knows about it. And if she did, there must be a record of it somewhere.' He nodded to Chris, who made a note. 'You've all read the post-mortem report. Did anything strike you about it?'

'She'd had a child.' Ashleigh thrust her chin forward, intrigued.

'Yes. I forget the exact phrase, but I think it tells us, specifically, that she gave birth. That means at least once, but possibly more than once, and it doesn't tell us whether the child, or children, lived or died. A son or daughter may still be alive. That's one mystery I'd like to sort out, and that means someone spending time looking at records of births.'

'A surviving child could be anywhere between about fifty and eighty years old.' Chris was scribbling away. Spotting the list of websites the constable was jotting down, Jude smiled at his enthusiasm. 'We can't rule out a child as the killer, can we? Especially if that child was given up for adoption at birth, or soon afterwards, and sees it as some form of rejection.'

'Yes. We don't know of anyone in the immediate area at that time who fits that age profile, unless it's one of her fellow residents. Theoretically that might include the woman who lived in the next room, who's seventy-four, but as she's currently in hospital, and has been for some weeks we can rule her out.'

He pointed a finger at a floor plan pinned to the board. 'Her room is here, next to Violet's. On the basis of what we've been told, there were a number of medical and care staff in that part of the building. The PM puts her death at roughly between two and five on Saturday afternoon, but Violet seems to have been found almost immediately after she died, which limits the number who could have done it.

She was found by a care worker, Klementyna Marcowics, known as Klemmie, who immediately called Becca Reid, a visiting district nurse, and then contacted the head nurse, Ellie Jack. Ellie's responsible for dispensing the patients' medication, and she was the one who pronounced Violet dead.'

'Do we have the toxicology results?' Doddsy said it with a cough, meant to attract Jude's attention, but Jude didn't meet his eye. Doddsy knew all about his relationship with Becca, but he didn't think any of the others did and he preferred not to discuss it unless he had to.

'Not yet. Let's look at the possible suspects. There's Klemmie, the carer who found her. There's Violet's niece, Monica Roland, who had left Eden's End shortly before Violet was found dead. She's listed in the paperwork as her next of kin. Aditi, I'd like you to chase up and see what the will says.' Because wills were often a source of valuable information when it came to motive.

'What you're saying,' Doddsy resumed, 'is our immediate key suspects are the carer, the head nurse and the niece.'

'They were the ones on the spot, though we don't yet know whether they had a motive. There may be others. The other two rooms on the floor were occupied by two people in their nineties. One is Colin Parsons, who is fit and mobile, though frail. He's also a possibility. The other is Marjorie Hodgson, who was having her leg dressed and categorically can't have done it.'

'What about the district nurse? Becca Reid?' This was Ashleigh. He wondered, fleetingly, what she'd make of Becca, but it was a waste of time speculating. It wouldn't be long before he found out. 'She was the second person on the scene. She was in the adjacent room, or claims to have been, at the time Violet died. She was alone with the body while Klemmie went to fetch the head nurse. What if Klemmie was wrong, and Violet wasn't dead when she found her?'

Internalising his sigh, Jude waited for Doddsy to help him out. His natural resistance to mixing his public and private lives meant he was careful never to mention Becca, but that train was about to hit the buffers.

Doddsy obliged. 'My understanding – I think I'm right in this, Jude? – is that Becca was the person who raised suspicions about the case in the first place.'

'That's correct.'

'I thought whistle-blower calls were anonymous.' Chris, this time. 'If you can get the number we can trace it. See if it did come from her phone.'

'There's no need.' Abandoning the whiteboard, Jude slid into the seat at the table. 'Okay, full disclosure. For those of you who don't know, I know Becca very well. We grew up together and we were in a relationship for eight years. It ended, but we still get on well.' Which was a lie, but at least they rubbed by, when they met, with reasonable civility. 'On Friday night Becca asked to meet me and told me she had suspicions about Violet's death. She asked for my advice and I advised her to report the matter, which she did. From my phone.' He forced a smile. 'That'll save you the effort of tracking the number, Chris.'

'Of course,' Ashleigh said, doodling a very complicated pattern on her notepad, 'that information has to remain confidential.'

'Yes. We'll be interviewing her like everyone else. She's a witness. I'd prefer to do that interview myself, though I'll take you with me, Ashleigh. You can correct any bias you detect.'

'I wasn't suggesting you're biased.' She turned that wide-eyed gaze on him. 'It's just as well she called you. Didn't anyone else suspect anything?'

'Not as far as I'm aware. And yes, if she hadn't reported it, Violet Ross would have been on her way to the crematorium by now.' Which was barely an exaggeration, because he'd picked up the impression the niece had been very keen to get the administration dealt with and her aunt dispatched. Too keen, perhaps? Or was she just efficient?

'Then we can rule Becca out.' Ashleigh was decisive about it. 'If she was guilty she'd have a hell of a brass neck, drawing attention to it when no-one else did, given there was no other reason for anyone to suspect. Did she spend much time up at the home?'

'I'm not that up on her movements. She's a district nurse. I believe she, or one of her colleagues, calls there a couple of times a week.'

'So if we rule out Becca,' said Doddsy, the faintest trace of relief shadowing his voice, as if he'd navigated his way out of potentially tricky waters, 'then who does that leave us with? If she was with the other resident—'

'Marjorie Hodgson.'

'Yes. Then Becca will vouch for the fact she didn't do it. There's the woman who found her, Klemmie. We know she must have had the chance, but we don't know how long she was alone with her. Then we have the head nurse. Where was she?'

Jude got up again, addressing himself once more to the floor plan of Eden's End on the board. 'In the residents' dining room, which the staff also use as a cafe on their breaks. It's at the back of the building. To get to these four rooms, which are in an extension to one side of the main building, you have to go up half a dozen stairs from reception, along a corridor with the dining room off it, and along again. She'd have been a matter of ten seconds away. We'll need to establish whether or not she had the opportunity to slip down to Violet's room unseen. She's a possibility. Then, of course, there's the niece. I'm interested to know more about her.'

'Karen said she'd left fifteen minutes before.' Ashleigh continued her doodling. 'But she had a key fob to get in and out of the building. The chances of her getting in the front unseen are nil. I noticed they have a CCTV camera up there. But Jude and I had a look round the back of the property and the gardens on our way out, and there's no CCTV camera on the door that goes out to the side.'

'Yes.' Jude marked a cross on the plan. 'Here's the side exit. There are quite a few cigarette ends here, so I imagine it's where the staff go out for a quick smoke. There's a hedge that borders the garden, and there's a public footpath down to the river on the other side of it.'

He drew a dotted line, down past the side door, from the road to the river – two clear escape routes. 'I haven't checked, because the CSI team hadn't been over the area when we were there, but from what I know of the path I think it's possible to get to the side door without being picked up on CCTV, as long as you approach it via the public footpath and through the gap in the hedge rather than walking across the front of the building. On that basis,

I think we have to leave Monica Roland in as a suspect, even though she'd already left.'

'Especially if she inherits.'

He nodded towards Chris, whose intervention this had been. 'Yes. And we need to look at Violet's belongings and see if there are any clues there. Aditi, you have charge of all those?'

'Yes.' She flipped up the lid of her laptop. 'All of her things are safely logged and secured, though obviously I've photographed everything. In actual fact she didn't have very much, so presumably most of her stuff was either disposed of or put into storage when she moved into Eden's End. What she had was mostly clothes, which we can probably return to her niece, if she wants them. She may prefer to let us hold on to them until this is all done. There's not much to learn from them, except they were all very expensive and some of them were hand-made.'

'I don't know for certain,' Jude said, 'but I think we can assume she was very well off. That makes me wonder if robbery could be the motive.'

'I don't think so, unless her attacker was interrupted. There was five hundred pounds cash in the drawer of her dresser. Her watch is expensive, too, and certainly worth stealing, if you've a mind. There were the shoes and the handbag. She had top-of-the-range cosmetics – she looked after herself. Maybe that's why she looked so good at her age. But it was the knick-knacks that really attracted my attention.'

'Go on.'

'The rings and necklace she's wearing in the photo. They were there. Real gems, I think. Given she treated them so casually, I'd say she was worth a lot of money.'

'Someone needs to find out where that money came from.' Mentally, Jude added that to his growing list of things to do. 'And the value of the estate. Anything else?'

'Yes. She kept a photograph.' A little self-consciously, as if she wasn't used to being the focus of everyone's attention, Aditi pushed her chair back and made her way to the board. 'It's funny how everybody keeps secrets. Here's a copy of it, blown up. The original was just a passport-sized snapshot, in a silver frame, and she kept it tucked away in the bottom of her bottom drawer.'

As if she was ashamed of it. Jude gazed at it in fascination. It showed a handsome young man in an RAF uniform, cap tilted to one side, a half-smile on his face. 'He's a bit of a heartbreaker by the look of it.'

'I'll say.' Aditi stuck the picture up on the board and returned to her seat.

Jude nodded. 'I know you should never assume anything, but there has to be a chance this is the father of her child or children. She certainly doesn't seem to have been keen to flaunt the picture of him, does she?'

'She doesn't. You'd think she'd keep the picture where she could see it.' Ashleigh stared intently at the photograph. 'Perhaps he was married. You can't see the hands, so we don't know if he was wearing a ring. And of course, morality was different in the war.'

'That's something else to ask her family about. It'll be interesting to know if they know anything about him. I'm going to guess not.' Jude resumed his seat once more. 'Okay. It's nearly time to head home. Tomorrow, we're going to be doing some serious interviewing of our witnesses. I think we'll do the key ones in pairs. That's the manager and the nurse, and the woman who found her. The niece, of course.' And Becca. 'Chris, you can go with Doddsy and Ashleigh will come to me. Aditi, I'm going to leave you in charge of finding out anything you can about Violet.' He shook his head. Because there was one question which really troubled him, and that was why anyone would want to kill an old woman when time, sooner rather than later, would do the job for them.

8

'This looks like an interesting one, doesn't it?' Brimming over with the boundless energy of youth, Chris Marshall hadn't yet been in the force long enough for cruel reality to blunt the edge of his enthusiasm.

'I'll say.' Sometimes it was hard to be objective. To Chris, a death like this – not shockingly violent and marking the end of a rich life well-lived rather than a promising one cut short – must seem like a puzzle to be unravelled rather than a dastardly crime to be solved. Ashleigh, who knew her weaknesses as well as she knew her strengths, felt otherwise and fought hard not to feel too much for Violet Ross, bedevilled, or so it appeared, by a secret love and a lost child. At best, love damaged you, and if you were unlucky, it destroyed you. She'd learned that from the bitterest experience, but there was nothing to be gained from feeling pain on behalf of someone already dead. 'The poor woman.'

'It's just as well Jude's district nurse spotted it. I wonder how many other people have been quietly shuffled off in their old folks' homes with everyone writing it off to old age.'

'Probably not as many as you might think.' Ashleigh, who liked Chris, smiled at him as they went down through reception together and towards the exit. 'There's no point. There are measures in place. And in this case I don't understand why anyone would want to kill her.'

'Inheritance is the usual one, but at that age all anyone needed to do is to wait until she shuffled off.'

'Exactly. She wouldn't need any help. Not at a hundred.'

'I suppose it depends how desperately you need the money, doesn't it?'

'Or you might be afraid she was going to change her will and leave it to someone else. A child, perhaps. But I suspect that's something we'll never know.' If she'd only been able to speak to Violet when she was alive, Ashleigh felt she might have teased that secret out of her, but there were still the living to question. In the morning, she and Jude would be talking to Monica Roland – and what an interesting interview that promised to be.

'There are plenty of other ways to find out who did it and why.' Chris came to a halt. He'd been in early enough to bag a parking spot close to the building and was reaping the rewards in not having to brave the elements to reach his car. 'See you tomorrow.'

'See you.' She pulled the collar of her coat up as she left him getting into his car, scurrying across the car park through the thin, chilling drizzle that was the best the weather had offered all day. November nights in the Eden Valley were brutal in their cold and in the numbing darkness, and she was a woman who loved light and sunshine. Winter was closing in and the burning Lakeland summer in which she'd arrived was a distant memory. She shivered and tugged her scarf tighter.

'Found a new man already, Ash? That was quick.'

'Jesus!' She jumped back, too wrapped up in her thoughts to have spotted the figure, lurking in the shadows. Her heart lurched, turned over, and then she took control. 'Scott! What the hell are you doing here?'

'You didn't answer my question.' He took a long stride towards her, swaying a little as he did so.

Fighting a rising tide of anxiety, Ashleigh swerved past him, flicking the key card to unlock the car, but he shouldered her aside and stepped between her and the passenger door. Her feet slithered on wet leaves and the stench of alcohol hit her as he stepped towards her.

'I was passing, so I came for a chat.' His speech was slurred. 'A wee talk about saving our marriage. Gonna give me a lift to your place?'

Regaining her composure, Ashleigh flicked the car door locked again, weighing up her options and finding them limited. If Scott got into the car, she'd never get him out again. He was irrational when drunk though he'd never been violent, but there was a first time for everything and this was the first time she'd seen him so angry. Apprehension fluttered in her veins. 'I hope you didn't drive here.'

'I'm not that stupid. I walked. But I knew you'd be pleased to see me. And now you can take me home.'

'I don't have anything to say to you.' She kept her tone crisp. The best option was to turn back to the office. Security would see him off the premises very smartly indeed, and if he were to react badly and cause trouble it wouldn't be her problem, but the best option wasn't always the comfortable one and too often in the past her head had failed to rule her heart. She owed Scott something, and helping him to get himself into trouble with the police would be an ignoble conclusion to their marriage. Besides, Jude's strictures against getting the personal and the business interwoven were a powerful reason to keep things separate.

'I'm not going anywhere until you talk to me.'

'Come on, Scott. This isn't getting us anywhere.' He wasn't going to make it easy for her. Should she offer him the compromise of a conversation? She decided against it. 'I'm not discussing anything with you when you've had a drink.'

'It's one drink. Are you calling me incapable?'

He'd had a lot more than that. 'Sorry. I don't want to talk to you.' She'd have to go back into the office after all, which wouldn't look good and would burden her with guilt.

Backing away for a couple of steps, with him shadowing her in real life when it was bad enough he did so in her memories, she came under the glare of the security light and into full view of the building as – she breathed in relief – Chris Marshall's car crawled along the wet car park and came to a halt beside them, window down. 'Is everything okay?'

She took a deep breath. *Sorry, Scott. I have to look after myself.* 'I wouldn't mind a bit of a hand, Chris. Thanks.'

'Sure. Just let me know the problem and we'll sort it.'

'There's no problem.' Belatedly, Scott seemed to realise his mistake. 'I was leaving. I came to talk to my wife.'

'Fine. But it doesn't look to me as if she wants to talk to you.'

'And what gives you the right—?'

'It's not about my rights.' Chris's tone was peaceable, but he made a move to get out of the car. 'It's about hers. Let's not make a big deal of this one, eh? Let's just not have any trouble.'

Jude watched the drama unfolding from the distance of the entrance for a moment or two before he decided to intervene. In fact his attentions had been a little less than pure, because he'd paused on the way to his car to indulge in the sheer pleasure of watching Ashleigh crossing the car park. Now matters had taken a different turn with a figure appearing by her car, her body language showing how unwelcome he was. Allowing himself a second to evaluate the situation before intervening, he judged it potentially serious and set off.

Chris – inevitably, because he suspected Chris of holding something of a torch for Ashleigh just as he himself was now forced to admit he did, and so they would both have been watching her – got there first. Still, there was no harm in additional numbers, even if his two junior officers had the situation under control. He reached the scene just as Chris swung the car door open. 'Is there a problem?'

Three faces turned to him. Ashleigh's showed relief, Chris kept his police-on-the-beat face of genial immovability, stopping in the act of getting out of his car, and the stranger, flicking a glance over him, to Chris, to Ashleigh and back again to him, seemed to have counted up the manpower and realised the inevitability of the situation. He took a stride backwards.

'No.' Ashleigh made light of it. 'This is Scott. He just came by to speak to me. But he's leaving.'

'That's right. He is.' Chris kept his smile, the one that dared Scott to take him on.

'Yeah.' Ashleigh's husband shuffled sideways under the streetlight, so that Jude saw his face for the first time. So that was the kind of man she'd chosen — baby-faced and blond, with a sheepish expression that could reinvent itself as a cheeky grin the instant circumstances required it. A man, now he came to see it, who looked not unlike Chris Marshall. 'I just wanted to arrange to talk to her. She hasn't been picking up my calls. I was worried. I thought there might be a problem.'

'You know I never take personal calls at work.' The first note of agitation crept into Ashleigh's voice.

'Yeah. Well. At least I know the number still works. I'll call you this evening. You won't be at work then.'

'Please don't. I'm busy.' She took the opportunity, stepped past him and opened the car door. 'I'll see you tomorrow, guys.' Sliding in, she closed the door and the unmistakable click as she locked it gave away her discomfort.

I'll follow her home, Chris mouthed, closing the door of his car. Jude, nodding at the wisdom of this, waited a moment until Ashleigh had pulled out of the parking space and Chris had pulled in behind her, and found himself once more picking up the pieces of someone else's problem.

'Okay.' The tail lights of Ashleigh's car disappeared and he turned back to confront Ashleigh's husband. 'I'm sorry, I don't know your name. Mr O'Halloran?'

'It's Kirby. She uses her maiden name.'

'Mr Kirby. Why don't I give you a lift back to wherever you're staying?' That way he'd make sure Scott went where he said he was going, and he'd be able to give Ashleigh the heads-up on where her ex was.

'You're okay, mate. It's not far. I can walk.'

'It's a foul night.' Jude tried to sound authoritative and, as he'd hoped, Ashleigh's almost-ex seemed to realise where he was and how many police officers might be within shouting distance, and fell into step beside him as he walked towards his car. 'Where are you staying?'

'Only at the Premier Inn.'

'Then I can have you there in five minutes.' Jude saw the man into the car and went round to the driver's door and started the engine, leaving him in peace for a couple of minutes while he negotiated the exit from the car park and made his way onto the main road. It would have been easier to leave Scott to walk, and it might have helped sober him up, but it would have left the matter hanging and that was never Jude's way. 'Are you staying here long?'

He sensed the sideways look without seeing it, guessed his passenger was trying to suss out who he was, why he was asking and how much to tell him. 'No. I came to speak to my wife, but as she doesn't want to talk to me it looks like I'll have to leave without having the conversation, doesn't it?'

'Your marriage is none of my business, but I'm going to advise you against trying to contact her if she doesn't want you to.'

'Right.'

Jude snatched a sideways glance in his turn and saw that Scott's face was surly and at odds with his apparent concession. He'd warn security to keep an eye out for this man. 'It's probably not a good idea to turn up at her office, either.'

'Good to see she's got so many men looking out for her interests.' They were approaching the roundabout that led to the Premier Inn, now. Scott's hands hovered over the seatbelt, as if he were keen to unsnap it but afraid of being hauled up on a technicality. 'Not that that's unusual. She's never short of a knight in shining armour. They seem to think she can't look after herself. The damsel in distress routine. She does it well. Don't fall for it.'

Jude drove on to the roundabout.

'Who are you anyway?' his passenger pursued. 'Her boss?'

'Yes.'

'She's made a good impression on you, then?' It was almost a leer.

'She's a highly competent police officer and a model professional.' Taking refuge in stiffness, Jude brought the car to a halt outside the hotel. 'Here we are.'

'Did she ever tell you why she applied for a transfer?' Scott clicked the seatbelt free, opening the door so that a blast of icy air blew in.

He should kick the man out of the car and spare himself, but he didn't. 'I don't interfere in my staff's private lives.'

'Maybe you should. Especially if you're married. She had an affair with her last boss. Warn your wife.' At last, Scott jumped out, as if afraid of the consequences of that parting shot, then stumbled across to the hotel and inside.

Jude watched him go, with narrowed eyes. He didn't need to know anything about Ashleigh's private life. He was her boss and the relationship ought to begin and end there. He should have turfed Scott Kirby out into the rain without waiting even for that piece of gossip, that shard of a warning, but he hadn't, because the part of him that was a man had trumped the part of him that was a professional. He wanted to know everything anyone could tell him about Ashleigh O'Halloran and the rest of it – the part so intangible it could be shared only between Ashleigh and himself – was something he desperately wanted to find out.

'Everything okay?'

You'd think she couldn't look after herself, needed someone – a man, inevitably – to ride shotgun for her. Despite her irritation Ashleigh was relieved to hear Jude's voice. 'You too, eh? I've just had Chris on the phone, checking Scott didn't turn up on my doorstep.' She tried to evaluate his tone, but it was impenetrably neutral. A pity.

'I take it he made sure you got home safely?'

'He did, and it was very kind of the two of you to be such gentlemen, but actually I didn't need it.'

'Of course not. I had quite a chat with your man. It's probably as well he wasn't staying very far away, or he'd have had time to tell me all sorts of things you'd probably prefer me not to know.'

Yes. Scott was like that. The tiniest chill ran along Ashleigh's spine at the kind of spin her husband, so lacking in self-awareness and so over-endowed with self-pity, would put upon the breakdown of their relationship if he were given the chance. The last thing she needed was Jude thinking badly of her. Professionally, of course. 'Don't take him on trust. I'm still very fond of him, and he didn't show himself at his best tonight, but he's never very reliable.'

'I can tell. However, he did make a point of telling me he accepts you don't want to speak to him and so he's leaving tomorrow. Do you reckon that's true?'

Who knew? 'It's true I don't want to speak to him. As for whether or not he goes, I expect we'll find out soon enough.'

'Right. Well if he gives you any trouble at all, make sure you call someone, whether you're in work or out of it. I'm only ten minutes away. Is someone with you right now?'

Lisa, whose earthy directness was always reassuring, was away in Carlisle, giving a talk about the Romans to a troop of Girl Guides, but she wouldn't be late back. 'Yes. And I promise I won't answer the door to anyone.' Even as she faked a laugh to make light of the situation, anger flared up within her. How dared Scott challenge her in a life she'd set out to build without him, leave her feeling vulnerable in her new home? It had been hard enough to make the break. Did he think he could change her mind, when all he'd done was prove she'd been wrong to marry him and right to let him go?

'Fine. And to be on the safe side, I'll pick you up tomorrow. We'll be doing the interviews together and we'll be out all day, so you won't need your car. I'll be round at half eight.'

'Yes, sir.' Out of the office she could be flippant with him. It had taken her two months to understand his sense of humour, and if his relationship had ended with a fraction of the bitterness hers had done, then it was no wonder he approached her with such caution. 'No, sir. Three bags full, sir.' And she was relieved to hear him laugh as he put down the phone.

When Chris had rung, his call to be swiftly followed by Jude's own, she'd been sitting at the table in the living room, telling the tarot cards. Not that it meant anything. The cards were her guilty pleasure, just as *Location Location Location* with a side serving of red wine on a work night was Lisa's. Their sole function was to help her relax. *Cheaper than shopping*, she justified it to herself, looking down at the cards laid out in a horseshoe in front of her, three face up and two face down. The first three represented the present, the past and the future. The clues to their significance were hidden in the two she'd yet to reveal.

Her right hand hovered for a moment above the fourth card. It was just as well she wasn't serious about the reading, because if she had been it would be a mistake to carry on. Scott's arrival had unsettled her and she'd intended to use the cards to channel some kind of calm, but there was no serenity to be had when his image kept creeping into her mind. That way, the interpretation of the cards became self-fulfilling. She'd loved him, and even though she'd stayed true to herself and what she knew was best for her, a worm of guilt ate away at her conscience.

And that self-fulfilment was happening. The first three cards she'd turned up – the Queen and Page of Cups and the Five of Wands, all reversed – hinted at discord and disharmony, betrayal and infidelity. The latter in particular caused her to frown, with its insinuations about a wrong decision. Which one was that? Loving Scott, or leaving him?

No. Once more she reminded herself that leaving Scott was no mistake. 'But it would be nice,' she informed the cards light-heartedly, as she turned over the next one, 'if you could give me a bit of positivity.'

It was the High Priestess. She smiled down at it. That was more like it, an instruction to trust her intuition. She always did, and it rarely let her down.

If only she'd trusted her intuition when it came to Scott, instead of falling for his charm and letting herself love him. Then she wouldn't be going through the pain of unpicking the effort she'd invested in him, long after she should have been free.

She never turned over the final card, because Lisa's key in the lock and her flatmate's cheery 'hello!' from the hallway prompted her to shuffle them all away. Lisa loved the cards, but she saw them as frivolous, as Ashleigh's party trick. When a reading wasn't going well, the worst thing to do was to bring in a sceptical outsider to laugh at its ignominious end.

'Come on through!' she called, thrusting the cards into their pack without ceremony and without respect, and hiding them down the side of the sofa cushion. Lisa would be proud of her and how easily she'd sent Scott on his way. 'Let me tell you all about the excitement of my day…'

9

'I can't stop thinking about this awful, awful thing. Constantly. I mean constantly. I've been lying awake at night and fretting about it. Not just about how it affects the other residents of our community, though of course that troubles me, too, and I'm the one who has to deal with it. But poor Violet. I can't believe that somehow we lost Violet. On my watch.'

Karen, who did, indeed, look as if she hadn't slept since the first suggestion of a suspicious death, paused for breath and sat back in her chair, the inevitable biscuit crushed between her fingers and spitting crumbs onto the table. The layer of make-up she'd plastered over her face failed to mask either her pallor or the dark rings under her eyes, and the smile she'd pasted on to welcome the police team into Eden's End had disappeared the moment she'd dispatched Doddsy and Chris to speak to Klemmie and guided Jude and Ashleigh into her office.

'It can't be easy for you.' Jude sat back a little. An interview with someone as on-edge as Karen had to be handled with care. Even on their first acquaintance, before the reality of the situation had had time to sink in and drag her down into its dark depths, he'd sensed a nervousness and excitability about her that would make her an unreliable witness. In the hours since, all the signs were that those emotions had intensified.

'No. It's anything but. I've the residents to think of. And their relatives. I wish I could lock the doors and keep them all out. The questions!' She rolled her eyes. 'Of course I welcome your investigation, and of course I'll do whatever I can to help.'

Taking advantage of the fact that Karen, as everyone seemed to do, had focussed her attention entirely on Ashleigh, Jude glanced down at the list of questions they'd prepared. Sometimes there was value in keeping a witness to the point and sometimes there was more to be gained from letting them ramble on. In his experience, if someone was lying they were as likely to catch themselves in a noose of their own making as they were to be caught out by a routine question from a detective.

'Yes?' He guessed Ashleigh, armed with the same list of questions, was thinking the same way.

Karen drew a deep breath and plucked at the sagging collar of her blouse. She wasn't in black, now, as if she'd worn it all and her mourning garb was in the wash, so she'd taken shapeless refuge in ill-matched shades of grey and brown, the closest she could manage to respect for the dead. 'It's obvious to me what happened. There must have been a mistake.'

The act of violence perpetrated on Violet Ross could hardly be described as a mistake, but they hadn't gone public with anything other than *unexplained death*. Knowing the way people's minds worked he'd have thought the sight of a police forensic team would have set the most restrained mind working along the theme of murder. It appeared not, unless Karen was in denial, laying the ground for her own innocence or desperate to persuade herself of a happier alternative. It wouldn't be the first time that had happened, nor the first time a witness had tried to be too smart.

'Our job is to investigate all possibilities. I'm sure you understand that.' Ashleigh engaged the manager face to face. 'What sort of a mistake do you think it could be?'

'It's obvious, isn't it? Ellie had been round with the drugs about half an hour before. She must have given Violet someone else's drugs.'

'Forgive me. I don't have all my notes.' Ashleigh was taking the gloves off, though Karen didn't seem to realise it. 'I'll have to ask Mrs Jack for the medical reports. But perhaps you can help. Did Dr Ross have an underlying medical condition? I didn't think she did.'

'I'm not a medical person. I don't think she did, nothing serious, anyway. She was frail but fit. She had arthritis. She got drugs for that. Methotrexate I think it is, once a week. I mean, she wasn't due to have it on Friday. But Ellie was very busy. Maybe she gave her a second dose, or something else.'

Jude stifled a smile, convinced Ashleigh wanted to give him a knowing look, a roll of the eyes. All the nice talk, the all-friends-together Karen had put up at the first meeting had been blown away. She must have looked in the mirror and seen a suspect, and now she was preparing to throw her head nurse under the bus to protect herself. Well, the woman might or might not have done it, but the post-mortem results told them if she had it hadn't been through an overdose of an arthritis drug. 'Why do you think Ellie might have made that mistake, Ms Grant?'

'She's very young to have that position. Sometimes she was very rushed, and not always as conscientious as she should be, if you ask me, although the doctors have never come back to me with any complaints about her. Not yet, at least.'

Ellie, Jude remembered, had been the one who'd been so adamant no post-mortem was necessary. How significant was that? He tapped a forefinger on his pad. 'We have a copy of the drugs book. I take it a doctor checks that regularly?'

'Yes, every week, and reconciles it against our stocks of drugs. But maybe nobody checked it last week. Or maybe she filled it in wrongly. Or she thought she'd forgotten to give them to her and gave them again. Something like that.'

'Are you alleging professional malpractice? That's a serious accusation.'

'Oh, no. Never. You mustn't think that. But anyone can make a mistake. And what about Becca? Those NHS nurses are always under such pressure. I know you're a friend of hers, Chief Inspector, but you can't account for people making mistakes—'

'Miss Reid doesn't dispense drugs, though.' Ashleigh allowed herself to sound severe and Jude, spared from having to compromise himself by defending Becca against a mistake she couldn't have made, was grateful for that. 'Surely you know that. Anyway, I believe she was in with Mrs Hodgson all that time.'

'Well, so she says. But Marjorie can get confused about time, even more than the rest of us. She's mostly sharp, but I'm not sure I'd say she was very reliable.'

'And what about yourself? Obviously you can confirm where you were at the time.'

'Oh... oh, of course. So I can.' The woman almost sagged with relief. 'I was on the phone. That's what I was doing. Ask Becca. I was on the phone when she came up from Marjorie's room, and then she went back down to get her car key. I was still on the phone when she came back to say poor Violet had passed away. It was some sales call, and I just couldn't get rid of them. So obviously I couldn't—' She ground to a halt. 'I'm sorry, Sergeant. When you came yesterday, did you say she'd been suffocated? Or am I making that up?'

'I don't believe we mentioned a cause of death.' Ashleigh's expression gave away no surprise at Karen's assumption.

The manager shivered. 'Suffocation would be so easy. I can tell you do think it was murder. Could she have fallen asleep with her face in the cushion?'

'We don't know what it was. That's what we're trying to find out. It's officially unexplained.'

'But surely—' Karen turned to Jude for a second opinion.

'As Sergeant O'Halloran said, we consider the death unexplained.'

'Yes. And as part of our investigation we're looking to find out information about Dr Ross.' Ashleigh chewed the end of her pen. 'Did you get on with her?'

'Oh, yes.'

'Did everybody?'

'Oh, yes. Yes, of course.' Karen reached out for another biscuit. The plate had been full when they started and Jude and Ashleigh had taken a polite single cookie apiece, but now there was nothing left but a sorry assembly of chocolate chips and a cascade of brown crumbs down Karen's chins and into her cleavage. 'Actually, no. Maybe not everyone. She could be very caustic.'

'About anyone in particular?'

'About everyone. It's an age thing, Sergeant. It'll come to us all. That didn't mean she didn't like people. Everybody knew it and nobody took it the wrong way. Sometimes she could be quite unpleasant, but it was never intentional.'

And yet the least likely people could react badly to the slightest insult. 'And anyone in particular?' Jude echoed the question Karen hadn't answered.

'I don't know where to start. She had something to say about everyone. She complained about Colin snoring, and his accent irritated her. She said it was common. She thought Marjorie was stupid. Ellie put her back up her because she was always rushed and never had time to be interested in anyone else's business. She was always on at me because I never spent enough time with her, even though I have the home to run. She seemed to think she paid all that money to have me as a companion whenever she was bored.' She took a deep breath. 'Old people can be as challenging as they're rewarding. Of course I wouldn't change my job, but it isn't always easy.'

She breathed, heavily, while Ashleigh continued to gaze at her. 'It must be tough for you. Do you have an assistant?'

'No. We only have a small staff. I try to please everyone. It's my job. But there are many people all wanting a piece of my time. I have to take a hard line. I wouldn't be surprised if Violet complained to head office about me. She threatened to get me into trouble, more than once.'

Jude smiled. Karen must have decided her alibi was sound

and so she could afford to be honest, or else she'd allowed Ashleigh's extraordinary gift for interviewing to hypnotise her into honesty. 'Obviously she didn't succeed.'

'I'm sure my bosses hear that kind of thing all the time. They'll have ignored it. We're one of a chain, you know. And Violet was unkind about Becca, even though she always made a point of stopping to talk to her, even when she didn't have time. In one breath she'd be telling her she'd never get a man if she didn't stop being so fussy, and in the next it was all about better having no man than the wrong one. She thought it was a woman's duty to have a husband, but she herself never married. I don't know whether that was just another example of her getting older, or whether she was bitter about the way life treated her.'

'Did anyone else get on the wrong side of her?'

'She had bad words to say to everyone, except perhaps Klemmie.'

'They got on well?' Ashleigh, seated next to Jude, pushed back her chair and uncrossed her legs, stretching them out beneath the table.

'I never quite understood that one. I was always a little bit worried, if I'm honest. She seemed quite devoted to the woman, and Klemmie's just a carer. A good one – don't get me wrong – but just a carer. And you have to be so careful these days that there's no undue influence exerted. I had to speak to Violet a couple of times, but she never took it well.' She looked at the empty plate, and sighed. 'Such a... self-confident woman. Always had to be right. I don't know what it was with Klemmie but Violet treated her better than she did her niece.'

'Did you ever speak to Klemmie about it?'

'No.' Karen got up and opened the window, looking at the empty plate with regret. 'I daresay that'll count against me at some point. What's the next question?'

'Dr Ross wasn't married, you say.' Ashleigh, looking down at her pad, went back to the original plan now Karen's random musings seemed to be over. 'Tell me what you know about her. You must have learned a lot. She seems to have been keen to confide in you.'

'Of course she did, as much as she did in anyone. But she was never free with her personal information. She told us all so much and no more. Mostly she gave us her opinion. I got the impression her past wasn't something she particularly wanted to talk about. A lot can happen in a hundred years, and she did live through the war. I always had the impression there was something missing in her life.'

'Such as?'

Karen shrugged. 'A husband, at a guess. Violet always had to have someone to order about.'

This tied in well enough with the interpretation suggested by the photograph Violet had kept hidden, but the very fact she'd hidden it implied she wouldn't have shared any deep secrets with Karen. Jude tapped his pad with his pen, notifying Ashleigh that it was time to get off the speculation and on to the facts, and picked up the questioning. 'Can I ask you something else? It goes without saying that Dr Ross was very well off. Do you know where her money came from?'

'I can't say for certain. Monica implied there was family money, and that Violet had made a number of wise investments along the way. Or lucky, one or the other.'

'How did she pay her fees? Monthly?'

'Yearly in advance, which isn't how we'd normally do it, but it was the way she liked. She said she liked to be sure she'd always have somewhere to stay. Say what you like about Violet – she never assumed she was going to die. The second year was almost up. I was going to talk to her about it. How callous, but I'll have to put together her bill.' She snatched at her pen and wrote something down. 'I think she realised investments on a regular basis. Her niece would know.'

Two years' care at Eden's End would cost a substantial amount. Jude did some swift calculations based on what he knew of the home's charges and the sum he came up with was astronomical. It would definitely be worth investigating Violet's finances. 'Thanks very much, Ms Grant. I appreciate you've got a lot to do, so we won't take up any more of your time, though we'll almost certainly want to talk to you again.' He pushed back his chair and got to his feet.

Ashleigh, following suit, made a point of softening the leave-taking. Not as hardened to the suffering of witnesses as he was – he'd learned that the ones who seemed the most upset could often turn out to be the villains – she seemed touched by Karen Grant's air of chaotic distress. 'I did enjoy the cookies. Thank you so much.' She reached out a hand to shake Karen's.

'Thank you. And of course, if there's anything you need...' The woman sighed. 'I really hope we don't upset any of our residents. I suppose you'll want to talk to them.'

'I'd certainly like to talk to Mrs Hodgson and Mr Parsons.'

'Oh dear. I suppose you must. Shall we do it now? If they're going to be upset, we might as well get it over with.'

'So that was interesting.' Ashleigh, getting into the car, frowned back at the care home. 'To start with I had the impression Violet was a lovely old lady who was friends with everyone, but that clearly wasn't the case.'

'No.' Jude started the engine and pulled away from the gravelled area in front of the building. 'So far we've spoken to three people and not one of them has a good word to say for her. If you discount Karen's singing from the corporate hymn sheet when she wasn't sure of her own alibi, of course.'

As she clipped her seatbelt into place, Ashleigh allowed her gaze to linger a moment longer than was professionally appropriate on Jude's fingers, curled around the gear stick. 'Marjorie Hodgson didn't like her, did she?'

'She didn't. Nor did old Mr Parsons.'

Like so many people, Colin Parsons had taken to Ashleigh, plaintively bemoaning his lot, mistaking her for his granddaughter and dismissing Violet's character with an old man's trenchancy. 'What was it he said? *Like her? God, no.*'

'*Too much like me wife!*' Jude finished, in perfect mimicry, and they laughed.

'On a serious note. She wasn't popular.'

'No, though I'll need a lot of convincing that either of those two old people is capable of suffocating her, so their dislike probably isn't relevant. But it's interesting she may have complained about Karen. That bears checking out.'

Ashleigh thought it through. There was definitely something about Karen that went above and beyond grief at the loss of a resident. She'd almost looked hunted. Finding out what lay behind would be interesting. And she'd not only quickly jumped to the conclusion Violet's death was deliberate but had come to the correct view as to the cause. 'You wouldn't think a vexatious complaint would cause her that much trouble, would you? Not if the complaints were unreasonable, which is what she implied.'

'It depends on what the nature of the complaint actually was, and how many previous complaints have been made. She certainly wanted us to think Violet made unreasonable complaints about everyone.'

Ashleigh inspected a chip in a fingernail. 'What was it she said about Becca? That she wouldn't get a man if she didn't stop being so fussy?'

It was out of her mouth before she thought about it, but once it was out, she held back on the apology, holding her breath for Jude's response, but he laughed. 'There's something in that.'

'Is she fussy?' she asked, out of curiosity. 'Or was that just Violet trying to stir?'

'Just because Becca got rid of me doesn't make her fussy. It just means she didn't see it as being a long-term relationship. Violet also said she'd be better with no man than the wrong one. That's probably sounder advice.'

Jude was always so uptight. His resistance to mixing work and personal life was rooted, Ashleigh was sure, in some kind of denial, but she sensed whatever upset him – maybe the humiliation of rejection, maybe even the fact he still held a candle for Becca – was fading. She stole a glance at his profile, sure he knew she was doing so. 'Did you think it was long term?'

'I think I probably thought it was for ever, but it wasn't. I'm over it.'

She turned her attention to the scenery as they skirted the southern edge of Penrith and headed west to Keswick. The ripple on the skyline grew into the lazy shapes of identifiable fells – Helvellyn with Catstye Cam as its outrider, the concave ridge of Blencathra. From a single cloud above them, rain spat onto the windscreen. 'That's very much how I feel about Scott. These things are wonderful for a time, but they end. Sometimes you don't stop loving someone, but it still ends.'

'You never had any more trouble from him yesterday?'

'No. I didn't expect any.' Which wasn't entirely true, because Scott's cheerful persistence was something she'd once adored about him, and now the cheerfulness had gone the persistence was beginning to look like obsession. But Scott was a sensible man, and all she had to do to steer safely through the wreckage was be more stubborn in her rejection of him than he was in his pursuit.

'Call me if you do, okay?' And Jude turned the car down onto the main road and headed towards Monica Roland's house.

10

'Take a seat, Miss Marcowics. I'm Detective Inspector Dodd and this is Detective Constable Marshall. We'd just like to ask you a few questions about yourself, and about what happened on Friday afternoon.'

It was always best to be composed, even when you lacked the courage to confront your destiny. As she took her seat at the table in the cramped room Karen had made available to the police, Klemmie knew Becca's advice was sound. Unseen by the two officers in front of her, she touched Violet's brooch, concealed in the pocket of her jeans, then placed both hands, empty, in front of her on the table. She'd exhumed her treasure from its hiding place intending to place it in front of the police with her brightest and most innocent smile, offering her explanation as if she expected them to accept it without question, but her good intentions fell away when she remembered how the police had come in and cleared Violet's room. If she handed it over, they'd take it away and, because there was no way to be able to prove it was a gift bestowed upon her freely, she'd never get it back.

'Yes. Of course.' She smiled at the two men, her strategy already formed. She'd treat this interview as if she were applying for a job, not being questioned as a witness and

– she wasn't stupid – the prime suspect in what was, no matter how much the police declined to give a firm response, undoubtedly a murder case.

'Why don't you start by telling us something about yourself?' The elder of the two smiled at her, encouragingly. He might be in his mid-forties, the same age as herself, but it was hard to judge because the receding hairline made him look much older, and yet when he smiled his face shed a decade and a half. Instinct prompted her to like him, although she suspected it wasn't in her interests to do so and if she was too receptive to his apparent good nature she'd end up giving herself away. Even so, he was much less intimidating than either the darkly glowering chief inspector or the blonde detective whose silent gaze threatened to see everything that went on in her soul. At least with this man asking the questions, she had half a chance of keeping her secrets.

Resisting the urge to touch the brooch again, for luck, she reviewed her life and career and found both stained with the stigma of underachievement. There was surely little of interest to them, and nothing that could incriminate her. 'My name is Klementyna Marcowics. I'm forty-three years old and I come from Krakow, in Poland.'

'How long have you been in the UK, Miss Marcowics?'

'A little less than a year.'

'What brought you here? Do you have family connections?'

Klemmie folded her hands in front of her on the table and stared down at them. 'It was the right time. I used to work with children. Sometimes as a nanny, sometimes with children who couldn't go to school with others. I did that for twenty-five years.'

'And now you work with older people.'

She nodded. Everyone had something they wanted to leave behind them, some emotional baggage they wanted to unload and walk away from. Not wanting to talk about it didn't mean she'd be compromised if she did. 'My father was a steelworker. He was injured in an accident and my mother gave up work to look after him. I supported them both. They died within a short time of each other, just two years ago.'

Daring a look at the detective, she found him nodding in sympathy. He wasn't taking notes, though his companion was scribbling furiously and the recording device, whirring in the middle of the table, warned her not to give away too much.

'I was unhappy in Poland. All my memories were sad.' For a moment she dwelt on it, the childhood in late-era Communist Poland. Life in Nowa Huta, the Soviet-imposed steelmaking suburbs that hovered beside glorious Krakow like a wolf at the edge of a shepherd's flock, had offered little when she'd been young and nothing but obligation where her contemporaries had found opportunity. 'Sometimes you need to change your direction.'

'A mid-life crisis?' The younger man smiled at her in his turn, as if he had any idea of what a mid-life crisis might be.

She had her own interests to protect, so she kept smiling at him when she'd have loved to slap him down. Violet had understood that just because life had been harsh it didn't mean you were a failure. 'That's what Karen called it. Change is how I get through. I was always interested in languages and I speak good English. I worked for an English family for four years. When I decided I needed a change of place, I thought I might try England.' Her dream of what Violet called a green and pleasant land had borne strange fruit. 'I looked for advertisements in the papers and saw this place.'

'That's very different from what you did before.'

'That's why it was good. I was lucky to get a job here, and I'm very happy.' Though in reality, it wasn't luck. She'd been given the job because she was prepared to live in, in not particularly comfortable lodgings, and do more than her fair share of late nights and early mornings for as low a wage as the management dared pay her. 'I'll give you a list of where I worked before. I don't have a copy of my CV – I don't have a laptop computer. But Karen will be able to give it to you, and my references.' She nodded, determined to be gracious, and switched the smile from one to the other, taking care to treat them equally in case they wielded equal power.

'Thank you. We'll follow them up.' The older man nodded to the younger one, who made a note on his pad. 'What's your job here at Eden's End, Miss Marcowics? Could you talk us through your responsibilities?'

'I'm a care assistant. I provide personal care to the residents, take them their meals, arrange for anything they need. I clean, if there's no-one else to do it.'

'And your hours?'

'My contract is forty hours a week.' Inevitably she did much more, unpaid. 'I work four ten-hour shifts or sometimes split shifts, early morning and evening. The shift patterns vary. Most of the time I work the evening shift.' That was when she'd become close to Violet, who slept little, stayed up late and craved constant stimulation, who could be savage to some but responded with joy to the few she identified as kindred spirits. A tear crept up into her eye at the thought of the old lady, laughing at something she'd said as they sat up after midnight while the rest of Eden's End slept. She'd been blessed to have such a friend. 'I'm sorry. I was thinking of Dr Ross.'

'You were close to her?'

'Yes.' She looked at DI Dodd, not troubling to hide her defiance. Why shouldn't she have been? Violet could stand on her dignity when she chose, and most of the time she did choose, which was why Klemmie was so proud of their friendship. 'She was old and she was lonely, though she would never admit it. When I wasn't busy in the evenings, she liked to chat. Is that wrong? Everybody needs a friend, and I was the nearest thing she had.'

'Do you have many friends of your own?'

'No. I left my friends behind me when I came here. I have colleagues and they're good to me.' She struggled to keep control. Emotion was the enemy.

'What do you do in your time off?'

'I walk in the country. I watch television. I read.' The question forced her to confront her loneliness. 'I wanted to leave Poland for a couple of years, to try something new.'

'You plan to go back?'

'Yes, if nothing happens to keep me here. I have no ties in Poland any more, but there's nothing to keep me here, either.'

'You don't have family there?'

'No. I never married. And Violet never married, either. It was something else that linked us. Something we could talk about and joke about. It's why I was so upset when she died.' Through eyes that swam with salt, she could make out the younger policeman's sympathetic nod.

'I know it's difficult, but I'd like you to talk me through what happened.'

So much for keeping control. Klemmie fought the tears. 'The lounge was being decorated so I took the tea trolley around to the residents in their rooms. Violet was there, and Mrs Hodgson and Mr Parsons. Normally there's someone else there, but she's in hospital.' Her tears under control, she folded the handkerchief back into her pocket. 'I was going to go to Mr Parsons first, then Mrs Hodgson, then Violet. That way I could find a few minutes to talk to her.' A watery smile. 'But Becca was in with Mrs Hodgson, so I went to Violet first.'

'Was anyone else down there, apart from the district nurse?'

'No. I passed Ellie in the dining room on the way down. She was there when I filled up the trolley. I took the tea tray in to Violet. She was asleep in her chair. That was unusual for her. She rarely slept in the afternoons.'

The younger of the two policemen leaned forward. 'What did you think when you saw her asleep?'

'I didn't think anything. She's old. I called her, to wake her up. And I expected her to wake up immediately, because she was always so alert. When she didn't I knew something was wrong. She just looked... odd.'

'In what way?'

Closing her eyes, squeezing her fingers tightly together, Klemmie recalled the moment when she'd seized Violet by her thin, old shoulders and shaken her, as if she could force the life back into her. The frail spirit had already fled, but she'd had to try. 'I shook her, to see if I could wake her up. And then Becca came in and sent me to call Karen.'

'And was there anyone else on the landing or the hallway while you were with Dr Ross?'

'Only Becca. I could hear Mrs Hodgson talking to her. She has such a loud voice. She was talking about the weather and telling her to get me to bring the tea.' Dipping into her pocket for the hankie, Klemmie's fingers brushed against the brooch, the comforting solidity of Violet's memory made real. It had been a gift. It belonged to her, and she didn't have to justify it to anyone, even to herself. She dabbed at her eyes again. Poor Violet, dead before her time.

'Did you hear anything? Apart from Mrs Hodgson.'

She stared at him. The door that went out to the side would be the perfect escape for a killer, or for anyone who wanted to come and go unseen. 'I heard a door.'

'Oh?'

'An outside door. Yes. I heard something click. It must have been the door.'

'You never mentioned it before.' This was the young constable again.

That irritated her. He must have read her initial statement and memorised almost all of it, in order to trap her, because that was what the police did, wanting to catch someone and not caring who, and it was always the person unlucky enough to find the body that they tried to catch. 'I'd forgotten. I was so upset. I'd never seen a dead body. And because I liked her.'

She pushed back her chair, an optimistic nudge to their subconscious minds that it was time to let her go, and was surprised when the older man took the hint. 'Thanks, Miss

Marcowics. We won't trouble you any longer today. But thank you for sparing us the time.'

As if she'd had the choice. But the man's old-fashioned politeness flattered her, and she smiled. 'Thank you, Inspector. If I can do anything else, let me know.'

'And if you remember anything else, do call us. Any time.' He got up to see her out of the room and, heart suddenly light, she skipped off down the corridor and back to work, the brooch still safe in her pocket.

Ellie Jack, next in line for an interview, had very little to add to Klemmie's account. Brisk, forthright and clearly rushed off her feet, she gave every indication of someone who had no time for nonsense and, in truth, not a lot of sympathy with some of her patients.

'Violet?' She tossed her dark hair in scorn when Doddsy asked her about the character of the deceased. 'Hmm. Bit of a cow, if I'm honest. I don't think she liked anyone. Except Klemmie, and God knows what was going on there. The two of them were as thick as thieves. I spoke to Karen about that more than once, told her she needed to watch and make sure Violet wasn't being taken advantage of.'

Doddsy, troubled by a strange stirring of sympathy for the dead woman, found himself compelled by his better nature to speak up for someone who could no longer defend herself. 'It's interesting you say that. I haven't heard anything that makes me think Dr Ross was particularly easily influenced.'

'Oh, God, no! She certainly wasn't. She knew her own mind and she always got her own way. I'd almost say she bullied the rest of us. She liked to assert her authority and everything had to be done her way. Which is fine and dandy, isn't it, if you're the only person around, but there are too many people paying the piper in this place. So she gave us grief if we did things any other way than hers.'

'Did she give you any particular grief, Mrs Jack? Did you find her, perhaps, a bit of a nuisance?'

Ellie put her shoulders back and stared. 'I wouldn't normally express myself like this, but yes. Patients are a nuisance, by definition. It doesn't bother me. It's part of the job. She was no more and no less of a nuisance than anyone else. And to be honest, apart from her arthritis drugs, I didn't have a lot to do with her. I expect if I had, I'd have thought she was a lot more of a pain in the backside than I did.'

Doddsy stifled a smile. He liked a challenge, and he was getting exactly what he was looking for – the complete, unpalatable truth. 'And you gave her the drugs as normal?'

'Not that day. The last she had was on Tuesday. She only gets one tablet a week. I'd been on my drugs round, as it happened, about half an hour earlier, and I'd been on that floor, but I hadn't been in to her. I was up in the dining room for a quick break when Klemmie came up to tell me she'd died.'

'And yet, Mrs Jack…' Doddsy looked down at his notes. The drugs record was exemplary. 'When you realised she was dead, you said you didn't think there should be a post-mortem. Is that right?'

She looked uncomfortable, but only for a second, and then she came back with spirit. 'She was a hundred years old!'

'All the evidence suggests she died of unnatural causes. Age doesn't take away your right to justice. Don't you think?'

'All right.' She drew her shoulders back and faced him. 'I'm a nurse, not a doctor, and definitely not a pathologist. I couldn't see any reason why her death wasn't natural. Yes, the extra paperwork was in my mind when I found her. But she was going to die sooner, rather than later. I didn't see anything suspicious about it at the time – only that it wasn't expected. So why put everybody through the stress and the hassle of a post-mortem?'

Doddsy did his best not to judge her, but it was hard. 'Were you surprised when you heard the PM uncovered something suspicious?'

'I was astonished.' This time, at least, she spoke with certainty. 'Totally astonished.'

'And you can't think of anything unusual about the time she died? Anything at all? You didn't see anyone you wouldn't expect to see?'

She shook her head.

'And visitors?'

'Her niece came every day. I've no doubt she was taking care of her investment. She's the next of kin, or so she says.' Her lips twisted in what could only be an uncharitable opinion of Monica Roland. 'In all the time she's been here, I don't recall her having another—' She stopped. 'Actually, yes. I think I do. She did have one visitor.'

'Recently?' Doddsy leaned forward.

'No, not recently at all. It was ages ago. I think it must have been last year. Yes. It was this time last year, I remember that. I was in with Karen talking about Christmas – not that Christmas events are really my job, but I have to show willing. I saw him arriving. He came in a taxi, which is what caught my eye. And when I asked — I can't remember who it was I asked — they said he'd been to see Violet.'

'What was he like?'

She shook her head. 'It was raining. He had an umbrella. I didn't see his face.'

'And did he stay long?'

'I've no idea. No idea at all. But it'll be in the visitors' book. Everyone has to sign in, for health and safety reasons.'

'Thank you, Mrs Jack. You've been very helpful.' Doddsy nodded to Chris to show the woman out, then helped himself to a cup of coffee and reviewed the notes on his pad. A mysterious visitor. He smiled. The challenge was on.

11

Monica Roland, who must have been sixty if she was a day, seemed immediately taken with Jude, twinkling an uncharacteristic and clearly unintended smile at him before she seemed to realise her weakness and suffered a flush of embarrassment in its wake. From her position on the sidelines, trailing behind like a bridesmaid as Monica escorted Jude into her aunt's living room, Ashleigh found it amusing, though the amusement changed to a spike of pity as Monica settled them in armchairs in the bay window that looked over the grey roofs of Keswick and the wintry blue of Derwentwater. Something about Violet's niece cried out to her, the eyes of a woman in whose life every twist and turn had led nowhere but disappointment, until it was no longer worth the effort of hope.

Monica poured them a cup of tea apiece – there was, it appeared, no coffee in the house – and offered a plate of stale biscuits. The room, long unused, was cold even though a fire blazed in the grate.

'I apologise for the state of this place,' she sighed. 'I was in Keswick seeing my aunt's solicitor this morning, and it seemed opportune to meet you here. No doubt you'll have questions about Aunt Vi, and I always think one gains more of a clue about people from the homes they've built for themselves than from the places they end up in. Do you have a sense of place, Sergeant?' She tore her eyes away from Jude and looked instead at Ashleigh, who'd been taking in the surroundings.

Abandoning her contemplation of Violet's dust-ridden mantelpiece – several photographs, three mismatched pottery candlesticks and a family of carved elephants, bookended by a pair of china dogs – Ashleigh gave their interviewee her full attention. 'I don't know if you'd call it a sense of place, as such. We're trained to adopt an observational approach.'

'Of course.' Pouring her own tea last, Monica took her seat, closest to the fire. She was a tall woman, thin and grey-haired, clad in a severely cut trouser suit of dusty black, and everything about her – speech, posture, expression, mannerisms – rang with rigid formality. 'Of course, Aunt Vi took her most precious items with her, and her valuable items were kept in the bank. What you see can only give you something of a feel for her personality. Nevertheless, with your skills, you may be able to learn something from it.'

In fact, the living room was exactly what Ashleigh might have expected of a woman who'd left it for the last time when she was almost a centenarian. The furniture was traditional, the three-piece suite chintzy, the standard lamps blighted by dark shades, the curtains heavy and in need of a clean. A thick, old rug, curling so much at the edges as to be a trip hazard, sprawled on the polished wooden floor. The accumulation of objects spoke of a life of travel rich in experience, and the bookshelves – perhaps the most telling

– revealed an eclectic but highbrow mixture of literary fiction, popular science, travel and history whose tattered spines suggested someone, if not Violet herself, had read almost every one of them. Polish history, she noticed, had a predominant place but Violet had also given shelf space to writers as diverse as George Orwell and Ayn Rand.

'Did your aunt live here alone?' Jude, too, was scanning the bookshelves with interest.

'Yes. She inherited the house from my grandfather, who was wealthy, though not extraordinarily so. He made his money in manufacturing – biscuit tins, as it happens.' She managed a smile. 'She lived in this house for more than fifty years, and I fear it shows.'

The house, if truth be told, wasn't that spectacular – a solid detached villa with a double front and large bay windows, not unlike a scaled-down version of Eden's End. It probably had four bedrooms and the grounds were modest and dank with winter misery, but its elevated position, its stunning views towards Derwentwater and its desirable address in one of the most popular towns in the Lake District meant the inheritance would have accumulated vastly in value over the past five decades.

'What did Dr Ross do for a living?' Jude turned back from his scrutiny of the bookshelves.

'She was a medical doctor. The war broke out and interrupted her training, so she didn't qualify until the late 1940s. But she was a very clever woman, with a wide-ranging intellect. Latterly, of course, that wasn't so obvious, though she retained most of her faculties. She worked in London initially, but settled here when my grandfather died, after which she worked as a GP in the town until she retired forty years ago. When she retired she amused herself with her hobbies – walking, painting and so on.'

'She never married, is that right?'

'That's correct. Like so many of her generation, she had an unhappy war.' Monica reached out a finger and nudged a coffee table book of Lake District views aside, smearing two years' worth of dust over an inch of the tabletop in the process. 'My aunt was very determined. She was also very loyal. She never talked about her war experiences, but something that happened to her long before I was born seems to have caused her distress. She once told me – on my wedding day, as it happens – that I was making a mistake, and I was better marrying no-one than the wrong man.'

Ashleigh saw Jude's lips twist into the semblance of a smile, surely an ironic one, as the advice had been the same as she'd given Becca. Violet never seemed to have been short of an opinion. 'What did you take from that?'

'I took it to mean that, for some reason, she had lost the love of her life, probably during the war, and she was far too stubborn to accept anyone else in his place. Of course, being the woman she was, she continually felt the need to justify her own approach by showing anyone who did things differently that they were wrong. And she was ruthless in that.'

Poor Violet. Ashleigh thought of Scott again, remembering how difficult it had been to admit to herself that the biggest decision of her life had been a mistake. It was no wonder Violet had become bitter in her old age, but astonishing she hadn't let it ruin the rest of her life. Or maybe she had. 'Did you ever ask her about it?'

'I'm not a coward, Sergeant O'Halloran, but if you had

ever met Aunt Vi you'd know it would take a very brave person to ask her about her secrets.'

The image of the handsome airman in the frame, hidden at the bottom of Violet's drawer, popped into Ashleigh's mind. A quick scan of the family photos on the mantelpiece showed no-one who might pass for him. Taking her cue from Jude, who nodded down at his notes as if to prompt her, she opened the folder she'd brought with her and extracted a copy of the photograph. 'This may give you a clue. Do you know who this man is? She kept his picture in her drawer.'

Lifting the pair of glasses that hung on a chain round her neck and perching them on her nose, Monica frowned at it for a moment, wrinkling her brow. 'No, I've never seen him before. But really, what a very handsome man.'

'Does he remind you in any way of anyone? Perhaps a family member?'

She laughed at that, perhaps a shade bitterly. 'Family member? The Rosses aren't particularly fertile. I'm an only child, and I have no children of my own. My mother and Aunt Vi were the only two children in their generation, which was most unusual for their class at the time. My grandfather and grandmother on that side of the family were both only children. And of course, as we know, Aunt Vi never married.' She looked down at the picture again. 'When I look at it again, I think he does remind me of someone, but certainly no-one in the family. A film star, perhaps. That's such a film star pose, isn't it? And the way he's flirting with the camera. A touch of the Errol Flynns about him, maybe.'

They were probably staring Violet's secret in the face as

they looked at the photograph, but unless someone could shed light on it, she'd taken it to the grave with her. Ashleigh looked at Jude for a prompt as to where they went next. His expression replicated Monica's, deep concentration.

'So your aunt never married. Was there any romance?' He watched Monica, keenly, as she laid the photograph down on the coffee table.

'Not to my knowledge, though as I say, I've no clear idea of what she did during the war, other than she was in the WAAF. Of course, knowing Aunt Vi it may just be she never talked about it because it was very dull.'

'Would it surprise you to know the post-mortem indicated she'd given birth at least once?'

Monica's first reaction was shock, but the expression blew across her face as quickly as snow melting from a dry stone wall. 'As my mother often used to say, nothing would surprise me about her. She was an extraordinary woman and not always conventional in either her views or her actions. But since you ask, I had no idea. I imagine it must have been a wartime pregnancy and she ended it in the time-honoured manner, rather than be disgraced. Not, of course, that she would feel any disgrace. I'm not aware she knew what it was to be ashamed. It's more likely she ended the pregnancy for her own convenience. That would explain her secret.'

'I think you misheard me. The post-mortem didn't say just she'd been pregnant, but specifically that she'd given birth. I'm keen to find out more about the child or children. Perhaps there's a clue in her personal papers?'

'I don't recall seeing anything when I looked through them.' Monica had something of the steel that must have characterised Violet, because the look she gave Jude was a very cool one indeed. 'One of the reasons I'm here today is to go through her private papers. Knowing her as I did, I'm prepared for more than one shock.'

'I wouldn't normally ask you this, Ms Roland, but would you be prepared to let us take those papers? We'd obviously return them to you as soon as we were able to take copies.'

'We're talking about murder. I understand that. So of course. I have no objections. I took them out of the filing cabinet this morning. I'll get them for you before you leave.'

Would Monica have an opportunity to hide anything she wanted to hide, or had she already taken the chance? It was obvious that Jude's line of questioning, or the brisk way in which he was choosing to pursue it, had unsettled her. She crossed and recrossed her ankles, uncomfortable even on the battleground of her choice.

'Excellent. Now, may I ask you a few more personal questions?'

'If it helps your investigation.'

'Good. I wondered about Dr Ross's finances.'

Monica settled her shoulders into a stiff line. 'There's this house. There were significant investments, most of which were liquidated to pay for her care. The fees at Eden's End are, as you'll be aware, extortionate. She had one or two valuable items of jewellery. No more.'

'Offhand, do you know the value of the estate?'

'Her solicitor has power of attorney.' Monica's look was much less friendly. 'He handles all Aunt Vi's affairs for her. And now, of course, you're going to ask me about the will and accuse me of helping her along the way so I could inherit.'

'I am going to ask about the will. Not because I'm accusing you of anything – far from it – but because it's part of the process. I take it you do inherit?'

If possible, Monica stiffened further. Hiding something, thought Ashleigh in fascination. Something she didn't like. 'I'm the sole legatee, apart from a bequest to a local charity.'

'Can you tell me about your own financial situation?'

She crossed and uncrossed the ankles again, the most obvious sign of her agitation. 'My situation isn't as comfortable as it might be. I might as well be honest with you. My mother inherited the same amount as Violet, but she was unfortunate enough to marry a man who spent money more quickly than he earned it. I took after my mother, as we so often do, and I chose a man who was just as much a spendthrift as my father. By the time he left me for a woman with more money – which was the better part of thirty years ago – there wasn't a lot of my grandfather's money left for me.'

'What was your job?'

'I was a teacher. Currently, I live off my pension and some savings. When my aunt first moved into Eden's End, I lived here in Keswick, but I realised cash by selling my house and moving to Langwathby.'

'Outside the National Park.' Jude's grey-eyed gaze swept over Ashleigh as he filled her in on the local information. 'You get much more for your money out there.'

'You do, and it meant I could continue to be close to my aunt. I was able to visit her every day.' She picked at her earring. 'Chief Inspector. You seem like a practical man, and I'm not a sentimental woman. I was very fond of my aunt, though I found her difficult and she took her frustrations out on me, but I put up with it, in the expectation that I would inherit. Don't look so shocked.'

Jude smiled. Ashleigh pulled herself up, stalling in her judgement on the woman in front of her. What she described was commonplace, practical even. The only shocking thing about it was that she'd actually said it. 'I appreciate your honesty.'

'Aunt Vi knew my feelings. She would regularly remind me of the situation, and I expect she told everybody else, too, though not in a derogatory way. I think if she was poor I would still have visited her as often as I did, and I hope she understood that. It isn't something people normally talk about but it's what you're thinking. That the money was my main concern. Isn't it?'

'Financial gain is the motive for far more crimes than I'm comfortable with. That's true.'

'I understand that. In my case, however, it isn't a motive for murder, though I expect it would make me your prime suspect. If I'd been there at the time.' She smiled, as if she'd checkmated him, as if her alibi was secure. 'You see, the gain from the will isn't as significant as you might think.'

Her fists were clenched tightly in her lap. Ashleigh understood. Violet Ross must have perpetrated some terrible prank – if you could call it a prank – over the will. 'Why's that, Ms Roland? The bequest?'

'Yes.' Monica kept her voice steady, but a quiver of her shoulders showed how hard it was. 'She left this house to a charity supporting single mothers. I am the residuary legatee.' Her thin lips contorted. 'Earlier, you mentioned the fees at Eden's End. My aunt insisted on paying yearly in advance, and the next year's fee was coming due. To fund that, the house was to be sold. It was to go on the market in the next couple of weeks.'

Ashleigh's mind whirred at the implications of that. 'Then if that had happened, the charity—?'

'Unless my aunt changed her will, which as far as I'm aware she had no plans to do, the charity would have lost out and I would have inherited the money.'

'And as things stand—'

'Once the funeral costs and solicitor's fees are deducted, I expect to inherit less than ten thousand pounds. Which removes any motive I might have had. It was very much in my interests that she lived.' The look she gave Jude was one of triumph, but he took the sting out the dramatic moment, merely making a note and nodding.

In the pause she'd generated, Monica sipped her tea. 'In the interest of balance, you should know I'm not the only person who stands to gain financially from Violet's death.'

'Oh?'

'There's the charity, of course. And not just them. My aunt had a very sharp eye and was a keen judge of character. She warned me that after she was dead I should check the statement of accounts from Eden's End very closely, which I will do. I should tell you her opinion of the manager was less than complimentary.'

'Did she say why that was?'

Monica sniffed. 'No. Don't misunderstand me. In my opinion Karen Grant lacks both guile and competence, but Aunt Vi certainly thought there was something about her. As soon as I heard there was something unusual about Aunt Vi's death I wondered if she might be the type of person who would panic if challenged.'

In both interviews, Karen had struck Ashleigh as a bag of nerves jangling far more loudly than the circumstances required, the very epitome of a guilty conscience. Quite whether she was capable of murder was a different matter. 'Do you know if your aunt challenged her about it?'

Monica, shifting her attention away from Jude, seemed to relax a little. 'I don't know for certain, but it wouldn't have surprised me. Aunt Vi was becoming increasingly short-tempered. Normally she took it out on me, but I could put up with it. Not just because it was in my interests.' She turned to scowl fleetingly at Jude. 'She was an old woman. But it was possible she might have threatened to report Karen, either to the police or to her employers. And she isn't the only one who might have thought she had something to gain from her death.'

'Oh?'

'Yes. The carer. The Polish woman. Aunt Vi had taken quite a shine to her. She met a lot of Polish refugees during the war, and she went there on holiday a few times. She liked it – the food, the culture, the people.'

'I see that.' The briefest glimpse around the room had betrayed it – a faded picture of the Tatras Mountains, a shelf full of books about Poland.

'Naturally, she became friendly with the carer. I don't blame her for that. And in fairness, I don't believe the woman was making up to her deliberately, or if she was I never saw any signs of it. But on the day after my aunt died, when I came to clear her things, before we heard there was to be a post-mortem, when I went into the room, the woman was in there.'

'Doing what?'

'Nothing. Just standing. But when I arrived she jumped like a startled rabbit. May I ask you a question, Chief Inspector?'

'Of course.'

'Did my aunt's effects include a gold and diamond brooch, about an inch across, shaped like a Polish Imperial eagle, with tiny ruby eyes?'

Jude sat back, as if he was running through the entire inventory of Violet's possessions when Ashleigh knew as well as he did that there had been no such thing in there. 'No. Should there have been one?'

'There should. She kept it in the top drawer, on the right-hand side. It was always there, and the last time I saw it was when I visited the week before. She'd asked to me to get her hairbrush from the drawer and it was there then. But on the day after she died, it had gone.'

'You think it was stolen?'

'Exactly that. It was the only valuable item she kept with her, apart from her rings, and it was maybe worth a thousand pounds. Whether the girl stole it, or whether she killed my aunt because she was interrupted in stealing it—'

'I don't think that kind of thinking helps us, Ms Roland.' Jude shut that source of speculation down as soon as it appeared. 'Thank you, though. That's a very interesting piece of information. Perhaps Ms Grant removed it for safekeeping.'

Monica's snort of contempt showed what she thought of Karen's trustworthiness. 'As long as it's found. I'm sure you'll think of everything.'

'Let's hope we do.' Jude, signalling the end of the interview, nodded to Ashleigh and got to his feet. 'We have another appointment. If you wouldn't mind showing us Dr Ross's private papers, that would help. And of course, I'll write you a receipt.'

'One other thing.' Monica stopped on the very edge of the interview, so far into the concluding formalities that Ashleigh and Jude were already down the front steps and onto the gravel drive.

'What's that?'

'I can't find my aunt's gun.'

'A *gun?*' Appalled, Jude spun on his heel. Ashleigh, clutching a carrier bag with Violet's personal papers in it, was staring at Monica, open-mouthed. 'Dr Ross had a gun?'

'Don't look so alarmed, Chief Inspector. Or you, Sergeant.' Monica's expression suggested that Violet's much-mentioned malicious streak might be a family trait. 'Surely you didn't think my aunt wandered round Keswick armed with an AK47?'

'Even a shotgun can cause a lot of damage.' Jude struggled to control a sigh. Violet Ross must have been a handful when she was alive, because she was proving to be plenty of trouble after she was dead. If she'd been shot, there might have been some obvious value in this information, but on first sight he couldn't see how it was anything but a complication.

'It isn't even a shotgun. It's a small handgun, a side arm I think she called it. She told me she had it during the war, when she was in the WAAF. I imagine they were allowed to keep them, though presumably they had to be disabled. It doesn't work, and I only saw it once. She showed it to me some years ago. But it occurred to me there might be some kind of paperwork associated with it now she's dead, so I looked for it. It wasn't there.'

'If she had a gun, it should have been licensed.' Jude stepped back into the fray, his exasperation with Monica now barely concealed.

'Then the licence will be in the papers you have.'

'Where did she keep it? Locked up?'

'There was nowhere to lock it up. When I saw it, it was in the drawer of the sideboard in the dining room, and it isn't there now. But I told you. It didn't work.'

'Are you sure it isn't there?'

'Positive. Should I be worried?' She looked at them, coolly.

Worried? If the gun was licensed then it should have been locked away, and if there was nowhere to lock it up then a licence couldn't have been issued. The best they could hope for was that Violet had disposed of it safely. In the worst-case scenario, a real weapon, one that might be disabled or might be capable of being reactivated, was going to end up in circulation. Jude felt a headache coming on. That meant warning his boss about the possibility, and that meant explanation and distraction and the allocation of time and scarce resources to find it. 'No. I'd leave it for someone else to worry about. With your permission, I'll send a couple of officers round to search the place for it. Then we can all set our minds at rest. Goodbye.'

'She has enough problems of her own, doesn't she?' Ashleigh deposited the bag of papers in the boot of the car and got into the passenger seat. 'How disappointed she must be at the way it's worked out.'

'Typical of you to think of her. I'm thinking of myself.' Jude let out the clutch and drove the car down the gravel drive, leaving Monica behind him with more than a degree of relief. 'I need a cup of coffee to make up for that vile brew she served us. We have three-quarters of an hour before we're due at her solicitor's. Good, because we've got plenty to talk about and a lot to follow up.'

'I'll get onto that right now.' Ashleigh had her phone out.

'Start by telling Doddsy to ask Klemmie Marcowics about the brooch while he's over at Eden's End. I've a suspicion she'll have it, and I'd love to hear her explanation. Then call Aditi and get her to get someone around to check the place for that gun. Ask her to check if Violet had a licence for it, though I'll bet Monica's inheritance on the fact she didn't.'

'She was something else, wasn't she? I don't just mean the fact she talked as if she'd swallowed a grammar book. I was expecting the odd nugget of information. There's always something useful that comes out of the initial interviews. But she didn't short-change us. The brooch, and the will, and finally the gun. Doddsy, hi. Are you still at Eden's End? Jude needs you to do something for him.'

While Ashleigh issued instructions to Doddsy over the phone, Jude negotiated the way down the hill into Keswick town centre, pulling up in the car park just a cut-through away from the town centre. It was early on a Tuesday afternoon in the first week of November, and the place was quiet. He led the way down a narrow alley and into the nearest cafe. 'Handily, this is just round the corner from the solicitor's.'

'I hope the coffee's good.' Ashleigh placed her folder on the chair beside her and looked out at the handful of walkers stomping off towards the lake shore. A council workman, scaling a lamppost outside, checked the Christmas lights, switching them on and off as Keswick prepared for the festive season.

'It is. What will you have?'

'An Americano.'

'I recommend that Lakeland plum bread. It's to die for.'

They placed the order with the waitress and paused. There was no point in starting the conversation since they'd only have to interrupt it when the coffee arrived, but he was strangely reluctant to get on to business. He stared at her, her long fingers resting in utter stillness on the table beside her notepad. It suddenly seemed a long time since he'd had to start a conversation with any woman but Becca on any kind of personal level and now the moment had arrived there was nothing he could think of to say. The silence persisted until the coffees arrived, and then he found he could slide back into work mode and the world became so much easier to deal with.

In the same instant, Ashleigh relaxed. 'So what do we make of Monica, then?'

He smiled at her. No matter how much he'd wanted to have the conversation, he was relieved the opportunity had passed and he was back on safe ground. 'Yes. Suddenly she offers us two options for people who might have killed Violet, and gives us reasons for it that we can't prove now her aunt is dead. Very convenient.'

'And she inherits.' Ashleigh sighed.

'But not much. Or I should say, not nearly as much as she was expecting.'

'She didn't say when she knew about the will. I bet

she didn't find out until after Violet died. You can see it in her face.' Ashleigh's weakness was always too much of a sympathy for the witness, her clear understanding of motivation made complex by the way she allowed it to cloud her judgement of right and wrong.

When he had a moment he'd speak to her about it, or perhaps get Doddsy to. 'Yes. And that suggests to me that, whatever she says and however sorry we might feel for her, it's effectively as good a motive as if she'd inherited the whole lot.' Because it was the expectation, not the actuality, that counted.

'I know there's no justifiable reason for killing someone, Jude, but some motives are easier to understand than others.'

'I agree. Inheritance isn't one of them.' Passion, at least, had a certain nobility to it, even if what had once been good became ultimately corrupted, but there was nothing good in the pursuit of money.

'I was thinking of the disappointment, if she did know. It sounds to me as if Violet treated her horribly.' She sighed.

'If she did know, as she said, it was in her interests for Violet to stay alive.'

'Yes. As it stands the charity, whoever they are, benefits from her death.'

'It sounds a bit far-fetched, but we need to look into that, too.' Jude picked up the cube of shortbread that had come with the coffee and crunched his way through it.

'We need to look very closely at the implications of the will, don't we?'

'We do. And at Karen Grant. And at Klemmie Marcowics, though even Monica seemed to understand that relationship.'

'She obviously didn't think Klemmie was a threat. And in the end, she wasn't. It was the cost of the care home.' Ashleigh lifted her cup and sipped. 'And then there's the gun.'

Jude groaned. 'God, I'm glad I didn't know Violet. She sounds just the type to wind me up. A gun? She must have known it was illegal, even if it wasn't capable of being fired. She must have known it needed a licence and she must have known the terms of the licence would require her to keep it locked up. Which all says to me there was never a licence. We'll just have to hope there was no ammunition, either.'

12

It had been too good to be true. When she'd marched out of her interview with the two detectives that morning, Klemmie's success had gone to her head. Neither Monica nor Karen could have thought to tell the police the brooch was missing and so, though she'd lost a friend – the only real friend she'd had in this alien country – at least she still had something to remember Violet by.

The wave of elation this knowledge brought with it carried her through the rest of her shift, not quite drowning out her grief but diluting it. Violet would have died sooner rather than later, and Klemmie was pragmatic enough to know their relationship was never going to be anything but brief, but that glimpse of fellow feeling had made up for her lifetime of drudgery. At six, just as she finished her last round of the day and headed towards the canteen to see if there was anything there worth eating or whether she'd have to forage in her own kitchenette, she saw the younger of the two detectives standing in the reception area and knew, straight away, that he was looking out for her.

'Miss Marcowics.' He stepped forward before she had time to think about flight.

Klemmie stopped, though the temptation to lift her chin in defiance and stride past him was strong. What would he do if she tried? Arrest her? 'Yes?'

'I wondered if you could spare us one final minute today.'

He was a polite young man with an appealing, apologetic smile, but she wasn't fooled. He was clever, but not in the same way as the others. His skills lay in chopping up what people said and did, rearranging it until their own words closed around them like a trap. People who allowed emotion into their thinking were gullible by definition, if only to a degree, but this man, a detective by numbers, was not. The police, whatever they claimed, weren't acting in her best interests, but in Violet's, as if the old lady could possibly benefit from their concern. Klemmie would have to look out for herself. 'I'm just going off shift.'

'It won't take a moment.' He opened the door to the office for her and followed her in, closing it more firmly than he needed to so it snapped shut like a prison cell. Inside the room his colleague was standing by the table, shuffling pieces of paper into a folder in preparation for departure, but the tape recorder in the middle of the table was still there, and he flicked it running the moment she came in. Her heart sank. They must have found something else. Who would speak up for her now Violet was dead?

'Miss Marcowics.' The smile didn't deceive her. 'I'm sorry to trouble you again. Something came up that we weren't aware of when we spoke this morning and I'd like to go over it with you. It won't take a moment.' He didn't invite her to sit.

She'd have backed towards the door if the younger detective hadn't been standing there with his hand resting on the handle, seemingly as eager as she was to be away. Maybe he had a date to go on, or a friend who'd be waiting for him in a pub. The tear that rose every time she thought about friendship and remembered she'd never see Violet again flared up and she dug into her pocket for a hanky. What a crybaby they'd think her. 'Of course.'

'I understand Dr Ross had a gold, diamond and ruby brooch, which she kept in her chest of drawers. It wasn't among her belongings when the room was examined after her death. We're keen to discover what happened to it.'

She swallowed hard, and nodded. It had been too good to be true.

'Did you ever see the brooch?'

Again, she could manage nothing more than a silent nod.

'When did you last see it?'

Without thought, Klemmie's hand went to her pocket and by the time she realised what she'd done, it was too late. Her fingers were clutched around the chunky metal of Violet's brooch and both of the policemen knew it. 'I didn't steal it! She gave it to me!'

'May I have it?'

She pulled it out and tossed it onto the table, hearing it fall but not seeing it through her tears. 'We were friends. She said she liked to be generous to her friends. She gave it to me. I'm keeping it to remember her by.'

'When did she give it to you?' He kept that ageless face free of expression, and that helped a little. No expression meant no judgement.

'Last week. I brought her tea in, in the morning, and she was talking about Poland and the wonderful times she had there when she was younger. She used to travel a lot. She went to Krakow, which is where I came from. She said she'd been dreaming about it. I showed her some pictures of my home and my family from before my mother died.' Violet's Krakow had been the tourist version, not the Soviet-era socialist realism that had shaped Klemmie, but it didn't matter. 'She gave me the brooch. She said she didn't need it any longer.'

'Are you allowed to accept gifts from residents?'

'Yes, but we have to… I didn't think.' Glinting in the artificial light, Violet's gold reproached her. 'There was no harm in it. I didn't think it was worth any money.'

'So you didn't clear it with the manager.'

'I told Becca about it. The district nurse. But not until after Violet had died. I didn't know anyone would miss it. I don't understand why she wasn't allowed to give me a gift. We got on so well.' Sometimes, in the spring or the summer, Klemmie had walked through the lanes in the countryside, down by the broad River Eden, and she'd always come back with a handful of wildflowers. They weren't much – and, she suspected, were probably stolen goods themselves, under some old law of which she was unaware – but they were all she'd had to give Violet, and the old woman had loved them, shifting them into pride of place ahead of the cut flowers that Karen ordered by the dozen. Klemmie had taken pride in seeing the roses and lilies, the whole host of other flowers so exotic she couldn't name them, put aside in favour of her jam jar full of weeds.

'You say you didn't know it was valuable?' The detective picked up the brooch and turned it in his fingers.

She nodded, watching as he slipped it into a small polythene bag and sealed it, writing a label on it with curly, almost feminine handwriting. 'When will I get it back? It's mine.'

'In the eyes of the law, the ownership of this piece has still to be established. Until that happens…' He shrugged at her. 'It's an exhibit. That's all.'

Knowing there was nothing she could do, she stared back. 'Then can I go?'

'Of course. Thank you for your time.'

Perhaps, after all, the senior detective, the one with the edge to his tone who struck her as if he'd benefit from anger management, was easier to deal with than this gentle man, who seemed to feel sorry for her, but they were all difficult in their different ways and all were working towards the same objective. 'Will I get it back?' she repeated, a futile attempt to get the right answer. 'In the end?'

'In the end, the brooch will be returned to its rightful owner.'

The constable stood aside and let her go. On autopilot, she headed for the canteen but turned back before she got there, realising the intervention had robbed her of any desire to eat. The police had left Violet's room sealed up, blue tape across its door, but she slipped down the carpeted ramp anyway, thankful they hadn't left an officer there, and paused in the silent darkness. Marjorie Hodgson, somehow discovering what had happened, had insisted on being moved so that three of the four rooms remained empty. When she'd come down the stairs, Klemmie had hoped to make some connection with her friend's spirit, but the blank door of the dead woman's room blocked her.

If she couldn't be with Violet, the next best thing was to be alone. Swiping her key fob at the lock of the outer door, she eased it open and stepped outside. The wind swirled round the corner, rattled through the thick hedge and hit her, and the swathe of rain it brought with it caught her full in the face. She shivered, yet felt no cold as she tiptoed to the window of Violet's room and peered, fruitlessly, in against the drawn curtains from outer to inner darkness.

Wrapping her arms round her, she strode swiftly around to the back of the building, where there was a little more shelter. The scent of nicotine alerted her to someone else's presence before she saw the orange glow of the cigarette, and the bulk of the figure on the steps gave the identity away at once.

For a second Klemmie stood unseen, but then decided to reveal herself before she was spotted. She'd given herself enough explaining to do already, without having to justify lurking around outside Violet's window, and she was realising, with growing weariness, that what she'd told the detectives that morning was true. She had no friends. All those around her, who might have offered her some support, were too busy looking out for themselves, too desperate to look back at their own uncertain, inexplicable actions and clear themselves of murder before the police's suspicions of them could stick. Any one of them would sell her to save themselves, and she must do the same to them.

But you could pretend to care. She walked along the path against the back of the house. 'Karen? I didn't know you smoked.'

'I didn't, until some god-damned criminal killed Violet right under my nose.' Karen, her face even more haggard under the lights spilling out from the kitchen than it was in kinder light, took a long drag. 'That's not true. I haven't smoked for five years. But the only other thing that'll get me through this is drink, and I daren't. Someone will need me and if I'm drunk as a skunk when they call, I'll lose my job.'

'I'd help you.' Being circumspect, trusting no-one, didn't mean you couldn't pretend. An offer of friendship, even to someone as wild-eyed and unreliable as Karen had suddenly become, might one day be repaid. Or it might not. Life at Eden's End had become a dangerous game. 'We could go up to my flat and get a drink. I have a bottle of wine.' And there was a bottle of cherry brandy there, which she'd occasionally sneak into Violet's room, sharing another secret.

'Oh, Klemmie, you're a sweetie. But no. Better not. After all those questions, we're all in enough trouble as it is.'

In her more rational moments, Klemmie understood that being questioned didn't, as Karen seemed to imply, make you guilty of murder, but she couldn't deny she, at least, had a lot of questions still to answer. If she couldn't prove the brooch was a gift she'd be dismissed for stealing, so she found it hard to be too sympathetic to Karen's interpretation of trouble. Sometimes she wondered what she might have done to stop her life taking this turn, but the alternatives would just have left her in different difficult straits. Some people were like that, doomed by their past to sabotage their future.

She dashed away another tear, unseen in the darkness, and tried not to be too brutal. 'You aren't in trouble. Are you?'

'I might as well be. It happened on my watch. I'll be the one who's held responsible. That Monica wants someone to pay for what happened to her aunt. You can see it in that hatchet face. If I was that detective, I'd be looking very carefully at where she was in the fifteen minutes after she left her aunt.'

Perhaps Monica could have done it. Perhaps the police were even now constructing a case for Karen having done it, or Becca Reid, somehow throwing her voice back into Marjorie Hodgson's room when Klemmie was in with Colin Parsons, knowing Marjorie was so confused that her account of anything would be unreliable. Perhaps Ellie could have sneaked down the stairs unseen and smothered Violet, for no reason she could think of. These were all possibilities the police would have to consider. And they'd be looking hardest at her, the one who'd found the body just after life had fled, working out ways in which she could have killed Violet, trying to think of a reason for it and coming back to the brooch she hadn't stolen, the only possible motive they'd be able to attribute to her. 'It isn't just you. They'll be looking at all of us.'

'Of course they will.' Karen, now obviously feeling the cold, shivered. 'Have you never done anything stupid, Klemmie? Not killed anyone – I don't mean that. But something stupid, or something really bad, that you don't want anyone to know about because you've changed?'

'Something stupid?' Klemmie shied away from the conversation, before it could take control of her the way destiny had done. 'Yes. Hasn't everyone?' She turned towards the door. 'It's getting cold. Let's go inside.'

When she was sure Karen was safely inside her flat, Klemmie acted. The police had taken the brooch off her hands but it wasn't the only thing of Violet's they might be interested in.

She'd wanted to keep the brooch but Violet's handgun, lodged under the mattress, had weighed heavily on her conscience and now, before she got into any more trouble, was the time to get rid of it. Lifting the package in which it was wrapped, she folded it in a plastic bag, put on her coat and stuffed it deep into the outer pocket. Closing the door of her flat behind her, she listened at Karen's door. The telly was on, loudly, and sitcom laughter drifted under the door. Confident she'd get out of the building uninterrupted, Klemmie ran down the stairs and out through the door of the empty kitchen.

The wind had picked up. She turned up her collar, regretting the lack of a hood, and crossed the garden as quickly as she could, dodging into the shade of the hedge and swiping the fob that let her out through the back gate and onto the footpath that ran down towards the river. A snatched look back at Eden's End told her she was safe. All the curtains at the back of the building were closed.

Giving herself a few moments to get used to the darkness she waited in the faint hope the moon would come out, but it only lit the clouds from behind, creating ghostly rags across the southern sky. She'd have to make do with the little light she had.

Following the dark shape of the hedge as it rustled with the wind and nocturnal wildlife, as something – a mouse, please God – scuttled across the path in front of her and an owl, interested, glided from one tree to another alongside her, Klemmie fingered the roll of plastic in her pocket. How far could she go before she was missed? How far did she need to go before she was far enough away from Eden's End for anyone to think it wasn't her who'd left it? How far off the path did she have to go before she could get rid of the parcel and be sure the wrong person wouldn't find it?

At the bend of the river a long slick of mud, glinting in the lights from the village of Langwathby just above her, answered all those questions for her. She'd go no further. To her left, bushes and brambles formed a tangled mat over the remains of a wall. Reaching into the dense vegetation, she rammed the plastic bag into the roots to her left and wedged a stone on top of it. The branches pushed her sleeve up her forearm and the thorns of the blackthorn bushes lacerated her skin. Even in the near-darkness, she could see the swelling beads of blood, blacker than the shadows that enfolded her.

Turning, she took a few steps back towards Eden's End before pausing to look back. The white plastic was invisible, a problem for someone else to deal with. Getting out her mobile phone — cheap, pay as you go and barely used — she checked it for battery and for credit. Low on both. It didn't matter. She only ever used it in emergencies, though emergencies like this weren't what she'd bargained for. 'It's Klemmie.'

'I thought I told you not to call me.'

She sighed, and pushed a strand of wet hair off her face. It was all right for him. He wasn't there. It was easy enough to sit and make plans but when something came spinning in to upset them, you couldn't always stick to Plan A. Trying to do so was, as her mother would have said with a sniff of disapproval, a very German way of doing things. 'Fine. I'll ring off. Then you won't get your father's gun.'

'Did you get it?' His tone shifted from irritation to eagerness. 'Where is it?'

Well done, Klemmie. Thanks for your effort, she said to herself with a sigh, then looked back down the bend. Maybe she'd hidden it too well. 'It's in a bush by the river.'

'Jesus Christ, Klemmie. What the hell did you put it there for? Anyone could find it.'

'I didn't have any choice. The police are all over the place. They might search my room, and if they do, I don't want anything to do with that gun. I got it because you wanted me to and you'll have to come and collect it. I'm done with this.'

'What about the brooch?'

Distance made Klemmie braver than she would be if he were nearer. 'Violet gave it to me. I'm going to keep it. The police asked me about it and I had to give it to them. But when this is all over, I'll get that back, and I'll keep it.'

'That brooch belonged to my mother.'

'I don't care if it belonged to the Virgin Mary. Violet gave it to me. I was fond of her. I cared about her, more than anyone else did. You can have the gun. I don't care about it. I never wanted to touch it and it's nothing to do with me.'

'Do the police know about it?'

'Why would they? Even Violet never told me about it. I only know because you told me.'

'That's something, I suppose. You'll have to put it somewhere safer than some hole in a hedge.'

Yet again, Klemmie looked back along the path. 'I'm not touching it again. It'll be safe enough. No-one ever comes down here. If you want it, you'll have to come and get it. I'll tell you where it is, but I'm done with it. And I'm done with you. You've got me into enough trouble.'

'We made a deal. You didn't have to agree to it.' At the

other end of the line, he laughed, but there was no humour in it. It was the kind of laugh people produced when they didn't know what else to do, when there was fear eating away at them and they didn't dare show it, even over the phone to a weak woman like her who'd end up taking the rap for someone else's crimes, because people like her always did.

'And I've done my part of it. I got you the gun, and I'm keeping the brooch, because I'm not going to get anything else out of it.' She snapped off the phone before he could argue, waited to see if he'd ring her back, but it remained silent.

Putting the phone back in her pocket, she made her tentative way back to Eden's End, shaking her head. A near-stranger's foolish sentimentality over the gun was going to be the ruin of her, even if her own weakness over the brooch turned out not to be, and somehow that wouldn't have mattered if she hadn't cared quite as much about Violet.

13

'So. We've a lot to get through, and I'm trusting in your collective brain power to solve this.' Assuming his usual position in front of the whiteboard, Jude frowned at the puzzle in front of him. 'With luck, we can come up with something together that's more plausible than anything I've managed to come up with by myself.' It had been a long and tiring evening the night before and ultimately an unproductive one. He'd been trying to get on with the paperwork for one of the many other cases he was working on, but he couldn't focus on it while his mind whirled with the mystery hanging over Eden's End — not who had killed Violet, because there was a very limited number of people who could have done it, but of what the old woman could have done to deserve death at the hands of any one of them. If he could understand why, he would surely know who.

He'd been tied up in meetings all morning but Doddsy had been on the case, rounding everybody up, making sure they knew what to do and all the information they had was ready for them to throw at him. 'Who's going to start? Is there any update on the technical stuff, before we have to move on to using our brains? Someone must have been crunching some numbers up at the lab.'

'We've just got the toxicology and forensic reports.' Doddsy shoved a piece of paper across the table. 'I've emailed you the full text, but these are the key points. There's one significant conclusion from the toxicology. Nothing unexpected came up. The only thing in Violet Ross's system was the arthritis drug, and that was meant to be there. The concentration was consistent with the dosage recorded in the drug book. For my money, that goes a long way to ruling out the head nurse. If she was ever really in the frame.'

Jude thought of Ellie Jack – irritable and over-efficient, totally intolerant, but nevertheless a woman whose professional conduct appeared unimpeachable and whose record-keeping was flawless. 'I wouldn't rule her out just yet.'

'If the nurse was going to murder a patient, surely she'd use the most effective means at her disposal. And I don't know that she has a motive.'

Chris Marshall, on the other side of the table, cleared his throat, tapped his pen on the desk like a man awaiting a major reveal. 'Jude.'

Jude raised an eyebrow. You could trust Chris to turn every stone. 'Well? Are you going to tell me you've found a motive?'

'Nothing as simple as that. But I did run a check on Mrs Jack. She has a bit of a history. Before she trained to be a nurse she worked as a volunteer in her local hospital. She was caught trying to steal some drugs and sell them on.'

'What happened to her?'

'Pleaded guilty. It wasn't a sophisticated crime. She never had a chance of getting hold of anything. She was given community service for it.'

Jude stilled. Ellie Jack, with a criminal record and a position to defend, rocketed up the list of possibilities, someone who might – even if she'd paid for her previous misdemeanours – yet lose perspective and deem an old woman's bad temper a threat worth hastening her on her way to heaven for. 'And she was still allowed to train as a nurse?'

'She must have persuaded them it was an aberration. Her record since then is excellent. She qualified with distinction. She's done well to have the position she has, at her age.'

'When did she start at Eden's End?'

'She fetched up there two years ago. I followed up with her current employers – the company that owns it – and they were unaware of her record. They'll be looking into it as a matter of urgency.'

And so they should. 'Email the disclosure stuff over to me. I'll have a look and then I think I may pop back to Eden's End after this and see what she has to say for herself. That's good work, Chris. Well done.'

'We have to look at her again, then.' Doddsy, this time, frowning. 'But there's still no motive.'

'That we know of.' Ashleigh, who had been quiet, looked up as she spoke and Jude, struggling to stop himself smiling, looked away. 'Violet was a doctor. Maybe she'd heard something about it on the grapevine. Or made inquiries.'

'I'd forgotten that. Good point.'

'So as I see it,' Ashleigh pursued, 'the question with Ellie isn't whether she had a motive. It's whether she could actually have done it.'

Sufficiently in control to turn back towards her, Jude considered. 'I think so. It's technically possible she could have got down there and back without being spotted. There was no-one with her in the dining room. We need to confirm neither Klemmie nor Becca saw her, but even if they didn't, she might have been there.'

'There are two cupboards and the fire door leading off that little area. The cupboards are shelved. She couldn't have hidden in either of those. In theory she could have hidden in the empty bedroom, though Karen said that was kept locked while the occupant was in hospital. She may have had a key. Or she could have been between the fire door and the outside door, but if she was she'd have had to get back up to the cafe without being seen.' On the far side of the table, Ashleigh wrote something down under a heading, which (Jude strained his eyes to read it) said: *Questions for BR*. 'Remember Klemmie says she heard a door.'

He managed a wry smile. Taking Ashleigh with him to interview Becca might not, after all, be the easiest thing for him. Doddsy would have been a more comfortable companion, but he needed Doddsy elsewhere and he wasn't a man to let his feelings dictate how he did his job. 'We'll check. Now, what about the rest of the forensics? Nothing again?'

'It's the old story.' Doddsy shuffled papers around. 'The place had been cleaned like an operating theatre — I suppose they have to — and what we did get from the armchair was all traceable back to Violet and didn't suggest anyone was there who shouldn't have been.'

'Anything from the rest of the furniture?'

'All the surfaces had been cleaned. There were some dabs from inside the drawers, mainly the niece's. Klemmie's fingerprints were in there too, but that's not a surprise. She looked after Violet. She brushed her hair and helped her with her make-up.'

Jude nodded. None of this surprised him. 'Okay, let's talk about the other possibilities. We know some of them could have done it. We know it's not inconceivable someone else, who we don't know about, did it. Bearing that in mind, let's look at what we know about the people involved. And let's start with Monica Roland.'

'She's an interesting case.' Ashleigh addressed the team. 'Jude and I went to see her yesterday. She was very up front. Wouldn't you say?' She flashed a glance at him.

'Refreshingly so.' To stop himself staring at her, he turned away from her and wrote Monica's name on the board.

'Yes. When Violet was first discovered dead, Monica seemed keen to let everyone know how much she adored her. By the time we got to her, she was a bit more realistic. I got the impression she was genuinely fond of her aunt, and did have a sense of both duty and obligation towards her. According to the visitors' book, and according to the statements Doddsy and Chris collected yesterday, she was a regular visitor, and she seems to have been very patient under a lot of provocation. But she admitted she had expectations from the relationship and that those expectations were financial. She was also quite up front about the fact she needs the money. She's not broke, but she lives on the financial edge.'

'No late changes to the will?' Chris, on rare occasions, let his imagination run away with him.

'No.' Jude shook his head. 'We called in on the solicitor. Monica inherits.' He wrote that on the board, too, and underlined it. 'Violet's solicitor can't say for certain, but as far as he's aware, Monica was expecting a lot more than she's actually going to get. And remember – it's what people expect that we need to look at when we consider crime.'

'The expectation of over half a million, which is probably what she thought...' Doddsy rubbed his chin, deep in thought. 'That's a very powerful motive for all sorts of crime.'

'Yes. But the question's the same as it was for Ellie Jack. Could she physically have done it?'

'When you've nothing else to do—' Doddsy raised an ironic eyebrow '—you can read over the witness statements from the other members of staff. Several people saw her leave the building fifteen minutes or so before Becca first identified Violet as dead, and CCTV confirms that. Both Becca and Ellie Jack thought she'd died after that time. You know the area better than I do, Jude. Is there anything to stop Monica parking her car a little way away, running back through the copse to the side door, letting herself in, smothering her aunt, letting herself out again and returning to her car?'

Jude shook his head. 'Anything but.' Someone had stuck up photos on the board, views of Eden's End from the road and of the road from all sides of the care home. Looking at them, he matched them up with what he knew of the area. There was no shortage of places you could pull a car in, and so little traffic passing by it would easily pass unnoticed there for a quarter of an hour. 'Perfect for it, I'd say.'

'Where was she when Karen phoned to tell her?'

'She says she was at home, but she only lives five minutes' drive away from Eden's End. Karen called her after she'd phoned the doctor. She could just about have done it.

There's bound to be a sweet spot that gave her the time to park, run back, do the deed, and get back to Langwathby in time to take Karen's call. It's a question of whether she did.' And of proving it. 'Chris, I think I'd like someone to look at Ms Roland's car and her shoes. If she'd crossed the fields, I'd expect there to be mud.' Though any mud would easily be explained away, because it was an easy walk from Langwathby to Eden's End and there had been plenty of rain.

'Next up. Klemmie Marcowics. Very interesting, this one. What did you make of her, Chris?'

'Very cool, to start with. Very bright, too.'

Doddsy nodded, as though Chris needed his approval and agreement. 'She talked like someone running away. No friends, no family, burying herself in the heart of the countryside in a place she's never been to before? I would have liked a bit more of an explanation than just a response to her mother's death.'

'There was definitely something about her that didn't ring true. Maybe because she was so nervous about the brooch. She just about cracked up when we asked her.'

Ashleigh twisted the end of her ponytail around her finger. 'Do you believe her story?'

'I'm not sure.' Chris looked to Doddsy, who shook his head, neither in agreement nor disagreement. 'Though I will say something about that. When she talked about Violet, it was the only time she showed any emotion.'

'And she said she'd spoken to Becca about the brooch.' Ashleigh added another item to her list of questions.

Jude, cursing Klemmie for having dragged Becca even further into the mire, adding another question that would prolong the interview he felt obliged to have with her himself because he didn't dare entrust it to someone else, moved the discussion on. 'Doddsy. Do you think there's any significance in the brooch?'

'In what way? I think Klemmie showed genuine attachment to Violet, and the other witnesses seemed to agree they were close. Even the ones who were a bit concerned about it didn't seem to think she was doing anything criminal – only that she wasn't handling Violet's fondness for her in an appropriate manner.'

'Except Monica, of course. But I suppose she'd see the brooch as a part of her inheritance.' And even Monica hadn't seemed particularly hostile to Klemmie as an individual, just as a staff member who'd overstepped a line. 'It would be interesting to find out a bit more about Klemmie, then. That's a job for you, Chris.'

'I'd be glad to.' Chris never minded being chained to his desk, happiest doing his detection among the highways and byways of the internet, unafraid of straying down its darker paths and well acquainted with too many of its tricks.

'I suppose it was just a coincidence she came from the same part of Poland that Violet had a picture of on her wall,' Ashleigh said, with a sigh. 'Maybe you want to check that, too.'

'That's the other thing. I'd very much like to know what Violet's Polish connection was, and where it comes from. In fact, I'd very much like to know the background to that part of her life, because if you listen to Monica none of her family seemed to know anything about it. Doddsy, I don't suppose anyone's had a chance to look through the stuff Monica gave us?'

'I got that done straight away, mainly to follow up what you said about the gun licence.'

'I'm going to guess there wasn't one.'

'No. I checked the records myself. She's never had one, and never applied for one. As you asked, I sent someone down to the house with a couple of uniformed officers and they combed the place. There was no sign of any gun. Are we sure it ever existed?'

'No.' Jude shook his head in frustration. The gun troubled him, so irrelevant to Violet's death and yet so potentially dangerous to someone, in the future. 'Monica says she only saw it once, and that was a while ago. There's no record of it. Monica can't describe it. It could have been an imitation. Maybe it was Violet's idea of a joke.'

'She was in the WAAF in the war.' Chris spilled a couple of pictures on the table, faded and monochrome.

'Right. I imagine she would have had it from then.'

'I followed that up. She wouldn't have had a side arm. She was a woman, and she didn't serve in the front line. Airmen would have carried a Webley or a Smith & Wesson, in all probability. But she wouldn't have had one.'

'I'd like to believe Monica's mistaken, but I don't think I can. Until we know for certain, we have to assume the weapon is out there, and we have to assume it works.' Jude turned back to Doddsy, still patiently sorting through the accumulation of half a dozen other officers' work. 'Was there anything else in the papers?'

'I haven't been through them myself, but from what I've seen there was nothing that leapt out. Most of it was newspaper cuttings about her role in the local community, and most of that dated from the later part of her professional career and her retirement. She was ahead of her time in the advancement of women in education and medicine and did a lot of speaking and even mentoring in local schools. She donated substantially to refugee charities.'

'Nothing caught your eye? Nothing about her war service?' Jude hated the idea of nothing. There was always something if you only knew how to spot it. Since his promotion he didn't have time to be as hands-on as he'd have liked. He had to trust others to do the basics.

'Only a reference in one of the newspapers to the fact she served in the WAAF during the war, as I already mentioned. But that makes a neat connection with the picture of the airman, doesn't it?'

Jude turned back to the board where the airman's photo, soft focus in black and white, seemed to invite every one of them to join him in his louche, exciting world of reckless fear, of life lived in the present, in the face of certain death. 'Yes. It would be helpful to find out who he was.'

'Nothing came up when I searched the internet for it. I'll get someone to send a copy of the picture to places that might have some idea. The MOD and the RAF, to start. Local museums, too, although there's nothing in her papers to suggest she was here in Keswick during the war, and the chances are she would have gone wherever she was sent.'

'See what Aditi can come up with. She's good at that sort of thing. There may not be a link, but if the motive isn't money, the chances are it's something to do with love.'

'A hundred's a bit old for a crime of passion.' Chris laughed at Ashleigh, in a way that annoyed Jude.

'It isn't too old for an act of revenge, however. It never is. That's another angle we need to look at. Violet seems to have antagonised a number of people, though it hardly goes to the level of total betrayal. She was an old lady with a sharp tongue, possibly with an increasingly suspicious nature, and a notable lack of charity. I don't think that's at all unusual.'

'She strikes me as having been the sort of person who squirrelled away every bad bit of information she heard about everyone and denied them the good.' A churchgoer, and the only one of the team with a truly charitable soul, Doddsy shook his head over this shortcoming. 'I can understand that gives a lot of people reasons to dislike her – but to kill her?'

Jude nodded his head in assent. Violet, it appeared, had had sharp things to say about everyone, from Becca, to her niece, to Karen. Everyone, that was, except Klemmie. Did the Polish woman remind her, somehow, of her younger self? 'Let's look at Karen.'

'She knew Violet had been suffocated before we told her.' Ashleigh, tapping fingers on the table, looked thoughtful.

'She certainly seemed to, but in fairness, that's the reasonable assumption once she knew the death was suspicious. Again, I'm interested in motive. Violet had complained about Karen to Monica, and Karen herself says she'd threatened to complain about her to the management. If she'd carried that through, it might have led to her losing her job. That's another thing to follow up. I don't suppose you've had a chance to do that yet, Chris?'

The young constable shook his head. 'I've put in the call and I'm waiting for a reply. But in the meantime, I've been tracking down Violet's mystery visitor.'

'You've found him?'

'Not exactly. I've tracked down when he came. It was late last November, the twenty-second. He's the only visitor other than Monica who ever came to see Violet, or at least the only one who signed into the visitors' book. He came at eleven in the morning and he stayed for an hour, almost exactly.'

'And his name?'

'That's the one thing we don't have. It's a scrawl you can't possibly read.' With an expression of regret, Chris pushed an enlarged copy of the visitors' book entry across the table. The signature, as he'd indicated, was illegible, written in thick black fountain pen whereas those above and below it were in blue biro. The letters in ink were tangled and smudged, as if deliberately. The box for the printed name was left empty.

'Well, well.' Jude frowned down at it. 'This gets ever more interesting. It looks for all the world as if he didn't want anyone to know who he was. Just as well you like a challenge, Chris, because this is a big one for you. I want you to find me that mystery man, and sooner rather than later.'

'Leave it with me. I'll get him.'

'Good.' Jude got up, his mind buzzing. Ellie had to be his next priority. 'Doddsy, you can come with me. I'm going to pop back to Eden's End. After that, Ashleigh, I think we need to go and see Becca. She finishes work early this afternoon. I've told her we'll call round about four.'

'I think you can guess why we've come.' Jude declined a seat, though Ellie had sat at the table in the interview room

Karen kept available for them and had helped herself to coffee and cake.

Though she must surely have been expecting her background to be uncovered, she showed no signs of nerves, wasn't remotely cowed. Instead she stuck out her chin and challenged him, with a look. 'Obviously you've discovered something important relating to Violet's death.'

'Not that. My team have done something your employers should have done, Mrs Jack, but it appears they didn't. They carried out a criminal record check.'

'I see.'

'You did disclose your criminal record to your employers, I take it? After your appointment, if not before.'

She shook her head at him. 'You can't accuse me of killing Violet Ross, Chief Inspector. Or if you are, you'll have to come up with something a lot better than that.'

'I'm not accusing you of anything. I'm asking you why you didn't declare your criminal record.'

She rolled her eyes at him, as though she found the question stupid and the required explanation tedious. Clearly she wasn't a woman with a great deal of respect for authority. 'I was never asked. If I had been, I'd have told them. It isn't my fault if they chose not to follow up my references, or do the background checks.'

'And what would they have found if they'd checked your references?'

She raised her eyebrows at him in a gesture that was almost contempt. 'I edited my references, Chief Inspector. I wanted a promotion and this was a good job. No-one's ever challenged me on my professionalism. I made mistakes.

I don't deny that. But they were mistakes I made when I was sixteen and under pressure from my peers. I've paid the price for them. Can't you understand that?'

Jude stared back at her, understanding too well. The situation Ellie described, that of a naive teenager under the influence of others, was exactly the same one Mikey had found himself in, and in his heart he knew that mercy was the most productive way of dealing with it. Beside him, Doddsy cleared his throat and Jude knew he must be thinking the same thing. 'That's a fair point.' He pulled himself back to the questions. 'And I take it the conviction is spent?'

She nodded.

'Was it spent when you took up this job?'

'Does that matter? I've proved I can do the job and do it well. Don't you dare try and pin a conviction on me for a crime I didn't commit, just because I committed a very different crime in the past.'

Jude caught Doddsy's eye, and wished he hadn't. His colleague seemed to find this funny, but there was little that annoyed Jude more than the layman who claimed to know the law, and his job, better than he did. 'I want you to understand where I'm coming from, Mrs Jack. Somebody killed a defenceless old lady and I need to find out who that person was. Because unless we find out who, and unless we find out why, then there has to be a chance it will happen again. What's significant about this is that you misled the investigating officer.'

'I don't recall being asked the question.'

'All right. I'm not unsympathetic to your position. I'm going to ask another question now, and I advise you to answer it, fully and honestly. Is there anything else you know, or suspect, that might be in any way relevant to the investigation into Violet Ross's murder?'

The word murder did the trick. It always did when he put a particular emphasis on it, and the people who flinched, as Ellie Jack did, were usually innocent. She'd been toying with her coffee cup but she put it down, squeezing her hands together in desperation. She didn't speak.

So that was a yes. 'Mrs Jack?' he prompted her. 'Anything? Anything at all?'

'Nothing important.' But she didn't look at him and her breathing increased in speed.

'Nothing important to you, perhaps. But I'd like to be the judge of whether it's significant.'

'About two months ago, Violet gave me something to keep safe for her. But it was only an envelope.'

'Only an envelope?' Out of the corner of his eye he saw Doddsy stiffen in irritation. 'Do you know what was in it?'

'No…I—' She reached for the coffee again. 'Obviously, it isn't relevant to what happened, but you said you wanted to know everything. A document. In Polish. I don't know what it said. She asked me to witness her signature on it.'

Inwardly, Jude groaned. Whatever it was, it was something he'd rather have seen earlier than later. A document in Polish that required a witness's signature, and Ellie didn't think it was important? 'May I see it?'

'I was to give it to Monica if Violet died.'

'Did you do that?'

'No. To tell you the truth, Chief Inspector, I completely forgot. What with everything going on in here, and me being quite wrongly suspected of professional misconduct, if not worse.'

'Where is this envelope? I take it you still have it?'

'It's in my locker, and has been all the time. If you come with me, I'll get it for you.'

14

Jude's sergeant arrived first, pulling up outside Becca's cottage and sitting waiting, as if she were too scared to approach the front door on her own. Hearing the car, Becca tweaked the curtains, only to let them fall when she saw the woman's blonde head, her face lit by the screen of her phone as she checked messages in the fading winter light, casting a furtive glance over her shoulder like someone afraid of being followed.

Becca was a gregarious soul, but it had been a tough few days, made tougher by the need to catch up on the time Violet's death had cost her. The last thing she wanted was to make polite conversation with a stranger when she'd barely had time to take off her work clothes and slip on a more comfortable pair of shoes. Letting the curtain drop, she turned her attention to setting a match to the kindling in the open fireplace. If Jude was determined to come along and make her uncomfortable, then at least she could take the chill off the cottage before he got there.

That done, she went to put the kettle on. The kitchen was at the back of the house, but the road through the village was quiet and she recognised the low rumble of Jude's Mercedes. It came to a stop outside, followed by the opening and closing of car doors and the sound of voices as Jude and his sergeant came up the path.

Nevertheless, she waited until they rang the doorbell before she moved to answer it, revealing the two of them standing there, with the woman on the step and Jude a little further back, scanning the lengthening shadows as they encroached on the path. She knew what he was looking for – any sign of her cat, Holmes. The man and the animal shared a deep understanding that excluded her, and she resented it, but this time Jude was doomed to disappointment. Holmes was asleep on her bed and unlikely to stir.

'Jude.' She put on her best polite expression and saved her smile for the sergeant. Jude had squandered too much of her goodwill over the years for her to waste any more. Until his inflexible conscience, his inability to cut some slack for a friend, had got in the way she'd thought she'd marry him. She'd been the one who'd ended it, but it was his fault. 'Come on in.'

Thank God, he'd decided to go for the formal approach, or largely so, keeping his smile under control. Nevertheless, used to feeling the full, warm force of that unconditional smile, she felt slightly cheated by its absence. 'Hi, Becca. Sorry about this. It shouldn't take long. It's just admin, really, but there are a couple of things we need to tie up.' There was a barely perceptible pause. 'I don't think you've met the newest member of my team. This is DS Ashleigh O'Halloran.'

'Sorry to cut into your valuable free time, Ms Reid.' Ashleigh O'Halloran, offering her hand, accompanied the friendly gesture with a searching look that Becca, confident in her innocence and on her own territory, returned with interest. 'I know we've taken up plenty of it already.'

'Not at all. Come through and sit down. Jude knows the way. The kettle's just boiled. Let me make you some coffee. Or tea?'

'Or I could make it,' he offered. 'Then Ashleigh can run you through the questions and we can get out from under your feet sooner rather than later.'

He was hard to read, especially when he composed his face into that almost expressionless mask and avoided her gaze, staring instead at a spot somewhere over her shoulder. The suggestion made sense, so she shrugged him aside. 'Go ahead. You know where everything is.' Leaving him to run riot in her kitchen as he used to do, she led Ashleigh O'Halloran through to the living room and settled her on the sofa while she herself took a seat in the worn armchair closest to the hearth. 'Fire away. I don't know how much help I can be. I don't spend a lot of time at Eden's End and I wouldn't claim to be privy to the inner workings of what goes on there.'

'But you're a regular visitor there, and an independent observer. You'll have an informed perspective on how the place functions. Jude's told me – off the record, of course – that you were the one who first raised suspicions about Violet Ross's death. Since then a number of things have come up, and we're hoping you might be able to shed some light on them.'

Despite her determination to be reasonable Becca found herself stiffening in hostility – not to Jude, which was what she'd prepared herself against, but towards this woman who couldn't resist looking towards the door as he emerged from the kitchen with a tray and mugs. And biscuits. He'd been into the cupboard and dug out the biscuits as if it were old times. It wasn't until she remembered this was exactly what she'd told him to do that she was able to suppress her irritation. 'I'm not sure how much help I can be.'

'You may be able to clarify a few things for us.'

Becca looked at the woman, assessing her. It was hardly surprising she was taken with Jude, whose charisma was undeniable, though maybe her own thinking was influenced by the years she'd spent with him. Certainly, when she'd brought their relationship to an end, it hadn't been because she no longer desired him. She folded her lips into a thin line as he placed a cup of tea on the table at her elbow and took his seat in the armchair opposite. When she'd seen Jude at Eden's End they'd been relaxed enough to joke, but Ashleigh O'Halloran's interested presence intimidated her. 'Fire away. I'll do what I can.'

'First up. Klemmie Marcowics. Do you know her well?'

Becca thought of Klemmie, careful and polite while remaining self-contained and withdrawn. 'No. I don't think anyone does. From what I saw, she keeps herself to herself, though I have to say she's always very helpful. The only person I ever saw her really relax with was Violet.'

'Did the two of them spend much time together?'

'I don't know. Usually the residents are in the lounge. When I arrived I'd wait in there while the staff took Marjorie down to her room for me to dress her leg. Klemmie would be taking the teas around at that time, and I often saw her sitting and chatting with Violet. Beyond that, I can't say how much time they spent together.'

'She says she confided in you.'

Becca lifted an eyebrow. All Klemmie had sought from her was advice, and that wasn't the sharing of a confidence, any more than it had been when she'd approached Jude for guidance and kicked the whole business off. Her relationship with both was purely professional. 'Oh. That. Yes. She spoke to me because she was worried.'

'What about?'

'Apparently Violet had given her a present, a brooch. She'd thought it was just a wee minding, but then she'd heard Violet's niece going on about how valuable it was. Strictly speaking, of course, she shouldn't have taken any gifts without checking with Karen first. But she won't have meant any harm.'

Jude and his new woman — his new colleague, she corrected herself in irritation, caught out by the fact he was so good at impounding his feelings when he needed to that she couldn't know what he thought about her, or indeed about Becca herself — exchanged glances, as if she'd shed light on some great mystery. She hoped she hadn't unwittingly got Klemmie into trouble. 'For what it's worth, I believed her. She'd have been so touched by the gesture she wouldn't have thought to ask.'

Ashleigh O'Halloran gave a tiny nod, and Becca felt judged in her turn. 'What did you say to her?'

'I told her she should own up to it. I take it she didn't?'

'Not straight away.' Jude smiled, leaned down and stretched out a hand. Holmes, ghosting his way into the room, perhaps alerted by a familiar voice, insinuated himself around Jude's ankles and then leapt lightly onto his lap with a squeak of complaint, as if scolding him for his long absence. 'But she did admit to it when we asked her directly. How well was the place run, Becca? Was it a tight ship?'

She considered. 'I'm not sure I'd say that. It certainly isn't regimented. When people pay all this money they — or sometimes their families — expect everything to be run to suit them, whereas dealing with so many people requires more than an element of regulation. Karen never quite got the balance right, so there's always something chaotic about it.' Taking a moment to think about it, she spent most of that moment staring at Ashleigh O'Halloran, her glossy hair, her blue eyes, her sheer and obvious availability. 'They don't pay their staff well, compared to the fees they charge, which means they can't afford to be too choosy about who they employ. I think that shows.'

'They certainly charge the residents enough.' In her turn, Ashleigh reached out a hand to fuss Holmes and exchanged rueful smiles with Jude when she was rebuffed with a hiss.

'Yes, but the money doesn't get to the people working there. Somehow it always feels understaffed, even though technically it isn't. But there's always somebody demanding attention.'

'Violet, for example?'

'Yes. Violet liked to hold court, and anyone would do at a push, but I think Klemmie was her favourite. I don't know what it was, but she always looked at her fondly. Violet spoke fluent Polish and they chattered away sometimes when I was there. And nobody else seemed to have the time for her.'

'It's the management that sets the tone in these places.' Jude flicked Holmes's whiskers, a liberty for which anyone else would have paid in blood. 'I get the impression you don't feel Karen's on top of her job.'

Becca shook her head, looking at the biscuits he'd

removed from the packet and arranged on the plate, and wondered if she'd feel any happier with life if she devoted more of her time to cooking and eating in an attempt to fill the void in her life. 'She wasn't on top of anything. Everything just about held together. I like Karen very much, but you're right. I don't think she's up to it. I can only imagine she got the job because no-one else would do it for the money. There's no deputy manager. She lives on site and she's always on call. I'm astonished it's allowed. It's obvious she isn't coping.'

'She says she suffers from stress.'

'I'll be surprised if that's all. And yet, for all she struggles, I think she likes the job. She's an odd woman. There's a lot about her I suspect nobody knows.'

'I believe Violet was scathing about her.'

'Yes, but Violet was scathing about everyone. Even me. She kept telling me—' She ground to a halt.

Jude cracked, a grin splitting his face as he scratched behind Holmes's ears. 'So I heard.' And the moment vanished; the smile disappeared. 'So. Tell me about Karen.'

'I think she's probably out of her depth, and I suspect she has personal issues that make it difficult for her to do the job as well as she's capable of. I don't know what they are. You'd need to ask her.' She was tired, and Jude and his sergeant, snatching half glances at one another, each when the other wasn't looking, were as tiresome as teenagers so she was desperate for the interview to end. 'That's about as far as I can help you, I'm afraid. Is there anything else?'

'Just one more thing. Did you ever see Violet with a male visitor, or hear her talking about one?'

'I'm afraid I never did.'

'Okay. Then that's all. If you think of anything else, you know where I am. Call me any time.' He got to his feet, manhandling the reluctant Holmes off his lap and onto the floor. 'Okay, Sergeant.' He flashed a grin across to the woman as she got to her feet. 'Let's get back to work. No rest in the pursuit of justice.'

'How's Mikey?' Determined to be sociable, not to allow him to think she was as small-minded as she believed herself to be, Becca also had a genuine fondness for Jude's troubled and troublesome young brother. 'Do you hear from him much, these days?'

'Not much. He comes back through from uni every now and again, and if Mum gives me the heads-up I pop by to see if he's okay.' Jude's look darkened, a reflection of uncomfortable thoughts.

She hurried to reassure him. 'You've done so well by that boy, Jude. He's turning out to be a lovely young man. And it's all down to you.' Because you had to give him his due. Mikey had gone off the rails spectacularly when his father left home, and it was Jude who'd had to deal with the fallout.

'Nice of you to say so.' But his tone cooled slightly, as if he didn't welcome the compliment. Mikey's wild period, and Jude's reaction to it, was what had precipitated the end of Becca's relationship with him. You could be too tough, take too hard a line in the pursuit of justice, so that other people paid too high a price. 'He's barely spoken to me since that mix-up over the flights in Ibiza.'

That particular incident, in which Becca had had to come to Mikey's rescue because Jude was occupied with work, was an unnecessary reminder of why their relationship had foundered. She and Jude had different priorities. That reminded her. 'There is one more thing.'

He must have sensed it was personal, because he waved at his sergeant. 'I'll see you outside, Ashleigh.' And when she'd closed the door, he turned back and subjected Becca to that deep, thoughtful scrutiny she'd once found delicious and had since come to feel as a threat. It was all very well to allow Jude to understand her, but she no longer believed he could be trusted to deal gently with her secrets. 'Okay. What can I do for you?'

Holmes had followed them into the hall and was rubbing around her legs in search of food, switching to Jude's in hero worship. Giving in to jealousy, she picked the cat up and held him close, calmed by his deep, long purr. It was bad enough to see Ashleigh O'Halloran fawning over Jude but to have Holmes join in was too much. 'It's Adam.'

He nodded. The expression didn't change.

'I heard a rumour he's coming up for parole soon.'

'That's right. I think the hearing was this morning.' He reached out a long finger to scratch Holmes under the chin. 'I expect he'll have got it. He was properly remorseful. And he should never have been in so long.'

She wished he'd give her some clue how he really felt. Adam Fleetwood had been a close friend of both of theirs, but when Mikey had got himself involved in drugs, he'd been revealed as his supplier. Jude, when he'd handed the matter over to the authorities, hadn't known that, but Becca couldn't quite be sure he would have acted differently if he had. That was the final straw, the note upon which she'd ended their relationship. 'He should never have been in at all.'

'That's a matter of opinion.'

'He deserves a second chance.'

'He's getting one. Regardless, if the hearing went the way I expect it did, he'll be back in town before we know it.'

They shared two decades of friendship, Jude and Adam, as kids at the village school, teenagers hanging out in the hills, young men making merry. It had stopped there, their paths gradually diverging and Adam taking one step off the straight and narrow. 'That'll be awkward for you.' As she stared at him in defiance, she felt a betraying blush creep up her throat, staining her face. There was a lot more that Jude hadn't known at the time, a lot that he didn't know now, and he'd think less of her if he ever found out. That was why it had had to end.

'I expect I'll cope.'

'Come on,' she said to Holmes, knowing that Jude had seen the blush and was bound to have misinterpreted it as weakness not guilt, 'let's get you fed. I've got tuna in the kitchen.'

'Tuna? You spoil that cat,' he said over his shoulder as he turned to follow the blonde out into the night.

'And why not? He's my child substitute,' she snapped at him, and somehow all her good intentions failed and her determination to be civil to him fell away, so this conversation ended, as every other seemed to do, in a cloud of bitterness.

15

'If you come on in,' Karen said, with a sigh that was worth a thousand words, 'we can have a drink. I don't suppose half a bottle will make me incapable of working tomorrow. But if you don't come in I'll drink the whole lot, and then God knows where we'll end up. So you'd be doing a public service.'

Klemmie acknowledged herself caught out. She'd paused on the landing to unlock the door to her tiny flat and she'd consciously tried to do it quietly so as not to attract any unwelcome attention, but Karen must have been listening out for her. When Klemmie had reached the landing her soft tread on the step must have given her away, and Karen was out there like a spider on a fly, overwhelmed by need.

Well, Klemmie was used to the needy, and good with them. And who knew? There might be something in this encounter she could turn to her advantage. If nothing else, now Violet had gone she realised just how little she enjoyed her own company. 'Maybe just for a quick glass. I'm on the early shift tomorrow.'

Karen acknowledged the reality of this. 'I don't know how I'd cope without you. You work so hard, so diligently.

Come on in. Are you hungry? I've made some banana bread.'

There was a leftover portion of lasagne waiting in the fridge for Klemmie to put it in the microwave, but it would wait another day. Karen's baking was so obviously an expression of her need to be needed that it would have damaged her self-esteem to refuse, and there were worse prices to pay for a good deed than a slab of home baking and a glass of good red wine. 'That would be lovely.'

'Come and sit down.'

Klemmie had been in Karen's flat before and coveted it – twice the size of her own, with a reasonably sized living room rather than Klemmie's cramped one and a view, in daylight, so awe-inspiring and calming it made you want to spend your life staring at it. If Karen's company wasn't comfortable then the sofa she'd squeezed along one wall made up for it. Sinking onto it, Klemmie's weary soul acknowledged how heavily the difficulties of the previous few days were taking their toll. One glass of wine, and she'd be asleep. 'Thank you. Isn't it all awful?'

Karen nodded, pouring the wine with the solemnity of a minister presiding over the blessing of the Host. 'They won't find who really did it. I know they won't. It'll be some stranger who sneaked in and stole her brooch, and killed her when she woke up. A vagrant. That's who it'll be. But the police won't believe that. It'll be too difficult to find him, and impossible to prove it. So they won't be looking in the right place.'

'Do you think so?' Klemmie yawned. Under Karen's rapidly accelerating speech she detected insecurity, fear and approaching breakdown. An idea flared in her head, one she dismissed out of hand, or thought she did, but it bounced straight back again.

'Obviously. It's all about targets. It ticks the boxes, blaming one of us. Maybe whoever it was got rid of the brooch. I hope they find it. Then we can all sleep more easily instead of worrying about being locked up for something we didn't do.'

Klemmie accepted the glass Karen offered her, but she pushed at the banana bread with an experimental finger. It had a leaden look, as if it was a product of its baker's desperation. Her heart felt just as leaden, so much so she couldn't even bring herself to pretend, the way Karen was pretending, that it wasn't someone in the home who must have done it. 'They've already got the brooch.'

'They have?' Astonished, Karen paused in the act of sitting down, lurched back and landed in the armchair. Wine splashed from the glass into her lap. *Unbalanced*, thought Klemmie, inspired. 'Where did they find it?'

'I had it. Violet gave it to me.'

'When did she do that? Why did you accept it, Klemmie? You know the rules.'

Klemmie had no time for common sense, for the explanations she'd been forced to trot out to the policeman who so clearly hadn't thought much of her justification. It was about so much more than that. It was about friendship. 'I didn't think it was worth anything. As soon as they told me it was valuable, I gave it to them. I only let her give it to me because I wanted something to remember her by.'

'So that's what you meant when you said you'd done something foolish. I understand, now. Thank goodness it was you, Klemmie. Thank goodness the police know. And thank goodness it's all sorted.'

Klemmie didn't recall her conversation with Karen going exactly like that, and *sorted* certainly hadn't been her interpretation of the policemen's reaction when she'd surrendered the brooch, but it was as good a way of tying up loose ends as any other. 'Maybe you're right. They do want to arrest one of us for it. That's why they're looking at me. I'm the easy target. The outsider. The foreigner. You don't know what it's like to be this lonely.'

'But I do know. I'm lonely too.'

'You've no reason to be.' Under a stealthy cloak of concern, Klemmie probed for Karen's weakness with the delicacy of a surgeon. 'Think about me. Separated from my family and friends.'

'It's so terrible your parents died, Klemmie. But at least they didn't reject you.'

'Did yours?'

'Not exactly. But they might as well have done. I wasn't what they wanted.' Karen fought back the tears. 'They wanted someone clever. They're both so clever, and so is my brother. But I'm not academic. I don't see them any more.'

'That's so sad.'

'No it isn't. They wouldn't want to see me and I hate the way it makes me feel. So stupid and valueless.'

'Surely they say—'

'Oh, they say the right things. But I know that's not what

they really think, so I didn't tell them where I am. They always blame me for everything. Like the police do.'

Interesting. It was time to up the ante in the self-pity stakes. 'But I'm the one they suspect of murder.'

'Poor Klemmie.' Karen's voice shook. She drank, deeply. 'It's awful. I know you didn't do it. But we still don't know who did. Do we?' Her tone cracked under the weight of self-doubt.

'What do you mean?' Surely Karen wasn't going to make an improbable confession of murder? Acting on a thought that wouldn't go away, Klemmie had been quite deliberate in attempting to tease out her colleague's problems, but she hadn't expected this. Still, why not test it? 'You don't mean you killed Violet?'

'No! No, of course I don't mean that. But there's an awful thing, Klemmie. If you do one thing wrong in your life… it breaks you.'

Klemmie considered. How close was Karen to breaking point? She fought to keep her face sympathetic. 'Awful. Especially if your family hate you.' Which they surely wouldn't, but Karen was displaying all the signs of the irrational, the fearful and the anxious soul for whom there was catastrophe round every corner and rejection lurking in every good deed.

'I'm a good woman. Really. But I'm so scared I may have done something bad without realising.'

'You think you might have killed Violet? Accidentally?'

A tear crept down through the folds of skin on Karen's heavy-jowled face. 'I'd never hurt anyone. I never would. Not deliberately.'

'No. You're a caring person. That's why you have this job. It's why you love the job.'

'I won't have it much longer. They'll look at me and think I can't cope. And I can't, but it isn't my fault. I have issues. It's getting worse. But even that isn't the worst thing. Do you know what the worst thing is?'

'No.' Klemmie closed her fist around the stem of her glass.

'Sometimes I forget what I've done. For hours at a time. I only know what I've done because I must have done it. Like signed for deliveries and left phone messages. Even baking. I must have baked this loaf, but I can't remember doing it.'

This was ridiculous. 'You didn't kill Violet. You can't have done. You were up at the desk the whole time. Weren't you?'

Karen put her glass down, reaching for a tissue and dabbing at her face with a shaking hand. 'But was I? That was what I told the police. But now when I think about it, I can't remember anything about that afternoon. Anything at all. It happens sometimes.'

'It'll be the stress.' Klemmie didn't want the banana loaf, but she bit into it anyway, and the strong tang of bicarbonate of soda bore witness to the chaos prevailing in Karen's mind. Normally the baking was professional in quality, and so obvious a mistake indicated not only a slip of the hand but one that had gone either unnoticed or uncared for. 'Stress does that to you. You blank out things that frighten you. Things you don't want to think about.' She took a deep breath. 'Bad things you've done.'

Karen stared at her, face white, mouth sagging into an expression of abject misery.

'Do you sleepwalk?' Klemmie asked her. 'Hear voices?'

'Voices.' Karen put her hands to her ears. 'Yes. All the time. Telling me how worthless I am. And sometimes that I don't deserve to live. As if I didn't already know.'

'That's not a good sign.'

'Oh God. Do you ever hear voices, Klemmie?'

'No.' Klemmie swigged at the red wine to drown out the taste of the banana bread. The only voice that ever troubled her was robust common sense, ticking her off for ever having come to Eden's End and got involved with Violet Ross, and even now she could see a way out of that. 'People do, though, if they're troubled. My cousin did.'

'What happened to her?'

Klemmie took a look out of the window, at the lights of Langwathby above the river, at car headlights heading past the bridge from the village and disappearing behind the low bulk of the woods where the predatory owl had swung low across the fields, hunting. Opportunity knocked once more, the last temptation to a bad deed. She succumbed. *May I be forgiven*. 'She went into the woods one day and hanged herself.'

Karen moved her hands from her ears to her eyes, each sense in turn causing yet more torment, and moaned. 'It keeps coming to me. I could have done it. I could have killed her. I don't remember anything, only what they say happened. Suppose I did slip down and smother her and then came back up to the desk?'

'You said you were on the phone.'

'I could have done it while I was on the phone. Couldn't I? I could have kept listening and then put the call on mute. And then I could have killed her and gone up to the desk.'

'But why? Why would you do that?'

'I don't know.' Karen put down the glass, bent forward and hugged her knees in desperation. 'There's only one reason I can think of. I've been afraid of it for ever and now it's happening. I'm going mad, Klemmie. Mad.'

16

Lisa had put a trap down in the kitchen of the house in Norfolk Road and a small scrap of adolescent mouse had walked right into it. Still squeamish about animals when experience had taught her to conceal her distress at dead and damaged humans, Ashleigh turned her back on it with a twist of the stomach and decided, after all, to take what passed for a meal through to the living room. Usually she and Lisa ate at the kitchen table, but Lisa was out and, as so often when Ashleigh was busy, supper was a sandwich, easily eaten with one hand while she flicked through endless documents on her iPad with the other.

'No doubt who's to blame for this one,' she said aloud, gathering sandwich, iPad and a glass of Coke. 'Sorry, little one. I'll leave you for the killer to dispose of when she gets home. Case closed. I wish they were all as easy.' Shouldering her way from the kitchen she left the recently deceased carcass in the cold draught from the back door and headed for the living room. Depositing the various items on the side table, she bent to switch on the fire and turned back.

Scott was outside the window.

For a second she stared at him, limbs still with shock, eyes locked on those of her husband, and he smiled.

It was the smile that did it. He thought it was funny. She swooped across the room as his pale figure vanished into the shadows cast by the yellow streetlights on Norfolk Road, and slammed the shutters closed. Then she stood with her back to them, her heart beating like that of a fool, hammering at her with fury. She'd let him frighten her. That wasn't how you dealt with Scott. You had to laugh and joke and never let him smell weakness because if you did, he'd be back.

Mr Persistent, she used to call him when that aspect of his character had amused her.

It didn't amuse her any more. She stood still for a few seconds longer, bracing herself for the ring on the doorbell that didn't come. That was how it would be all night, so even the sound of Lisa returning from work would send her heart jumping in fear, but she wouldn't let him win and she wasn't too proud to ask for help. Thrusting her hand in the pocket of her cardigan, she pulled out her phone. 'Jude.'

'Is everything okay?'

He was so unlike Scott. He had no charm and no patience with fools, and he split the opinions of people who knew him with no-one left ambivalent, but he was reliable, he was dependable, and when he'd said she could call him, she'd believed him. He was everything her ex-husband wasn't, the opposite in both the good and the bad. 'Yes. Just a little local difficulty.'

'Your husband?'

'It's probably nothing.'

'Is he there?'

'I thought I saw him outside in the street just now, but if it was him, he's gone.' She was already feeling foolish. It had been the briefest of sightings, maybe a subliminal one, a mental victory he'd won through his ambush of her earlier in the week, and the more she replayed it in her head, the less sure she was of what she'd seen. 'Something spooked me. No, I'm being ridiculous. I don't think it was him.' *Call yourself a police officer, Ashleigh O'Halloran.* But with Jude's voice, supportive and authoritative, at the other end of the phone she didn't regret making the call.

'Okay.' There was a pause, a rattling noise as if Jude, too, had been eating his meal and had pushed the plate aside. 'Is your housemate home? Or will she be home soon?"

'No.' Ashleigh's heart rate had slowed once she'd realised Scott wasn't going to ring the doorbell, but now it was inexplicably on the rise again. 'She's somewhere up near Hadrian's Wall, at a public meeting. Telling them no Roman roads are going to be destroyed by a small-scale wind farm or something.'

Now she was rambling. She breathed slowly, deeply, listened for Scott's footsteps at the door or in the street and heard nothing. Because it hadn't been him, but a trick of the light on a stranger stopping to check his phone outside, and after the first second she'd known that. 'Sorry. I'm rambling. And I'm sure it wasn't him.'

He laughed. Jude didn't laugh often, and the warmth of it always surprised her. 'Don't worry. I'll come round and check the place out for you anyway.'

'Thank you, but it's okay. I don't want to disturb you. I shouldn't have called.'

'Nevertheless, I'll come round and check for you.'

'I don't want to put you out. Or get him into trouble.'

'I'm not doing anything else. And if he wasn't there he

won't get into trouble.' She heard his front door open, a car rolling past, a dog barking. 'I'll be with you in five.' He ended the call.

Ashleigh stayed still, furious with herself for allowing Scott to spook her when he wasn't even there. A watery smile crossed her face at the irony, the hunter hunted. Even without intending to, he had her on the run, taking up space in her head now she'd evicted him from her heart.

She shook her head, ruefully. Why had she called Jude? Because he was the perfect example of how to behave in the circumstances? He'd managed to let Becca go with a proper degree of respect. He was still in love with her – anyone with half an eye in their head could see that, possibly including Becca herself – but he was living proof you could be grown up about an unwelcome break-up. And in any case, it would suit her fine to date a man whose heart was given elsewhere: it meant there was no risk she'd end up with someone else like the man she'd married and still had to fight so hard to free her heart from. She still had to lay the marriage to rest, but a strong letter from the solicitor would do it, and if that didn't send him back to his boats and the temptations of bikini-clad beauties with his tail between his legs, she'd be applying for a restraining order on him. She'd do it if she had to.

A car, outside. Jude lived in Wordsworth Street, almost within sight of the front door, but even so he'd made good time. She waited for the doorbell and when it came she hesitated, just in case, but then she went to the door. 'Jude. Sorry – I didn't mean to drag you out.'

'No worries.' He gave her a cool look, a sidelong one rather than the direct and challenging stare he gave her in the office. Caught out just as he seemed to be by how easily their relationship had shifted from colleagues to friends, Ashleigh went pink. Now she understood why she'd called him. 'You know what I said. Want me to have a look?'

'If you wouldn't mind.' From the safety of his shadow, Ashleigh stepped down from the doorstep and onto the street. As she'd known it would be, it was empty.

'Is there access at the back of the house?'

'Yes, for the bins. There's a lane.'

He made his way to the kitchen, thrust open the door and stepped out into the darkness, rattling down the path with his long shadow stretching ahead of him. Another mouse, bolder and smarter than its dead associate, pelted across the path behind him. She'd suggest to Lisa that they get a cat.

'No sign of him,' he said, coming into the light with a cheerful smile. 'And that's a good solid lock you have on that back gate.'

'Yes.' With hindsight it had been ridiculous to trouble him. Even if it had been Scott, he'd meant no harm, had only been desperate not to let their marriage go. Perhaps, after all, the best thing would be to talk to him, for his own and for old times' sake. 'I'm sorry I called you out.'

'Not at all.' He let himself back into the kitchen, locking the door behind him, looked down at the mouse in the trap and didn't insult her by offering to get rid of it. 'Are you coming?'

'Coming where?'

'I don't imagine he'll come back, but if he does then he can't hassle you if you aren't in. And I don't know about you, but I need something to eat. Hop into the car and we'll go down into the town.'

She stared at him for a moment, before she saw it made perfect sense. 'Okay then.' And, picking up coat and bag, she stepped out of the house. Close by, the express train rumbled northwards through the station and the street was empty. *Scott*, she thought to herself, *you're too late. Too late. I've left you behind.*

'Do you reckon your man will have gone home yet?' Jude put his pint down, the glass empty, aware it was a work night and he had plenty of things to do, but he was a man who seized opportunities, no matter how slender. If you didn't, you were left with regrets. Sometimes, of course, you were left with regrets anyway, but that didn't mean you shouldn't try. The chance to talk to Ashleigh about something other than work was rare, and he'd hardly consider himself a man if he didn't want to prolong it.

And he did consider himself a man. If he'd had any doubts they'd vanished with the way she looked at him. Daring, he placed his arm along the back of the seat behind her.

'I expect so.' She shifted, but towards him not away. 'If he was here he'll have jumped on the next train and be almost back in Manchester by now. Anyway, Lisa will be back.'

'Then I'll walk you home.'

She turned those blue eyes up towards him. 'You're a proper gentleman, but there isn't any need. You saw Scott at his worst the other day. He's fine when he's not drunk.'

'He may or may not have been drunk if he was there two hours ago, but even if he wasn't, he might be now. And he might not have got the train. The walk will do me good.' He'd left the car in town, where he could pick it up in the morning, and Ashleigh lived barely twenty minutes' walk from his front door.

'If you're sure you don't mind.'

'Not remotely.' He strode off too quickly along the pavement, too used to walking by himself, and had to moderate his step to allow her to catch up. 'It does me good to have an evening off from time to time.' That was what Becca always said. He smiled, wryly. 'I'm glad you called me, if you were worried.'

'I wasn't really.'

He smiled in the darkness. 'Then why call me? Because you enjoy my company? I hope so. I enjoy yours.'

Was he rushing in too quickly? Were those few sentences something he would come to regret? There was still a lot about Ashleigh he had to find out before he made a fool of himself over her. Because he would; he knew it. It wasn't a relationship that would last, or could possibly last, but it was a relationship they'd have to have. Ashleigh, so vibrant, so attractive and so interested, was pulsing around his body like his blood and there was only one way to get her out of his system. A part of him understood exactly why Scott was so reluctant to lose her. 'Why did the two of you break up?'

She shrugged, keeping close beside him as they walked up Castlegate. 'It was his fault. He keeps his brains in his trousers.'

Hopefully the darkness hid his wry smile at something he himself was guilty of. 'Did he play away a lot?'

'Oh, all the time. That's the trouble. No matter how hard he tries, he can't resist temptation. He was away from home a lot. He's a sailor – he crews proper boats, on the

Med – and there was plenty of opportunity with people looking for a holiday fling. It wasn't as if I didn't know. I made the mistake of thinking he'd settle down when I married him, but of course he didn't.' She turned swiftly away, as if to hide her face. 'That's what happens when you love someone.'

'Yes.' Jude thought of Becca. Had she thought she could change him?

'Now I realise he'll never change. I think he does love me, as much as he's ever loved anyone, and he was upset when I left. He probably just assumed I'd come back. But he's going to have to learn to live without me, because I'm not going to spend the next forty years of my life with someone I can't trust. It's not about love any more. It's about self-preservation.'

They paused to cross the road outside the Station Hotel. A breeze, springing from nowhere, blew from her to him and left him the gift of a breath of perfume. 'And did you live a blameless life all the time you were married?'

She looked up at him, tilting her head in reproach. 'That depends on what you mean by blameless. He's been talking to you, hasn't he? When?'

'If you remember, I gave him a lift back to his hotel the last time we met.'

'He rambles a lot when he's drunk.' She thrust her hands deep into the pockets of her Barbour jacket against the cold. 'Did he tell you anything interesting?'

'He warned me against getting involved with you on the grounds you have a penchant for your bosses.' He grinned down at her, resisting the temptation to take her hand, reminding himself that, even though he knew what he wanted, knew what he had to have, it wasn't always good to get it too soon. The only way to prove to himself he wasn't obsessed was restraint. 'Is that right?'

'It's a version of the truth. It happened once, and I was on the rebound at the time. It was when I'd realised the marriage was over and I wanted him to know how it felt. Do you think less of me for wanting revenge?'

'No. I can quite understand it. And is that the reason you left your last job?'

'Yes.' She laughed. 'It's always the way. Scott slept his way through all his firm's pretty female customers and no-one turned a hair. I had one affair with my boss when I was hurting like hell because I still cared about him, and there was hell to pay.'

'Was your boss married?'

'Yes.'

'And what did his wife think?'

The lights changed and she strode off across the road leaving him in her wake. 'Her husband was most put out,' she said, over her shoulder.

'A woman? You're bisexual?' He lengthened his stride, catching up with her.

'Does it make a difference?'

Jude drew a long, deep breath. 'No. Why would it?' Everything about her, so rich, so alluring, indicated discrimination yoked to unconventionality. If the usual rules of relationships as he'd always played them before didn't apply, that only made her more attractive. 'I don't even think I'm surprised.'

'I wouldn't call myself bisexual. I really dislike labels. You see someone, you fancy them, you sleep with them.

It doesn't matter to me whether they're male or female, as long as I'm attracted to them.'

Jude replayed his conversation with Scott. 'That explains it.'

'What?'

'He told me to warn my wife about you. Now I see what he meant.'

Her lips twitched into a smile. 'Your wife wouldn't be the one at risk. That was a one-off. I like men most. You know how it is. No rhyme or reason. Some people turn you on and some people don't.' And she turned her head towards him with a look that said: *and you do*.

Jude got a grip. There was a time and a place for losing your head over a woman and a weekday night, when he had work to do before the morning, wasn't it. Was it a good thing or a bad thing they were so close to her home? As they rounded the corner he could see lights burning in the living room. 'Looks like your housemate's home.'

'Yes. She'd have called me if Scott was there, so it'll be fine.' She paused. 'Why don't you come in and meet her? You'll love her. But she's a bit scary.'

He couldn't see her face, couldn't read her body language. He'd love to go in, but not to meet her flatmate. 'Maybe another time.'

'Things to do, eh?'

With any luck someone would have found a translator and there'd be a copy of Violet's document, in English, waiting in his inbox. He was dealing, he reminded himself, with life and death. 'You know how it is,' he excused himself, confident she did know, but he had to be certain she knew he was interested.

A delicate moment of hesitation hovered between them, one so riven with difficult silence that he could think of only one way to end it and that was a way he didn't dare go. Neither made a move. Eventually, Jude's courage left him. He leaned forwards, brushed her into the briefest of hugs and let her go. 'I'll see you tomorrow.'

'I'll see you, Jude.' And she turned and went up the steps to her front door.

He stood on the pavement for a moment in front of the closed door. What had that been about? Ashleigh was surely more than capable of handling the situation if Scott had turned up, but he had a strong sense she herself didn't believe what she thought she'd seen. So why had she called? Because she wanted to see him?

If that was the reason, it was more than good enough. He turned and headed out of Castletown with a spring in his step.

17

'Okay.' Arriving in the incident room slightly later than the others, Jude headed straight over to the desk where his deputy was flicking through a document on his iPad. 'Doddsy, I'm going to leave you to deal with the briefing this morning. I have to go down to Eden's End.' He flicked a quick look around the room, trying to decide where the path of professionalism took him. At one level it would be most unwise to take Ashleigh, with the parting of the night before still unresolved between them, but the needs of the job won out. Intuitive and sympathetic, blessed with a capability to open up the most distrustful of suspects, she was the best person for the job.

'Something up?' Ever-inquisitive, Chris popped his head up from where he sat at his desk.

'Yes.' Jude broadened his comments to include him. 'When I went to speak to Ellie Jack yesterday afternoon, she remembered an envelope Violet had given her to look after.'

'Remembered?' Chris laughed. 'Aye, right.'

'I suspect she was holding on to it to see if there was anything in it for her, then thought better of it when we started asking questions, but whatever. She claims Violet had asked her to witness her signature on a document. It was in Polish. God knows why. Because she could, I suppose, and because she could be sure Ellie couldn't read it. I got the translation through late last night.'

'A will?'

'You guessed it. I've just come off the phone to Violet's solicitor. You can imagine the reaction I got.'

Doddsy ran a narrow, thoughtful finger along the line of his chin. 'I haven't had a chance to look. I was just checking my emails there.'

'You don't need to read it. Any of you can guess, given what we know about her. She's disinherited her niece.'

'The more I see of people's decision-making when it comes to their disposable assets, the more I despair of human nature.' Doddsy, so charitably inclined he must have to fight his better nature every day when he came to work, shook his head.

'In fairness, there are ninety-nine fair and reasonable wills for every malicious one. But yes. If Monica did kill her aunt thinking she'd get herself out of financial difficulty, she's monumentally misjudged. Though if she didn't, I think it's reasonable enough for her to feel aggrieved.'

'What does she say about it?'

'She doesn't know yet. I decided it wasn't for me to tell her.'

'So why are you off to Eden's End? To speak to Ellie?'

'You're lacking your usual sharpness, Inspector.' Jude raised an amused eyebrow at him. 'I want to see the reaction of the new beneficiary when I tell her a five-figure sum has fallen into her lap.'

'Klemmie?'

'Yes. The terms of the will are as before, except she's now the residual legatee.'

Sitting back, Doddsy contemplated the collage of information on the whiteboard. 'Well, well. Do you think Monica will challenge the will?'

'I'd think very carefully if I was her. Violet was of sound mind. We know she was fond of Klemmie and there's evidence she'd given her gifts in the past. And on a more practical note, ten grand isn't worth fighting over. It'd be eaten up in legal fees before she knew it.'

'Klemmie, eh?' Doddsy was still thoughtful. 'Do you think she knew?'

'That's what I want to find out.' Jude turned away to where Ashleigh was sitting back, staring at her computer screen and tapping her fingers. What was she thinking? About work, about Scott, or about the might-have-beens of another day? 'Ashleigh. Are you busy just now?'

She spun round on her chair, and the look she gave him was professionally dispassionate. Just as well, because Doddsy's cool gaze was upon both of them. 'No more than usual. Do you need me?'

Did he need her? He stifled a laugh, saw a sudden flicker in her eyes that showed she'd seen and understood it. 'I'm off down to Edenhall. Fancy a jaunt?'

'Of course.' She turned away again, unhooked her jacket from the back of the chair, reaching down beside her for her bag.

Conscious of the temptation to stare at her and equally conscious he mustn't allow Doddsy to see him do it, Jude turned back to the activity in the rest of the incident room. 'Has anything else come in I need to know?'

'Yes.' Chris, jumping up, snatched a piece of paper from the printer by his desk. 'You'll want to put this on file. It's from Eden's End's parent company. As a matter of routine, they passed the information about Ellie's criminal record to their accountants. It looks as if we aren't the only ones working hard. They must have been up all night working on it. They've found…' he frowned down at the paper '…*discrepancies in the accounts*. They're looking closely at them.'

Ellie had nothing to do with the accounts. 'Jesus. That must mean Karen's been cooking the books.' It was amazing what you found when you lifted a stone, and if Becca was right Eden's End's operating company would have much more to learn about the perils of running a business on the cheap. 'She's in charge of all the financials at Eden's End, isn't she?' Jude shook his head again. 'I wonder if Violet knew? She told Monica Karen couldn't be trusted. Maybe she told someone else, too.'

In two minutes, circumstance had presented him with two new motives for the murder of Violet Ross, black marks against the names of both Karen and Klemmie. 'Come on, Ashleigh. Let's get on.'

'I take it Scott never reappeared?'

Jude, Ashleigh noted with amusement, had waited until they were turning up the drive of Eden's End before he brought the conversation round to personal matters. A full briefing on new developments had taken him all but the last few seconds of the ten-minute drive from the police headquarters to the nursing home, so finely timed she thought he must have done it deliberately, leaving himself long enough for the bare minimum he needed to say.

She smiled. Poor Jude. His rigorous professionalism wasn't as necessary as he seemed to think it was, so she was beginning to suspect it was a self-defence mechanism. She'd seen enough of him in their conversation the night before to know there was more to him than a man driven only to succeed in his chosen career. Hurt once, he didn't want to be hurt again. It followed as night followed day, as break-up follows marriage. 'No.'

'I made a couple of calls on your behalf. I hope you don't mind. I couldn't find out where he was last night, but he's certainly back in Cheshire this morning.'

'I'm coming to the conclusion I imagined it. I'm sorry for wasting your time.'

'You did anything but.' Was that the ghost of a smile? 'If he does turn up again, make sure you let me know. And even if he doesn't, you know you can call me any time you need me.'

'He'll be fine.' Ashleigh dimpled a smile towards him. 'I'm friends with all my exes. He's the only one who's cut up rough, but that's because he was the only one I ever committed to. He'll get over it.' And in time, he would. She just had to find the stamina to outlast him.

Jude stopped in the act of getting out of the car. 'Do you have many exes?'

'At least a dozen. I have them round every Christmas for sherry and mince pies.'

'Sorry.' He turned round with a grin. 'It's none of my business.'

'Ask me about Scott next time we get a chance to go

out for a drink. I'd be happy to tell you all about it.' And she'd offer him more overt encouragement at the end of the evening. She'd underestimated his strength of purpose the night before.

'As long as he isn't bothering you.' He unfolded himself from the low seat of the Mercedes and uncurled his long, lean body, stretching in the pale sunshine. 'Let's go. I've a funny feeling this could be a little bit awkward. Ellie last night was difficult enough, but this could be worse.'

She followed him across the gravel frontage to the door, stepping back while he leaned on the bell and looking at the end of the building, where closed curtains in Violet's room testified to the continuing investigation into her death. When no-one answered after a couple of minutes, he rang again, turning to her with a slight frown. 'They're normally quick to answer around here. I wonder if something's up.'

They waited another moment, while the sun faded in and out and a pair of greenfinches descended to the birdfeeder that hung from a low branch of the chestnut tree. It took a third ring before someone answered – one of the other care workers, looking harassed. 'Come in. I'm sorry – Karen usually gets the door. She must be busy. In the office, I think. Oh, here she is. It's okay, Karen. I'm off back to work.' She scurried off along the corridor.

Ashleigh sensed Jude's sigh. Karen was a complication they could do without. 'Ms Grant. Hello there.' His tone was guarded. 'You'll be glad to know we haven't come to disturb you, today. I was hoping for a word with Klemmie.'

Karen had been crying – no, was still crying, and the expression on her face held vestiges of rage rather than grief. 'Just as well. I'm not in a position to help you.'

Too soft-hearted to be a police officer, let alone a detective, Ashleigh cursed herself. She couldn't help it. Her heart touched by Karen's wobbling lip and ravaged features, she shuffled half a step forwards as if to comfort her, only to be stalled by Jude's fierce gaze. He, it appeared, had less sympathy for Karen's predicament than she. 'It's all right. We won't stay long.'

'Stay as long as you like. Do whatever you like. It's nothing to do with me. I don't work here any more.'

'Is that right? I'm sorry to hear it.' Jude managed, at least, to sound sincere.

'Are you? It's thanks to you I'm going to lose my job. It was you, wasn't it?'

'Again, I'm sorry.' Jude lowered his voice. He could be tough enough in private, or when an interviewee gave him any kind of grief, but he was never a man to humiliate someone publicly. 'I assume you're talking about your employer looking at the accounts. No-one in the police pointed them in that direction, and they'd have got there themselves, in time.'

'The pay's crap.' Karen's nostrils flared in the face of unbearable injustice. 'I was only taking what they should have paid me to start with. They deduct a hundred pounds a week for that shoebox I live in, and they charge me for the electricity. And I pay tax on everything. They call it a perk.' She sniffed. 'I didn't even take much. Just enough so I could get away, if I ever needed to.'

These things always came out. If it was true Karen was snipping a little bit here and there off the accounts, then there was no alternative to dismissal. Even now a clear motive had emerged for murder — the fear of discovery

– Ashleigh struggled to harden her heart against someone so clearly fighting a losing battle. For Karen, cheating the accounts for a few pounds wasn't grand larceny, but bore all the hallmarks of a cry for help.

'Will you be staying on here, Ms Grant?' It wasn't the most tactful question but it had to be asked, and she was confident she could handle it better than Jude – who was already displaying his desire to get on – would do. 'We may need to be in touch.'

'I suppose I should be grateful they've decided not to throw me out straight away. No, I can stay here while they check the books.' She seemed to be taking dismissal as a foregone conclusion. 'You'll need to know where I am for when you want to lock me up for murder, won't you?' She took out a hanky and scrubbed at her eyes. 'At least then I won't have to worry about where to live, or where my next meal might come from. Let's look on the bright side for that, at least.'

Jude shrugged her self-pity aside. 'So who should we speak to if—?'

'I don't care. They're sending someone from an agency, and someone from head office is coming up to read me the riot act. You do what you want. None of this is my problem any more.'

Karen was a suspect in a murder case. Under Jude's fierce stare, Ashleigh resisted the temptation to swoop on the woman and offer her sympathy. 'Can you tell us where Klemmie is? Then we can leave you alone.'

She smiled, and the smile crept under Karen's guard, sympathy catching her weak spot. 'I'll go and get her for you, if you want. I don't have anything else to do. Just go on through to the office.'

Ashleigh followed Jude through to the room they were accustomed to using as an interview space. 'Sometimes I hate this job. That poor woman.'

'That poor woman appears to have had her fingers in the till. If Violet was on to her, and especially if she threatened to tell her bosses about it, that gives her a good reason to commit murder.'

'People like that don't usually steal for money. It's obvious she needs help.'

'I don't dispute that. But we're not the social services. We're the police. I'm sticking to my job, and that's finding out who killed Violet Ross.' He laid the folder he'd been carrying on the table and strode across to the window, staring out at the garden while they waited for Klemmie's arrival.

She came within a minute, but she was uncertain. Ashleigh's sharp ears picked up footsteps, hesitant and slow, along the wooden floor of the hallway, pausing outside. As Jude turned, she caught his eye and he nodded. He must have heard it, too. Then there was a knock at the door and in came Klemmie, head held high and confident, just as Doddsy had described her. And, relating that self-assured personality to the hesitant steps outside the door, Ashleigh knew the inspector had been right and something about Klemmie Marcowics rang like a badly cast bell.

'Chef Inspector. Sergeant.' She nodded from one to the other, smoothing down her blue plastic apron. 'I'm sorry I took so long. I was busy. We're understaffed today.'

Ashleigh stepped back and left the talking to Jude. This wasn't the time for sympathy. Sometimes you had to be cruel to get to the truth, although her better self shrank away in shame whenever she thought about it.

'So I believe.' Jude turned to face Klemmie, but he didn't ask her to sit. Clearly it wasn't to be that sort of interview. 'I won't keep you long. This isn't about interviewing you, though perhaps I do have a couple of questions. It's more for your information.'

'I'll do everything I can to help you.' Klemmie maintained that perfect mask of polite control, but she kept on picking at the plastic apron.

'Thank you.' Crossing to the table, Jude extracted a photocopy of the original document Ellie had surrendered from the folder, and handed it to her. 'I wondered if you'd seen this before.'

With obvious — perhaps over-obvious — curiosity, Klemmie took three steps towards him and stretched out her hand for the paper. Studying her face intently, Ashleigh registered the sequence of horror that set in — the draining of blood from an already-pale face, the shaking hand, the widening eyes. 'I don't believe it!'

'You've answered my first question, Ms Marcowics. You obviously didn't know.'

'Know? If I'd known I wouldn't have let her do it. I don't want her money!' Distress creased Klemmie's face and she spun round on her heel like a wild animal, cornered and seeking to break free.

Ashleigh stepped forward. She could just about bear Jude putting one witness under pressure but two within five minutes was too much for her. 'Let me get you a glass of water.'

'I don't want water. I don't want anything. I don't want her money! Why did she do that? It'll destroy me. I just want Violet back!' Klemmie put her hands to her head, sank into a chair at the table. 'It's a mistake. It must be. It'll all get sorted out. I don't want her money!' And she burst into tears.

18

'What do you reckon?'

'I think there's something very wrong about Klemmie Marcowics.'

Jude smiled at Ashleigh, the only recognition he allowed himself of the subtle change in their relationship. A week before – even the day before – the smile would have been a frown, and who knew where they'd be in another week? 'I thought that.'

'But when I say wrong, Jude… I don't mean criminal.'

'An interesting observation.'

Ashleigh frowned at him, and the frown amused him in a way it shouldn't have done. 'You must have seen it. She really cared for Violet. She cared that she died; she misses her. She doesn't care that she's inherited ten thousand pounds.'

'Yes, okay. But for someone on her wage, that's a lot. Was it just to spite Monica?' Without knowing Violet he couldn't judge, but something about the friendship between the rich English doctor and the Polish steelworker's daughter intrigued him. 'I think we need to look a bit more closely at her background, don't you?'

'Yes.' Ashleigh picked her bag up, turning her back on

him as she headed to the door, and he took a second to enjoy watching her. A sense of optimism overcame him. After the pain Becca had put him through, he was learning to move on. Not to love – he was still hurting too much to dare commit himself to any woman in that way again – but with Ashleigh in a similar position, did he need to?

Out in the reception area the bell was ringing, and ringing, and ringing. In the deserted front office, where Karen had been accustomed to sit and carry out her day-to-day business as the public face of Eden's End, there was trouble. A man in a navy blue rain jacket, glistening with moisture, was standing by the desk leaning on the bell.

'At last.' Clearly annoyed, the stranger greeted them with a ferocious, sarcastic smile. 'I thought no-one would come. This place is like the *Mary Celeste*. Where are all the staff these rich people pay all that money for?' His accent, a curious hybrid, was unidentifiable on those few words but its strongest component was American. 'You guys better get this sorted before someone raises hell. And that someone's gonna be yours truly.'

'We can't help you with that, I'm afraid. We don't work here.' Ashleigh shook her head at him, even as Jude stared at him in fascination, the germ of understanding growing in his mind.

'Maybe we can help.' The idea took over, feeding on the man's thin face with its full head of silver hair, on the dark eyes, on the narrow, unsmiling lips. 'Are you here to visit someone?'

'My mother.' The man picked his briefcase up with a shrug of impatience. 'Don't worry. I'll go find her myself. If you see anyone, tell them I'm here, would you?'

'Do you mind if I ask who your mother is?'

The stranger spun round again. At last Jude got a good look at him, and knew he was right. 'Sure. She's Violet Ross.'

Jude looked towards Ashleigh, who was already moving in on the stranger, in full family liaison mode. 'Oh, goodness. This is so unfortunate. I'm afraid there's nobody about from the home to talk to you, Mr—'

'Kava. Stefan Kava.'

'Mr Kava. I'm so very sorry. There's some bad news.' She kept steadfast eye contact with him. Of all the parts of the job, Jude most hated breaking bad news and Ashleigh, who hated it so much she sometimes let herself down, seemed determined not to shrink from it. 'Unfortunately your mother passed away last week.'

He stared at her, then at Jude, then back to Ashleigh again. 'Guess I shouldn't be so surprised, only sorry I just missed her. Was she ill? If I'd known, I'd have gotten myself up here a bit sooner.' He looked at the date on the calendar that sat on the desk as an aid to the forgetful, residents and visitors alike. 'Looks like I'll be extending my trip by a few days.' He looked back at them. 'Not staff, you say. So you are?'

'I'm Detective Sergeant Ashleigh O'Halloran. This is Detective Chief Superintendent Jude Satterthwaite.'

Jude took over, stepping forward, composing his expression to one of appropriate grief when in fact what he felt was a thrill of excitement. Stefan must be Violet's mystery visitor. 'I'm sorry to tell you your mother's death wasn't accidental.'

There was a long silence. 'You're saying she was murdered.'

'I'm afraid the evidence points to that. Yes.' Jude took a look around. 'Perhaps we should go somewhere a little more private. I'm sorry no-one told you. We didn't know anything about you, or we'd certainly have sent someone to break the news, but I assume the staff of the home—'

'There's no need to apologise. The staff didn't know, either. My mother was keen to keep me a secret, and I guess I can understand why.' Stefan's lips twitched into a cynical smile as he cast a look around. 'You're right. This isn't a great place to talk. Who's in charge here? They can find us somewhere comfortable.'

The meeting room Karen had made available was anything but suitable. 'The manager's had to take leave of absence.'

'You don't say. You can tell Mom's dead. She'd never have stood for that kind of nonsense if she was alive. We'll go back to my hotel. I came by cab. Did you drive?'

'Yes. We'll give you a lift.' On balance, getting out of Eden's End was probably the best option.

'I'm staying at the George in Penrith.' He turned towards the door. 'It's going to be interesting talking to you. Don't think I won't have questions.' There was a dry irony in his tone.

Pausing to sign out in the visitors' book, Jude led the way to his car. Giving Stefan the short time it would take them to reach the hotel to collect his thoughts would be both sensible and kind, but he had to ask himself just how much a man might grieve for a mother who wouldn't admit to him, who failed even to acknowledge him in her will and who, it appeared, he rarely saw. Taking half an opportunity to glance in the driver's mirror to see his unexpected passenger's face, he caught an expression of deep calm.

'If you'd like a little longer to compose yourself.' He pulled the car into a convenient space right outside the hotel's front door. 'We can wait.'

'No, thank you.' Getting out of the car, Stefan stretched off the stiffness of a transatlantic flight, suppressing an accompanying yawn. 'You can see for yourself my heart isn't broken. I didn't know my mom well, and she was a hundred years old. I'm shocked you say someone thought it was worth the effort of taking her life, but I sure can't shed any light on why they might have done it.' Picking up his case, he headed to the hotel entrance. 'We can get a table in the lounge. I don't expect it'll be busy.'

Following him through the stained-glass door, Ashleigh and Jude exchanged glances. 'He's our mystery man,' she breathed in his ear as they came into the lobby, side by side. 'Isn't he?'

'Looks like it. And very confident.' A couple of long strides took him away from her and into the lounge where Stefan was already making himself comfortable in front of the fire.

'I'll order tea.' He flicked a casual hand for the waiter and a gold signet ring flashed in the light. 'You English always have tea, don't you?'

'We both drink coffee.' Ashleigh smiled at him, as if this were the most artificial of social occasions, as if small talk would get them somewhere.

'So I just learned something about the English. Mom was English as apple pie, and it always had to be tea for her. That's two coffees and a tea.' He nodded the waiter on his way. 'I'm a New Yorker. Now, can we get to the point? What happened to my mother?'

Sitting by the fire, Jude outlined the tale of Violet's death in as few words as he could, choosing the information to reveal and to withhold with extreme care. 'I'm sorry to have to be the bearer of bad news. Until just now we didn't know about you, or we'd have broken it too you a little less suddenly.'

Stefan surprised him, flicking a forefinger across his narrow chest in the shape of a cross. 'I'm sure you'll catch whoever did it. My cousin, perhaps? A mercy killing? Was my mom in any distress before she died?'

'On the contrary. She was fit and well, and fully *compos mentis*.'

'Maybe she wanted to die before she got...' he looked for the right word '...not old. She was already old. Too old. I don't think anyone in their right minds wants to live for ever.'

Yet all the signs were that Violet had resisted her killer. Jude kept that piece of information to himself. 'Perhaps.' He stretched his legs out towards the fire. 'Tell us a bit about yourself, Mr Kava. I have to admit to being intrigued. Nobody I've spoken to seems to have any idea she had a child, and as far as we know, she never married.'

'She never did.' Stefan got a packet of cigarettes out of his pocket, looked at them with regret, turned them over in his hands and put them away again. 'My mom wasn't perfect. I barely knew her so I don't know how her mind worked. Let me tell you about me, and then you'll see.' He patted the pocket with the cigarette packet in it, as if for comfort. 'Your generation might find my story astonishing;

but I can promise you, for someone born in my time, in my place, it's nothing out of the ordinary.' He tapped his fingers on the arm of his chair. 'History's a curse. There's lots of mine I don't know myself, and all I can tell you is what I've been told by others. I can't even be sure it's true.'

Jude waited.

'I was born in London, just after the war. Guess that must be where Mom was from, or where she was living at the time. I don't know who my dad was, or anything about him, except the only thing that matters. He died before I was born.'

'Do you know how?'

'I never heard.' Stefan shrugged, accepting the pot of tea the waiter placed at his elbow with an aristocratic wave. 'People died. No-one cared. It was war. Guess I don't want to know.'

He turned his hands upwards, in a gesture of regret.

'Guess it didn't matter. Whatever the circumstance, she couldn't or wouldn't keep me, but I lucked out. I was adopted by a Polish widow with a boy my own age. She married a Polish refugee and we moved to America. My adoptive father was hard-working and entrepreneurial and America suited him. He invested wisely and he built a business in construction. It was all very American, and yet at the same time, my parents never forgot their heritage and we were a Polish family, though they never returned to their homeland. When the Cold War ended, I did go. I bought a flat in Warsaw, and a holiday home in the Tatras. I spend a lot of time there. I regarded myself – and I still do – as Polish-American.'

He fell silent again and the ticking of the clock timed his moment of reflection. Ten seconds. Fifteen. He sighed.

'And your mother?' Ashleigh prompted him.

Stefan's fingers tapped impatiently on the arm of the chair again. 'I never spared my mom a thought. I knew who she was, I knew she'd given me up, and I had some idea of the circumstances.' He laughed. 'She must have been some girl. Wartime affair, no husband – maybe the man was married. Society was pretty judgemental back then, I guess, but I didn't hold it against her. I understood how these things happened. I thought I didn't need to know. But when my adoptive parents died, the inevitable happened. I started thinking too much, until my grieving process made me want to find out who I was.'

'When was this?'

'A long time ago. My adoptive mom died twenty-five years ago, my dad a couple of years later. I resented my real mom – Violet – for a long time, because she'd made no attempt to reach out to me. I was in England often, and I never passed through without thinking about her. I never looked her up, but I knew she was still alive.'

Behind the bar someone dropped a glass, and from outside in the lobby there was laughter, but Jude and Ashleigh were silent as he picked up his tea and sipped. 'There's a bond between a mother and a son that defies description, and it ate away at me. Last year, I stopped over in England as I often do, and something came over me. I weakened. I looked her up and found out where she was. It was so easy. It was like it was meant to be, all tied up, the great reconciliation. So I came north to introduce myself to her.'

Silence played again around the three of them. A group of walkers rumbled in and occupied the seats to the other side of the fire, but Stefan sat alone in the sealed bubble of his memories and his regrets.

'It didn't go well.' He shook his head. 'Guess I was wrong to expect it to. I thought she'd be glad to see me, tell me everything about herself and about my background, about my dad. I see now that if she'd wanted to keep in touch with me, she'd have done that. It's the kind of woman she was. She chose to keep me a secret, ashamed of me when she should have been ashamed of herself. When I turned up here, no-one knew about me. She told me I have a cousin I've never met, and who probably still doesn't know I exist. I should have been coming home, and she made me feel like a stranger.'

Jude looked at him. His sudden arrival must have raised traumatic ghosts for Violet, too, but Stefan didn't seem aware of that. Or he didn't care. 'How did you react?'

Stefan raised an eyebrow. 'I guess I see your thinking. Yes. I was bitter about my mother, Inspector. She treated me badly and I let her know it. We had a fight, and I was angry when I left. I might have killed her, if I'd lost my temper and shaken her, and God, I was tempted to do it. But I didn't. And that isn't why I came back.'

'Why did you?'

Stefan shrugged, turning his gaze from Jude towards the leaping flames of the open fire. 'I guess, after all, I have a better nature. I never meant to. I planned on taking the moral high ground and doing my duty from a distance. I sent flowers for her birthday, but when she never bothered to reply, I swore I was done with her. But it kept nagging at me. I knew she couldn't live much longer. If she was ill, no-one would tell me. If I didn't keep in touch, I'd never find out when I lost her.' As indeed had happened. 'I'm on my way to Warsaw to visit family and I stopped over. I flew into Heathrow yesterday morning, spent the evening trying to nerve myself to see her again, and took the train up first thing this morning. I checked into my hotel and went straight to visit her. And from there, you know the story.'

Jude nodded. 'Again, let me say how sorry I am for your loss.'

'It's no real loss. I just hope you find who did it.'

'I'd like to ask you a few questions about your movements, for formality's sake, if I may.'

'I guess I understand that. Sure – I can give you the details of my flights.' Getting a small notebook out of his pocket, Stefan scribbled some notes down in tiny handwriting, then tore it out and handed it over. 'Keep me updated. I guess the least I can do for her is stay for the funeral. And if I could see her, I'd appreciate it.'

'I'll arrange that. I'll get someone to contact you about it.' There was one last thing, one last question to which Jude already knew the answer. Reaching for the folder he'd laid on the table, he lifted the copy of the will he'd shown to Klemmie, bringing out from underneath it a blown-up version of Violet's secret photograph. 'I don't suppose you recognise this man?'

Stefan took the picture, holding it at arm's length. From the inside pocket of his jacket, he brought out a pair of glasses and slid them on, staring, then held the picture up beside his face. 'It's not quite like looking in a mirror, but it's close enough.' He laughed, a laugh without humour. 'Guess she did know who my dad was, after all. Who is he?'

'We don't know.' But Jude already knew his next priority was to find out.

When the police had gone, Stefan sat alone in the bar while the walkers laughed and the pain and pressure of too much transatlantic travel bore down so hard on him he couldn't work out whether he was tired or whether he genuinely felt bereaved. But he did know he was angry. Not with the detectives, who were doing the best they could to find the killer and looked as if they were making a spirited attempt at it, but with himself.

He got up and left the bar, stumbling over the step so someone coming in looked at him with disapproval for the drunk rather than sympathy for the exhausted, and shuffled along the street, turning into the churchyard. When he'd visited Violet the year before, he'd come here afterwards, not because he was a religious man but because the church had seemed the most likely place to come to terms with fury and rejection, with the overriding regret he hadn't taken the coward's way out and killed her when he had the chance, instead of slipping away into the darkness and out of the country. He circumnavigated the church, his feet dragging through the drifts of damp, dead leaves.

If he'd killed her he wouldn't have been there, with those two detectives looking him up and down as if he were their perfect suspect and had been too smart for them. He'd have been safe in New York, unidentified and unidentifiable, and

Violet would have shuffled off the Earth with no mourners but her niece.

It wouldn't have mattered so much if he'd arrived in time to get from Violet the things that really mattered to him. Not money, which he didn't need and didn't want, but the two things that obsessed him for their connection with his history: his father's service revolver and his mother's gold brooch.

19

If she stood on her tiptoes and craned her neck, Monica could just make out the grey bulk of Eden's End, squatting on the open ground above the river like an animal, watching her. Resentment rose like a tide in her soul, spilling out as tears. Violet had been so controlling. That was bad enough, but she'd turned out to be a liar, with it, promising that Monica would inherit and then reneging on it, leaving everything to the Polish carer who'd only spent time with her because it was her job. One never knew with Violet whether her motives were genuine or cynical, but what did it matter when the result was the same?

Now, so one of the girls had told her when she'd called in at Eden's End to challenge Klemmie (who, fortunately for them both, hadn't been around) there was a new character on the scene, a late entry into the *dramatis personae* of Violet's life story. The girl hadn't known who he was but Monica could guess, and she both hated and envied him for having no need to scurry around after an old lady's whims for the sake of either his wallet or his conscience.

He must be Violet's son. Her lip curled at the girl's description of him – elderly, handsome, and apparently wealthy enough not to care that he, too, had been cut out of

Violet's will in favour of both a charity and a nobody. With his arrival Monica, at the end of everything she'd done for her aunt, would not only be left penniless, but relegated at the funeral, expected to play second fiddle to a man whose name she didn't even know.

I may not get the money, she said to herself, *but some appreciation of what I did for her would have meant something.*

An abstemious woman, she poured herself the smallest gin and tonic in which to drown her many sorrows and returned to the window, weighing up life's injustices while the last of the late autumn light died away in the west. Darkness and the deep shadow of trees enfolded the swirling river in the middle distance and the lights flicked on, one by one, in Eden's End as Monica fought her better nature. No matter how much she wanted to, she couldn't blame Klemmie. It was so obvious the woman was fond of Violet, and even if she'd been foolish over accepting the brooch Monica couldn't, in her heart, believe she'd pursued Violet with the intention of inheriting. It was far too believable, however, that Violet's twisted sense of fun had prompted her to leave the money to the Polish woman just to make it awkward for them both.

No-one could think it unreasonable for Klemmie to share the money, or at the very least concede her claim to the brooch. She must see the injustice of what Violet had done. Maybe a quick line to ask her about it would do no harm. If not, then Monica's cousin could pay her, reasonable compensation for all she'd done for Violet.

A stranger, stealing the limelight. Klemmie, getting the money. Either way, somebody owed her. It must, surely, be either Klemmie or the stranger, Violet's son, who'd killed her aunt. It would need only the faintest hint to flush the murderer out and so, surely, it was worth a gamble to see if one of them would pay her something for keeping any knowledge she pretended to have to herself.

Taking a ladylike sip of the gin, Monica carried the glass over to her desk and set it down on the polished tabletop, before reaching into the drawer for a pad of paper and her fountain pen.

I am sorry to contact you like this, she wrote, *and I hope you will treat my letter with appropriate discretion. Thanks to you, among others, I have been cheated out of what is rightfully mine. I'm not a greedy woman and I don't seek to ruin anyone, but I do feel that you owe me some effort, at least, to repay what I've lost. Perhaps we could meet, sooner rather than later, and with a little luck I won't have to tell what I know to keep you out of jail.*

It was a suitably ambiguous note. When she'd finished writing, she sealed the letter and placed it in an envelope. Then, as the full, fat moon brightened in the sky, she put on her coat, opened the front door and, getting into her car, set off in the direction of Eden's End.

'Fill me in.' Lisa slid into the seat next to Ashleigh on the sofa and reached out a tentative hand for the pack of cards her friend was shuffling. 'Shouldn't I feel a bolt of electricity when I touch them?' She grinned.

When Lisa was there everything in the world felt good. Buoyed by her friend's goodwill, Ashleigh laughed. 'Why would you? They're a pack of playing cards.'

'But shouldn't I feel the force? Shouldn't the cards be channelling the earth's electro-magnetic field? Come to think of it, shouldn't we be doing this sitting in the middle of a stone circle on a ley line somewhere?'

'At midnight on the winter solstice, by the light of a full moon?' Ashleigh shook her head and smiled again at the way no-one seemed able to shed their preconceptions about the cards. 'No. How many times do I have to tell you? This is about rationalisation and making choices and accepting guidance. The magic goes on in your head, not in the cards. Think of it as a form of meditation.'

'I definitely need to learn to meditate. I need calm. I've had a horrendous day at work and my head's in a whirl. Teach me to read the tarot and it'll make it all right.' Lisa tilted her head to one side, a pleading, wheedling look.

Ashleigh's good humour asserted itself. Lisa never took her seriously and maybe Jude, who couldn't hide his cynicism whenever her unconventional hobby came up in conversation, was right and she should learn to treat it a little more lightly herself. 'You've caught me at a weak moment. Okay. We can try it. But you have to promise to treat it with respect.' Ashleigh tucked the folds of her scarlet kimono around her knees and carried on shuffling the cards.

'You're looking so cheerful, my girl.' Settling herself on the sofa Lisa stretched long skinny legs out, her feet too close to the electric fire. 'What's happened to you?'

'Nothing.'

'It'll be to do with a man. It always is.' Except with Lisa herself – curiously asexual, comfortably androgynous and emotionally content. 'Has Scott left town?'

'Yes, if he was ever here. Last night must have been a figment of my imagination.'

'If it was, it just shows how badly it affected you when he turned up before.'

'Yes, but he's not here now. It looks as if that little storm has blown over.'

'And that's enough to make you cheerful? Are you sure you haven't fallen in love with someone else?'

Sometimes, when she looked at Lisa and felt the way she understood everything, so easily, Ashleigh couldn't believe how lucky she'd been to land up in Penrith with her old school friend as her housemate. Now there was Jude. There was only one way that relationship was going, in the short term at least. She preferred not to think beyond that. 'I'm not falling in love with anyone. That's the road to ruin. There's a lot more to life than love.'

'Oh, I get it. I get it. You've caught the eye of some nice young man in a uniform. Is that it?'

'Here.' In a distraction tactic, Ashleigh laid the pack of cards on the table, seized Lisa's long thin hand and laid it on top. 'Stop prattling on for a moment and concentrate. You won't feel the force, or anything silly like that. Don't expect to. The whole point is to calm you down. So do as you're told, for once, and stay still if you can. It'll do you good.'

For a moment Lisa sat there, fingers resting lightly on top of the pack of cards, a frown of concentration on her face, sharp cheekbones casting shadows in the lamplight. 'Okay. Now what?'

'Normally, I'd lay several cards out and we'd interpret them, both individually and as part of a spread. But as you're just starting, we'll keep it simple. Cut the cards. Let's see what you've got.'

'What's this?' With a frown of perplexity, Lisa turned over a card. 'What does it say? The Two of Cups. What does that mean?'

'It means you need to think carefully about relationships.' Ashleigh smiled. She liked the Two of Cups, a card whose strength and common sense offered something to aspire to. 'It means you know when a relationship is balanced and healthy. That's a good pick. I think that's a pretty good description of you. Eminently sensible.'

'It isn't sense. It's self-preservation. What about you? Let's see what you come up with.'

Ashleigh picked up the pack and shuffled it, with a certain degree of reluctance. At a time when she thought she had things under control, it could be a risk to look too closely at the situation, to have to consider the down side of life as well as the up, but that was part of wisdom – understanding there was a cloud for every silver lining. Placing the pack face down on the table, she cut it and turned up the face of the card.

'And that one is?'

'That's the Three of Swords.' Her lips twitched. If she'd had Jude sitting beside her instead of Lisa, she knew exactly what he'd say when she explained what it meant. He'd say: *coincidence is a wonderful thing*. 'I've had this pack a long time. I think it knows me too well.'

'Why? What does it mean?' Lisa leaned forward to examine it, wrinkling her nose in faint distaste at the image of three swords through a bleeding heart. 'That's... creepy.'

'Not at all. What do you think it means?'

'Nothing good, that's for sure. Broken hearts and a love triangle? Surely that can't be healthy?'

'This card is telling me to think about what's behind me. It's all about betrayal and deceit and divorce.'

'That doesn't sound like something to smile at. And I'll tell you something for nothing. If Scott's a part of a triangle, it's going to need a hell of a lot more than three sides.'

That was a valid point and if she'd listened to Lisa's advice — or anyone else's — in the beginning she'd never have married him. 'The important message for me is that I have a tendency to make my own problems. That's also been true in the past. In the future it'll be different. I can learn from the card you drew, and I'll be making my own solutions.'

'Oh, hey. That sounds very positive.' Lisa was tired of the cards already. 'The only thing I'm planning to make in the near future is a cup of cocoa. Do you want one?'

'Oh, go on then.'

When Lisa had gone through to the kitchen, Ashleigh could resist it no longer. The cards didn't tell fortunes, but she was looking to concentrate her thoughts on the future, not on the past. If there was guidance to be had, she'd be both foolish and arrogant to turn it down. Shuffling the cards once more, too quickly, she set them down on the table and turned up the top one.

The Moon. She looked at it in perplexity. The Moon could mean so many things, depending on its context, but the interpretations that sprang first to her mind were negative — yet more secrets, deceptions and lies.

That must be Scott again, lurking in the future when she thought she'd locked him in the past. That was it. Folding the card back into the pack in case Lisa should see it and demand an explanation, she got up and crossed to the window, lifting the curtain. The rain that had persisted through most of the autumn had given way to a clear, cold night, offering the first frost of winter, and the moon, the real one, hung large and low in the winter sky like a fruit ripe for picking. *Reflect upon history*, the card had warned her, and she shook her head. What was her history? Scott? She'd spent far too long reflecting on him.

But as she heard Lisa's step in the hall and dropped the curtain, it wasn't Scott who sprang to her mind. The Moon, like all the cards, had an alternative explanation and could mean something wasn't what it seemed. And as she turned away from the window, she couldn't help thinking of Stefan Kava, whose secret history almost certainly held the key to murder.

'Things on your mind, Jude?' asked Doddsy, his habitual opening gambit on the occasions the two of them managed to get together for a pint, and Jude parried it with his standard lie. 'No. My conscience is clear as a bell.'

The formalities over, they settled into a moment of companionable silence near the fire while Jude occupied himself with running through all the things that were on his mind in the secure knowledge Doddsy would pick them off, one by one, before it was time to go home. He drew a deep draught from his pint and the yeasty flavour of the local brew hit home.

'Another one of those weeks, eh?'

'I'll say.' It had been chaos, not just with the puzzle of

Violet Ross's death but with a dozen other things that had landed on Jude's desk and required an immediate response. Now, at least, they had a chance to escape. They'd headed out of Penrith and down to Pooley Bridge, camping in the corner by the window where, if he squinted hard enough through the window and into the darkness, Jude could see the reflections of the ripples of the River Eamont as it raced its enthusiastic course from Ullswater and on to Penrith and the sea. These days unless he was out of the office on business he never got to see the place in daylight, let alone take a turn along the lake path for a dose of fresh air.

'Any thoughts on our killer?' Doddsy had the same one-track mind, the mentality that couldn't leave a victim unavenged and a killer at large. Violet's death might not, in the great scheme of things, have been a huge loss to the world or to anyone other than Monica and Klemmie, but there was a principle at stake.

'Not yet. We're certainly not short of suspects.' Jude, reviewing the list in his head, couldn't recall such an unlikely collection of potential murderers. 'All women. All in a certain age group. All of them in the so-called caring professions. I don't think I've ever seen a collection of possibilities quite like that before.'

'Let's not forget our old friend, the random stranger.'

'Do you believe in an unknown killer?' Doddsy sat back while the waiter delivered their meals. 'I don't. Someone wanted Violet dead because she was Violet. I'm not sure of much in this case, but I'm pretty sure the motive was personal.' But they'd been over this, over and over again, and the information they had wasn't going to fall into any new shape during an evening in the pub. 'I'm convinced the answer's to do with her past life, and probably with Stefan's father.'

'Let's see if Aditi can find out, shall we?'

Jude had packed Aditi, the most junior of the team, off down to the National Archive in London, with a remit to dig about until she found out everything she could about Violet and the child she'd given up – a job, he'd thought, Chris Marshall had coveted, but he preferred having Chris's technical and research skills close to hand. 'I can't see anything we can do until we hear from her.' He turned his attention to his plate, spearing a crispy sweet potato fry with his fork and adding a savoury slice from the fat curl of Cumberland sausage that was the first decent meal he'd sat down to all week.

'If there's anything to find, I expect we'll hear about it soon.' Doddsy, looking delicately over at the roaring log fire as if he couldn't quite bring himself to approach the subject, lifted the puff pastry top from his vegetable pie and inspected the innards with care. 'You didn't think of sending Ashleigh down there?'

Jude stiffened slightly. If there was one thing about Doddsy that made him uncomfortable, it was the permanent threat of his disapproval. 'No. I think she's better employed up here. And she has plenty of other things to do.'

'You think she's settling in?'

Ashleigh had been with them for two months. 'She fits in very well.'

'You won't like this, but I have some concerns.'

Jude sighed. A creeping feeling came over him that his friend was about to lecture him on elements of his personal life he hadn't got to grips with himself, and yet he knew a lecture was what he needed most. 'She's very professional. I hope you aren't going to suggest otherwise.'

'About her? Or about you?' Doddsy burst out laughing. 'Not that. No. For God's sake. Did you really think that was what I was going to say? Do whatever you want in your own time, Jude. It's nothing to do with me. And for the record, I don't think I've ever seen anyone so inhumanly determined to stay professional as you are, so don't take it to heart.'

Jude allowed himself a rueful grin. He must, indeed, be inhuman if he'd managed to hide his increasing obsession with Ashleigh O'Halloran, even from his best friend. 'I'm going to take that as a compliment. So what's your reservation?' As if he couldn't guess.

'I'm all for sympathy, even with the devil. All for giving people the benefit of the doubt. You know me. I'm a charitable man. But I don't bring my charity to work.'

There was live music in the bar that night. If the conversation got awkward, it might be a useful distraction. 'Maybe you should. Maybe we all should. It works for her. She gets people to talk.'

'What's the story there, Jude? She's a woman with talent. I'll give her that. But don't you ever worry she gets a little bit too emotionally involved with some of our witnesses?'

Attempting to be dispassionate, Jude considered. It was impossible to overlook Ashleigh's vulnerability – the reaction to her husband's first visit, and to what he was certain was the delusion of his second, told him that. But her warmth and intuition were part of the attraction, secondary to her more obvious attributes but attractive nonetheless. 'She's interested in them.'

'She can't be any more interested than you or me or any of the rest of us. I can see you twitching like a ferret's whiskers whenever a suspect starts to talk. Part of the reason we're all in the job is because we're nosy as hell.'

'She gets better results.' Jude flinched as the guitarist plugged in his amp and treated the audience to a debilitating blast of distorted sound. 'Even by just being there. She makes people feel at ease. You can't deny that. People want to talk to her.'

'I can't for the life of me work out why. She seems to use the same techniques as the rest of us. But people talk to her in a way they don't to us.'

'Maybe that's the upside of getting closely involved. Empathy.' Jude considered the froth on top of his pint as if it were a crystal ball. 'It's more valuable to me the way it is. Professionally speaking. You've seen how witnesses respond to her. Even the uncooperative ones.'

'Have it your own way.' Doddsy didn't shrug, but he might as well have done. 'She fits in with the team. I rate her highly. I just had my concern about a possible emotional vulnerability, that's all.'

'I suppose you're right. There's a part of me thinks we'd all be better people if we showed a bit more empathy and a little less cynicism. But that wouldn't get the job done.' And getting the job done sometimes made you into someone who wasn't a pleasant person to work with. Becca would have vouched for that.

'Are you finding it tough, always being the bad cop?'

Jude had been thinking about Ashleigh, in a way he felt free to do when he wasn't at work, and Doddsy's telepathic intervention sent him straight back into a place he didn't want to be – a past in which Becca had turned him out for doing the right thing. 'No. It's what I was born to do.'

The guitarist, finally in control, shook out a few experimental chords and the customers in the bar rearranged themselves, facing towards him in expectation of some old favourites. Jude cursed the choice of pub. It was his suggestion, and he'd picked it for all the wrong reasons. And so, because you couldn't hide things from everybody, because Becca, who would once have understood, was part of the problem and Ashleigh, who would have turned that renowned empathy on him was, he hoped, a part of the solution, he came out with it. 'Did you hear Adam Fleetwood got his parole?'

'Aye, I did.'

'He and I used to come in here, back in the day. We'd hike around Ullswater.' It was twenty miles and the two of them could do it easily in a day, even without an early start. 'We'd treat ourselves to a pie and a couple of pints as a reward, and we'd get Mum or Becca to come and pick us up.' With Adam's impending release this looked like it might be the last time he'd go into this pub, or any one of a dozen others, knowing his past wouldn't be waiting for him, in a corner or behind a door. Thank God you could lose yourself in the outdoors with ease. 'He'll be back under our feet. He'll be out of jail by the weekend.'

'You'll adjust. It'll be difficult for you, Jude, but you know you did the right thing. He has to take responsibility for what he did, not you.'

Jude didn't answer, tapping his fingers on the table and pretending to listen to the strains of *Wild Rover*. Adam's return wasn't just a trial for him, but a potential risk for Mikey. He hadn't spoken to his brother but he'd know. Adam, who could charm the birds from the trees when there was something in it for him, had been a hero of Mikey's. Was he still?

'Any regrets?' Doddsy persisted.

Maybe he wasn't as effective as Ashleigh at extracting information, but it wasn't for want of trying. 'None,' Jude said, after too long a pause, and wondered if Doddsy was smart enough to realise he was lying.

'There had better be a good reason for this.' Shivering, Klemmie pulled her coat tight over her pyjamas and wished she'd bothered to get properly dressed, but Stefan's phone call had had an urgency about it, and she'd bolted out of Eden's End without thinking things through.

That was nothing new. If she'd thought things through she wouldn't be there, would be much poorer in some ways and very much richer in others.

'There is. I can't find that gun. If you've cheated me of it, I'll break your neck. If you haven't, then get it for me.'

She sighed. 'Is that all you dragged me out for?'

'If someone's found it—'

'If someone had found it, the place would be crawling with police. You just aren't looking in the right place.' She dropped to her knees in the mud, reaching into the guts of the bushes where she was sure she'd left it, marking the place in her mind by a break in the hedge and a tuft of sheep's wool snagged on it. For a second she groped around in wet grass and felt nothing but a void and her heart skipped in fear, until her fingers closed on the loose stone she'd wedged on top of it, touched the slippery plastic beneath, and she hauled it out in relief. 'That's it. I've done my bit.' Scrambling to her feet, she delivered the package into his outstretched hand with relief. 'Now can I go?'

'No.' He flicked on the torch on his phone and shone it into the bag as if he didn't trust her. 'The brooch. Where is it?'

The beam flashed across her face, dazzling her. On the bank of the river in the dead of night, Klemmie felt both horribly exposed and desperately isolated. 'I told you. The police took it.' A sudden burst of defiance broke from her soul. 'But I'd have kept it anyway. Because that's all I wanted from her.'

'That and the thousands of pounds she left you.' He laughed and, seeming to recognise the risks of the situation, turned the torch away from her and down to the ground. It shimmered around her filthy shoes, the claggy red mud on the hems and knees of her pyjamas.

Klemmie rolled her eyes to the heavens, unseen. Stefan didn't seem to grasp, any more than Monica or Karen or the police, that it wasn't about the money. That was how it had started, but the last year had taught her how little she needed it and how much more important other things were. 'When I get the brooch back from the police, I'm going to keep it.' Because you couldn't do deals in friendship.

'If you get it back, you give it to me. It was my mother's.'

'It belongs to me. I've risked jail and my job for your sentimental pride. You've got your father's gun and getting it for you nearly got me into more trouble than I'm already in. Take it, and go.'

She turned away, but his arm shot out and long fingers clamped around her wrist. 'One more thing. What have you been saying to the niece?'

'Nothing. I don't talk to her. She doesn't think I speak good enough English. And anyway, she despises me.'

'Then how do you explain this?' He felt in his pocket with his free hand, and had to let go of her wrist to unfold the piece of paper and thrust it into the pool of light.

Massaging her wrist, where bruising was already rising to add to the second load of scratches she'd picked up from the brambles, Klemmie allowed herself a sigh as she read. It hadn't taken her long to get Monica's measure. 'That's nothing.'

'She knows.'

'No, she doesn't.'

'Then how did this appear under the door of my hotel room this evening?'

'Because she's a chancer. Because she's clever. Because she doesn't know you can't have done it so she wants you to think she can prove you did. So you pay up.'

'Right. And since you're so smart, you can tell me what I should do about it.'

'Nothing.' She didn't bother to suppress her yawn. It had been a long day and a stressful one, and she was on the early shift again in the morning. 'Go back to your hotel and stick to your story. Pretend you never saw it.' And then she had a better idea, twitching the piece of paper out of his hand. 'Leave it with me. I'll get rid of it. But there's a deal to be done.'

'You don't seem to like the terms of the deal you've done with me already.' There was contempt in his voice.

The deal she'd struck with him was possibly the most stupid move she'd made in her life, and there was plenty of competition, but it was done and it wasn't too late to try and retrieve something from it. 'I'll get you out of this mess.' She waved the piece of paper at him, like a white flag. 'And you get me out of here.'

'You can get yourself out. You have the money.'

'Do you think I'll ever see the money? I don't. I'm ready to cut my losses, and I have some savings.' She'd never spent much, sitting in her room with only Karen and the television for company. 'But you'll have to get me out of here. Get me a plane ticket. Get me to the airport. They can look for me all they like, after I've gone.' She folded the paper and placed it in her pocket. 'Okay?'

20

Aditi Desai sat in the corner of the reading room at the National Archives, waiting while the archivist, intrigued both by Jude's introductory email of the day before and the warrant card Aditi had presented with all the pride of a newly fledged detective, prioritised her request above those of a roomful of dry academics.

Leaving the coffee on the desk, she stepped out into the lobby to put in a quick call to the office. It was Ashleigh who answered the incident room phone. 'Any news?'

'Not yet.' Aditi shuffled sideways to allow an earnest young woman with pink hair and a matching backpack to pass her. 'They're hunting out Violet's file now. I just thought I'd check in and see what's going on.'

'No movement.' Ashleigh sounded cheerful enough. 'It's all desk work at the moment. Take your pick from the suspects. Colonel Mustard in the library with the candlestick, for me. Although I was never any good at Cluedo.'

Aditi had been exceptional at Cluedo, unbeaten for so long that the rest of her family gave up playing with her before she was fourteen. It was funny, the things that set your life on a particular path. Now she was helping to solve mysteries for real, but Violet's death was the closest she'd come to the classic board game mystery. 'I'll be back in touch when I've had a look at the file.'

'Okay. You probably won't get me. I'll be out of the office. It's always nice to get a break.'

Seeing the archivist moving towards the desk and looking around as if for her, Aditi slipped back in to the silence of the reading room. The man had something of the look of Detective Superintendent Groves about him, yet somehow contrived to be anything but alarming. It was extraordinary how your intentions gave shape to your actions, how one person's words could be reassuring and another's carry an implied threat. With Violet, surely, it was a question of what she'd said and to whom to make them take an old woman's trenchancy and interpret it as a slight sufficient to prompt murder.

An involuntary smile crossed her face as she approached the desk. By all accounts Violet wouldn't have stood for any nonsense from anyone.

'Okay, Constable.' The archivist smiled at her. Under his serious exterior she sensed a little excitement. The archives must hide a hundred thousand secrets, some of them never to be revealed or their significance ever known. Violet was by no means the only murder victim whose story was filed away in the vaults and yet the involvement of the police brought something new to this otherwise serene environment. 'You're lucky to be able to get this. It was only made public a few years ago.'

'I thought documents were available to the public after thirty years.'

'Not all of them. The really secret ones are locked away for a century. This one might be pretty special, too. It was kept secret for seventy years. Here's the file. Take it away and have a look. If you need anything else, or if you need copies made, let me know.'

'Thanks.'

'I hope it's what you're after.' The man's eyes followed her across the room but it was almost certainly a specialist's interest in what she was about to discover rather than a sleazy interest in herself. Taking the brown paper file, Aditi carried it across to an empty table, past the pink-haired woman who was typing rapidly and a man who was sitting with his glasses on the end of his nose and poring over what looked like a very old letter. She sat down by the window, listening. The hum of the heater, the bleep of a delivery van reversing nearby and the rattle of a passing train only seemed to accentuate the stillness.

From inside the folder Violet's face looked up at her from a black and white photograph. Her war record. Enthralled, Aditi leafed through details of her war service, jotting down notes, pulling together a picture. And, lifting the record sheet and turning it aside, she found herself staring down at a handwritten sheet with a typed card pinned to it.

Violet M Ross.
A Confession

'So here we are again. I don't think I need to recap on very much. You're all aware of our progress. And so,' Jude grinned at Chris, who was always the most enthusiastic, 'for once we beat you to it. We've tracked down Violet's mystery visitor, and a very interesting story he had to tell us. But he didn't kill her.'

'He can think himself lucky he was in the States when she died.' Doddsy was looking at the picture of Violet's mystery airman on the board, frowning. When you looked at the picture next to the one of Stefan that Chris had dredged up, the connection was clear. Stefan's face might be well fed where the airman's was regulated by rationing, and his thick silver hair was incomparable with the Brylcreemed crew cut of the man in the photo, forty years his junior, but the eyes gave them away.

'Yeah. He'd be a gift of a suspect if he didn't have that convenient alibi.' Chris, too, contemplated the photograph, deep in thought. 'He admits he fell out, badly, with Violet on the one occasion they met. He admits he doesn't grieve for her. Why did he bother to come halfway across the world to see her?'

'He didn't. He came up from London.' Doddsy snorted in contempt. 'Though we may look half a world away from there. He said he came on a whim, but as for his motives, who knows?'

'He claims it's because he couldn't stay away.' Ashleigh was picking at her curl again, like an anxious schoolgirl. 'I don't know if I believe him. That's not just a gut feeling.' She shot Jude a look. 'It's because of the time lag. Klemmie says she left home as a reaction to her mother's death, but that was only two years ago. I can believe that. But twenty-five years seems a long time to do nothing about finding your mother, especially when he knew the clock was ticking on her. He left it long enough as it is.'

'Okay. So he's the perfect suspect, apart from two things.

One is that he couldn't have done it. The other is that he was convincingly surprised when we told him she was dead.' Jude turned back to the table. 'Onwards and upwards. Chris, I have a feeling this meeting is going to be all about you and what you've found out. What can you tell us about Klemmie? Anything?'

'Nothing we don't already know. Everything I've followed up ties in exactly with what she told us. Date, place of birth, parents' death, previous employment, arrival in the UK… There's not a weak link. She's exactly who she says she is.'

'So until we hear otherwise, do we just assume her story is correct?' Ashleigh was frowning. 'Not that we should ever assume anything, of course. But we can be sure she was working where she said she was, doing what she says she was, certainly for the past decade or so.'

To his discomfort, Jude found he could read her mind. 'You've got a theory. Do you want to share it?'

She shook her head. 'I did have, but it's bitten the dust in the last thirty seconds. In my wilder moments, I thought Klemmie might be Violet's granddaughter, but Chris has killed that idea stone dead.'

'Just doing my job, Sergeant.' He gave her a mock salute.

'That idea had crossed my mind.' Jude ignored the byplay. 'On balance, I think if there is anything sinister about Klemmie, she must have acted opportunistically. I suppose it's possible she might have met Violet in Poland, but it's probably thirty years or more since Violet was there. It's more likely she discovered Violet had happy memories of the place and played on it.'

'That makes sense.' Doddsy nodded. 'If her son's adoptive

parents are Polish, it's a reasonable bet his father would be, too.'

'We'll get to that in a minute. I might be inclined to treat Klemmie more seriously as a suspect if I could get my head round the motive. She certainly seemed to have no idea the money had been left to her, and she also claimed not to want it.' There the shadows of suspicion that had troubled him when they told her still lurked.

'She may well get over that, when she stops to think about it.' Doddsy was in one of his less charitable moods.

'Yes. I'm inclined to agree. But let's leave Klemmie just now, and move on to the interesting stuff. And this is really interesting, and possibly significant, too. I'll let Chris talk us through the reason for Violet's fondness for all things Polish.'

'It was Aditi who did the digging.' Chris sat back, twisting his pen between his fingers and addressing himself primarily to Ashleigh. 'She just phoned in. She went down to London last night and turned up at the National Archives first thing this morning. They have a file on Violet. It was previously classified, presumably because it related to her war work, and it's interesting it was held for seventy years rather than thirty. It was released three years ago.'

As Chris took a sip of his coffee and prepared to read from his laptop screen, Jude settled back to listen. He knew what was coming, or the gist of it, but hearing things a second time, in someone else's voice, often gave a different perspective, so you could see behind the words to the sense – and the motive. 'Go on then. Tell us. We know she was in the WAAF.'

'Yes. She worked in intelligence – not one of those girls

who pushed planes around on maps, but proper intelligence. She was involved at a very high level in processing the information received about military operations from, and involving, Biggin Hill airfield, which is where she was based. She encrypted and decoded messages in the operations centre. All the contemporary reports indicate she was highly regarded and entirely trustworthy.' He paused for another sip of coffee.

'I can see why she might have kept that secret,' Ashleigh said, with a sigh. 'Or not even so much a secret, but just something she didn't want to talk about. They must have been scary times.'

'Yes. In 1943, while she was serving at Biggin Hill, she became involved with an airman who was based there. He was a pilot, and he was married with a child. His name was Zoltan Franc, and he was from Krakow. He'd left immediately before the war broke out, along with his wife, and joined the RAF. He served with distinction during the Battle of Britain.'

'A lot of Poles did that, didn't they? But I thought most of them arrived as refugees, after the declaration of war.' Jude rubbed his chin, thoughtfully. 'History isn't my strong point.'

'Nor mine, but you're right to question it. As the war went on, Franc's behaviour, especially his pursuit of Violet Ross, raised some concerns and he was suspected of being a German agent. Although there's nothing to suggest Violet ever shared any classified information with him, both her bosses and his were sufficiently concerned about the affair to restrict her access to key documents and to investigate his activities. In spring 1944, they decided they had enough evidence to arrest and charge him. Because he was serving in the RAF, he would have been charged with treason and almost certainly hanged if found guilty. When they went to arrest him, they found him dead in his bed.'

'Suicide?' Ashleigh asked. 'Did Violet warn him?'

'No.' Chris's voice was unusually hushed, as though this story from seventy years before had touched even his unsentimental heart. 'He was murdered, and she did it.'

Silence, broken eventually by Doddsy's long, low whistle. 'Well, well.'

'Yes. I have a copy of her confession. It was in the archive.' Chris laid a sheet of paper on the desk, the scan of an original document – handwritten, a shaky but legible signature at the end. 'Shall I read it out? It isn't long.' He picked up the paper. '*I, Violet May Ross, of Biggin Hill, confess to the wilful murder of Zoltan Franc. On hearing Zoltan was suspected of treason, and realising that he would hang if convicted, I went to his lodging. We drank wine. I had obtained some potassium bromide and placed it in his drink. After dinner, Zoltan complained of feeling sleepy. When he fell asleep, I placed a pillow over his face. He woke up and he struggled with me, but under the influence of the drug, he couldn't resist. I held the pillow over his face until he died. I fully confess myself to be guilty of murder, an act I committed in the knowledge that he would otherwise hang, and that by killing him I helped him to avoid justice. I loved Zoltan, but I love my country more. Signed Violet M Ross. Dated 13 March 1944.*'

Silence greeted him as he laid down the paper and looked around.

'So he was an enemy of the state.' Ashleigh dipped her head, as if to hide an unwelcome tear. 'That mattered more to her than the fact she loved him. But she still loved him enough to spare him conviction, death and disgrace. Imagine living with that for seventy-five years.'

'It's hardly surprising she never told anyone.' Doddsy had a softer heart than he let on. 'What happened to her?'

'She went to prison but was never tried. The papers relating to the case are missing, or at least not immediately available, so we don't know why not. We don't have access to anything about the investigation into Franc's activities, either. But we do know she was pregnant when he died, and while she was in prison she gave birth to a boy. She was released at the end of the war, and considered sufficiently rehabilitated to go back to her work in the WAAF. She was posted to Germany, where she spent two years, before returning to her medical studies and qualifying as a doctor.' Chris laid the papers down. 'I'm no historian and that's the bare bones of her story.'

'And the child?' Ashleigh's tone was anguished. 'Stefan. No wonder they didn't get on. That ties in with his story.'

'Even more than you think. Zoltan Franc was married with a baby son, Tomasz, and after his death his widow – who, by the way, always maintained his innocence – offered to adopt Violet's child.'

'The child of her unfaithful husband and the mistress who killed him? That's extraordinary.'

'Yes. There are still some checks to make on Stefan's story, but it all fits in with Violet's.'

'It's probably all we need to know.' Jude allowed himself

a wry smile. Whatever had come about between him and Becca because he'd chosen to place his job above his relationship was trivial in comparison to Violet's tragedy, played out against a background of war. 'So, we have a motive. We have Stefan, who didn't get on with his mother, from whom he was estranged, and who may know more about his father's death than he led us to believe. And we have this extraordinary coincidence that she died in the same way as she murdered her lover. But Stefan, who is the obvious candidate, wasn't in the country when she died.'

'And he could have killed her when he visited last year, if he'd wanted to.'

'Yes.' Jude frowned. 'Zoltan died in exactly the same way as Violet did, and that information has only been in the public domain a short while. You all know I don't believe in coincidence. So I want to know who else accessed that file.'

'Leave it with me.' Chris made a rapid note. 'I'll get Aditi on to it.'

Jude pushed back his chair. 'We should probably let Monica know about Stefan. If Violet never told her, it'll come as a shock to her that she isn't the next of kin. And it'll probably make her revisit any idea she might have of challenging Violet's will. I don't imagine that will go down well. Even if Klemmie doesn't want the money, there's someone else with a claim to it, and he doesn't strike me as the sort of man to turn it down, even if he doesn't need it.' And Stefan, by the look of it, could afford a Pyrrhic victory over the cousin he'd never known existed.

'I'll take a run along there and tell her, if you like.' Ashleigh looked down at her watch. 'It's half five. I can pop in to Eden's End, too, and just see if there's anything else happening there. I'd be virtually passing the door.'

'I'll come along, too.' Chris flipped down his laptop. 'It'll be interesting to see if this jogs her memory. Come on, Ashleigh. Let's go.'

21

It was cold and it was dark, but Karen's heart and mood were colder and darker and her mind was the coldest, darkest place of all. Wrapping her coat around her in a half-hearted attempt to tackle the physical elements, the only thing she could do anything about, she touched her lighter to the end of her last cigarette and drew in long, rasping puffs, but even that act of conscious self-harm couldn't do anything to ease her misery and confusion.

Dropping the still-lit cigarette onto the sad slick of mud that was all that remained of a summer flowerbed, she wandered along the garden path at the back of Eden's End, her steps uncertain. At the corner of the building the wind hit her as she turned into it, welcoming the misery. A gust of cold rain slapped her face, plastering her hair across her forehead and, lowering her head against it, she pressed her way along the hedge that marched with the side of the house, past Violet's dark and shuttered window, into the shadows of the car park and on to the path that took her to the swirling River Eden.

Red mud squelched under her feet, breaching the seams of the light shoes she hadn't bothered to change out of. A nightmare came upon her, the one she'd had the previous night in which, against a background of wind and water, she'd stood on a stage in front of an assembled group of police, of judges, of a limitless jury of her peers, and had smothered Violet Ross to the soundtrack of their disapproval.

But why had she done it? Why? And, having done it, how could she keep herself out of jail?

I don't want to go to prison, a little voice whimpered in her head. *Prison will break me.* But so would being out in the wild world, with her conscience grating daily on her peace of mind, touching that raw nerve of knowing she had killed without understanding why and so – and she shivered at the very thought – she might do it again.

I can do something to keep you out of jail. The words in the letter that had slid beneath her door jumped about in front of her half-closed eyes as she stumbled down through the woods. Was it worth it? What would be the price of keeping her out of prison? Did she dare pay it, leaving herself free to roam the world and kill again, without reason or understanding? Or was it better to do what Klemmie's cousin had done, and hang herself from a tree?

She moaned, stumbling over the dark path, catching her bare legs against the night patrols of ragged brambles as she strayed off line, into the hedge. The trees beyond, young and slender, lacked the strength to bear her weight, just as she herself was too weak to carry her invisible cross.

Down at the river's edge, the water sang to her through a cloak of fog, the only comfort she had. When times got tough at Eden's End, this was where she came, taking the opportunity to escape from the pressures and sit by the water's edge until she somehow managed to drag herself back and carry on. There was a stone bench there, but she couldn't see it in the darkness, feeling her way until she cracked her shins against it, sank down onto it, and breathed again. But this time, she could see no way forward.

She didn't know how long she sat looking at the dark sky, losing herself in the soothing rush of the water, but it was long enough for the rain to ease and the cloud to break, long enough for lights in the houses on the opposite bank to go on and off as people moved through their houses, long enough for her to become soaked through, so much so that she no longer shivered.

It's over. The thought grew louder, burst out of her brain; became a voice that was joined by a dozen others, a chorus that assailed her even over the wailing of the wind. *It's over. You're mad and they'll catch you. They'll lock you up and never let you go.*

The moon, limbering up for its full phase the next night smiled down on her, its chubby face beaming in benevolence. At that point, she understood she couldn't put off her invidious choice any longer, that she was damned to either a nightmare in prison or a nightmare out of it. She got up and stumbled along the riverside towards the bridge that led up to the village of Langwathby.

'Any chat from up at Eden's End, then?'

Karen had been hoping the surly, silent man would be on at the village shop, but she was disappointed. Instead, it was the gregarious woman who loved to engage, who always had something cheerful to say and never seemed to grate on anyone else's nerves the way she did on Karen's. 'No, no more than usual.'

'There was some chat there were police up there.' The woman turned behind the counter to serve her with a packet of twenty cigarettes and a half bottle of vodka, placing them on the counter without so much as a raised eyebrow.

'Routine.' Karen's fingers twitched as she handed over a twenty-pound note. 'Unexplained deaths. Post-mortem. They keep changing the rules.'

'All that red tape, eh?' The woman folded the bottle in tissue paper and thrust it into a carrier bag with the cigarettes, then handed over the change.

'Strangling the care industry.' Karen didn't quite understand how she was having the conversation. Wasn't it obvious she was mad? Wasn't it obvious she'd killed Violet Ross, choking the life out of the poor woman as she slept in her chair? The care industry needed more red tape, not less. The innocent needed protection from people like her.

'Not a lot we can do about it. It takes me hours to do my accounts every week. At least they're not still talking about quarterly tax returns. God help us.' The woman handed over the carrier bag. 'It's a foul night out there.'

'Yes. It didn't look too bad when I came out.'

'Oh, I know. Still, the fresh air does you good after being inside all day.'

'Goodbye.'

'See you later.'

Karen escaped, with relief. On the other side of the green, Monica Roland's cottage sat half-hidden behind a straggly privet hedge. Karen looked at it for a while, with another shiver, and then made her way slowly back in the direction of home. As she descended the steep hill to the bridge, she paused. The lights of the village of Edenhall lay on the brow of the hill away to the left, Eden's End sitting in isolation away to the right. She turned her back on them, sliding onto the wet bench that looked northwards over the Eden and its sodden string of riverside villages. Lit the first of the cigarettes, dangling it between her fingers. Twisted the top off the bottle of vodka at the second attempt, swigging the first, comforting shot of Dutch courage. The neck of the bottle clinked against her chattering teeth.

Mad, the voices sang to her, to an upbeat tempo that only maddened her further. *Stark staring mad. Look how Klemmie looks at you. Look how she pities you. Look how she's afraid to meet your eye. Scared of what you'll do.*

'I don't want to hurt Klemmie,' she argued with them. But Klemmie lived next door. Maybe she'd sneak into Klemmie's room in the dead of night and kill her, too. 'I've no reason to hurt her.'

She'd had no reason to hurt Violet. She drank again, dropped the cigarette from shaking fingers, lit another, drank again, shivered. Somehow, just as she was struggling to get her life back together, just as she was trying to be someone who was a success so that she could be proud of herself if no-one else was, it had all gone wrong. She couldn't understand how she'd become a killer. Her life had moved towards a conclusion, and now she was facing the ending. She'd never expected it to be a happy one.

The rain had eased. She heaved herself up from the bench, sending the empty bottle tumbling down into the long grass, and stumbled the last few precipitous steps down onto the pedestrian carriageway of the bridge. In the middle she paused and looked down to where the dreamy silver rope of the Eden wound its way in an endless plait, flowing to eternity.

Jump!

Jumping was easy. You didn't have to be brave to jump. Years before, the last time she'd been this close to a breakdown, she'd stood on a different bridge and pulled back from the edge. Here, the sides of the bridge were higher to stop people from falling in but she wouldn't even have to make much effort to jump. All she'd have to do was lever herself upwards with the strength she'd gained from moving people around, leaning forward until her weight toppled her forward and the river claimed her. Then she couldn't kill again. She tried it, looking down into the dizzying water, lit by headlights at the end of the bridge. She waited for the lights to pass and the darkness to rise up again, but it didn't. A car door closed.

'Ms Grant? Karen?'

She tightened her grip. The blonde detective with the blue eyes. They must have found out, be coming to take her away. The last trace of hope ebbed from her heart.

Jump! She didn't recognise that voice. Was it hers? Was it anyone's?

'Karen. It's Ashleigh O'Halloran. I'm here to help you. I've got one of my colleagues with me. Step back and let us help. If you let go of the edge I'll take you back to Eden's End and we can fetch a doctor.'

If she comes any closer, Jump! 'I'll jump!'

'It's okay, Karen. Let us help you. You'll be all right.'

All right? She'd heard that many times before, but to her what other people called *all right* was just a break in the battle, and she couldn't bear the thought of taking up that constant fight again. 'Don't come any closer!' She heard her own voice, pitched high, ringing with stress. 'I'll jump. I swear I'll jump.'

'No. Please don't jump. Tell me what's the matter. I'm here to listen to you. I'm here to help.'

'Listen? You always want to talk to me, don't you? You're the police. You always want to talk to everyone. You ask questions and try and trap people. You're trying to trap me because you think I'm evil. How can I trust you? How can I trust anyone?'

'I want to listen to you. Karen, it's okay.'

The woman had shuffled a little closer. Taking her eyes off the river, Karen stared at her silhouette. How had that happened? 'I told you not to come any closer.'

Her hands tightened on the rail. How deep was the water? Deep enough for her to drown? Would she break her neck? Would it hurt? But if it did hurt it would be brief, and dying must surely hurt less than living on under the burden of guilt, sane enough to suffer, mad enough to be out of her own control.

'Karen. Tell me what's bothering you and we'll see if we can find some way to sort it out. We'll get you some help. I promise.'

'You don't understand. You people just don't understand.' Karen braced herself to spring over the edge. Another car came over the bridge. 'You don't understand what it's like to hate yourself. You don't know what it's like to be a bad, dark person, with an evil soul. I lie awake in the night and think I'm mad. Then I wake up and I know it's true.'

'Karen. My dear. Let me come and help you. You must

be so cold. Let's get you somewhere warm and find you something to eat. Then you can tell me what's bothering you, and we'll get help.'

'You know what's bothering me. I killed Violet.' A wild, twisted moan broke from Karen's lips. 'Poor Violet. She never did anything to hurt me, and I murdered her.'

'You need help. Let me help you.'

'Everything's always been my fault, all my life. I've always let people down. I want to do the right thing, and it's so hard. I'm so weak. All I did was take a little money from people who didn't need it so I could get away if I had to. Nothing's ever forgiven. When you do something bad, everyone turns on you. The whole world hates me.'

'That isn't true.'

'How do you know what's true?'

'I don't hate you. I can tell you're a kind and caring person. You do a wonderful job, and it's such a difficult job to do well.'

'But I don't do it well. I want to die.'

The girl made another inch towards her. 'The river's only a few feet deep, here. You won't drown. But you'll be hurt, and I don't want you to be hurt. You've suffered enough pain already.'

'I deserve to be hurt. I deserve people to hate me. I'm an evil bitch. I killed Violet.'

A touch on her hand, warm, soft fingers. Startled, Karen looked down. Ashleigh O'Halloran, ghosting her way so gently along the bridge that she'd barely seemed to move an inch, had somehow reached her. 'I killed Violet. I must have killed her. That's why you're here. To arrest me.'

'No,' Ashleigh said, with the most believable smile Karen

had ever seen. 'It's just chance we saw you. Chris and I were just coming along to see Monica. He's called for an ambulance. We can get you to hospital and get you to some help. Isn't it funny? I think we were meant to find you. It'll be all right.'

Monica. Monica who'd threatened her. Monica who would tell the police what she'd done and get her locked up. Monica, whose aunt she'd killed.

Some people aren't meant to be forgiven.

Karen pushed forward, thrusting her bulk up and over the parapet, lunging out into the darkness. Gravity took her and she crashed down to the river.

Ashleigh hated water. She feared the chill grip that it cast on your body and the shock that could stop your heart, and in the damp of November that shock broke the rhythm of her blood as it flowed round her body. Even as Karen's tumbling form dragged her downwards, even as she gasped for breath, she didn't dare let go and the two of them hit the water together.

The River Eden, barely four feet deep even after weeks of rain, closed over her head and broke her grip. Free to save herself, she pushed upwards and breached the surface of the dark water. Her feet touched ground but the shifting, stony riverbed gave way underneath her and she slipped beneath the river again.

'Ashleigh! I'm here! Keep hold of her!' Chris was in the water too, up to his waist. Buffeted by the swift, strong current, she struggled to her feet, slithering and turning. 'Karen. Where is she? I can't see her.'

Karen, wallowing in the shadows under the bridge, wasn't even trying to fight as the current dragged at her, tugging her away. Hampered by her wet clothes, Ashleigh struggled out of her coat and lunged at the mass of Karen's body, her fingers catching in the short blonde hair. *Jesus*, she thought. *I'm going to break her neck*. But she held on anyway, yanking Karen's head up out of the water. She spat out cold water. 'Karen. I've got you.'

Chris was beside her in the water, one hand reaching out for her, the other stretched out in a precarious attempt to save his balance. 'Get to the bank and keep hold of my hand. I'll get her.'

'Stop struggling!' Ashleigh yelled, as Karen tried to fight her off. Still with her fingers entwined in Karen's hair, she pulled as hard as she could, one hand reaching out for Chris.

A surge of water came riding under the tall Langwathby bridge. She saw it a second before it reached them, carrying the heavy branch of a tree just in front of it like a bulldozer. It sideswiped her as it passed, so her foot slipped from under her and Karen's leaden body broke free, tossed ahead of the running wave, rolled into the fast-flowing centre of the stream, before Ashleigh could regain her feet. Diving past her into the current, Chris snatched at empty water and Karen's body swirled down the river out of their reach and into the darkness.

'Thank God you're okay.' Jude opened the door to the room where Ashleigh sat on the bed, knees drawn up and a white hospital blanket round her shoulders.

'What about Chris?' She lifted a pale face to him, the eyes

appearing even more blue than usual. 'Is he okay? He tried to get to her and I thought he was going to be swept away. I thought—'

'He's fine. I've just been up to see him. They're keeping him in overnight just to be sure. He seems to have swallowed half the Eden. It was just as well you'd already called the ambulance for Karen.'

'It's funny the things you don't know about people, isn't it? I didn't know he was an open-water swimmer. Just as well he is.' Ashleigh shook her head. 'I was always the first to wriggle out of swimming at school.'

'He's a fell runner and a triathlete. But open-water swimming is one thing. The river in the dark is another.' Jude dropped the bag he'd been carrying onto the seat. 'I've brought you some clothes.'

'You have? Where did you—?' For once she lacked her natural sharpness.

'Your housemate. When I heard what had happened I called her to let her know. She said she'd already spoken to you and she was going to pick you up, but as I was coming up anyway I said I'd save her the journey. Didn't she tell you?'

'She may have tried.' Ashleigh swung her legs off the bed and leaned over to pick up the bag. Jude looked away, but not before he'd got a glimpse of her breasts under the ill-fitting hospital gown. 'My phone's at the bottom of the river. I had to use a payphone.'

'I'll let you get dressed. Then we'll get you home. Just as well you've got someone to keep an eye on you.'

'Lisa will do a grand job. But Karen. Oh, Jude. I don't know what to say. We lost her.'

'Chris told me.' Hands in pockets, he lingered a moment longer while she unzipped the bag and rifled through it. 'It wasn't your fault. You did everything you could.'

'Yes, but we nearly had her. I thought we did everything by the book. We managed to get hold of her. We managed to keep her afloat. But we couldn't get her to the bank, and then a wave came down. I don't understand how it happened. It isn't even deep.'

As his contribution to keeping her spirits up Jude allowed a false smile to play over his face. There was something to smile about in that neither of his staff had been hurt, but that was never the whole story. 'It isn't deep at that point, no, but you don't need much water to drown, if you get knocked out.' The river, swollen by autumn rain, had been flowing fast on its way to the sea and there was every chance Karen hadn't wanted to be saved. 'I'm proud of you both. Though I'd expected nothing less of you.'

'We were just doing our job.'

'Chris said you were brilliant. He thought you'd managed to talk her down, but there's only so much you can do for someone who's determined to die.'

'Has she been found?'

'Not yet. I went down to Langwathby myself, and there are people looking along the river, but there's a limit to what they can do in this weather and in the dark. Doddsy's out coordinating the search operations but realistically…' Jude shrugged. 'If they didn't find her straight away, the chances of saving her are slim. I haven't heard any good news.'

'We're looking for a body, then.'

'I'm afraid so.' He turned, checked the clock. Almost nine. He'd told Doddsy to ring him the moment he heard anything. Karen had been in the water, or washed up, soaked and cold on some isolated bank, for over three hours. She might still have a chance, but it was leaching away with every minute that passed. 'I'll go and check in with Doddsy while you get dressed, and then I'll get you home.'

He stepped out of the room, straying out into the main waiting area of the A&E department in an attempt to get a signal, but when he finally managed to snatch a brief word with Doddsy there was no joy to be had from it.

'I'm ready now.' Ashleigh appeared beside him. 'Have you heard anything?'

'No news yet.' She was paler, in the harsh light of the waiting room, than she'd seemed in the side ward. Lisa obviously hadn't thought to pack a hairbrush, so Ashleigh's hair, though dry, was matted and a smear of mud marked her cheek. A tangle of waterweed was caught up in the blonde wreckage of her ponytail and he reached out without thinking and pulled it free. 'Come on. I'm parked just out here.'

She followed him through the door and into the car park. 'We buggered up. Jude, I feel so awful. I could have saved her.'

'It doesn't sound like it to me.' Reaching the Mercedes, he took the bag from her and put it in the boot before sliding into the driver's seat, turning the heating up. 'Karen was in despair. From what Chris was saying, it sounds to me as if she had a breakdown. I don't think we'd have been able to save her even if we'd been able to get someone there with proper training. You did well to try and talk her down and you were more than brave going in with her.'

'But we let her down. She was desperate and she needed help. We didn't give it to her.'

'I don't know, but it's a fair bet there was no-one who could. Not the stage she was at. You mustn't beat yourself up about it.'

'I managed to get a hand to her. Chris did, too. But she didn't want to hold on.'

'We can go over that tomorrow. Or later. But as far as I'm concerned, the two of you did your best.'

'Did Chris tell you why? That she confessed?'

'Not in detail.' He hadn't been paying attention to the minutiae, too aware that the welfare of his staff had to come first and any kind of debriefing could wait now there was nothing to be gained from it that could help Karen Grant. 'Exactly what did she confess to? And in how much detail?'

'She said she'd killed Violet. That was it. She thought we'd come to arrest her for it. I tried to explain we were on our way to visit Monica, and I tried to tell her I wanted to help her, but I couldn't make her believe me.'

'Don't let it bother you. There will be plenty of time to talk about it later.' Talking to Monica was another thing that would have to wait until the morning, probably before or after Jude had tackled a report on the evening's events, and there would be a dozen things that would back up with Chris in hospital and Ashleigh probably not in the next day either. When Karen's body was found there would be a post-mortem and explanations to her family, more chaos at Eden's End and probably a degree of understandable but intrusive press interest. 'Nothing else?'

'Only that she didn't deserve to live. I don't suppose there's a bright side to any of this, really, but at least now we know who killed Violet, even if we don't know why she did it.'

Did they know, or did they only think they did? 'Indeed. But that's a discussion to have at the office, I think. Right now, it's time to get back home.' Jude turned the car onto the main road and headed towards the motorway.

It was half an hour from the hospital to Penrith, and they completed the journey in silence. Pulling up the car outside Ashleigh's front door, Jude got out and retrieved the bag from the boot. 'Here.'

'I'm not hurt. I can manage to carry my own bag.'

'I know. I know.' He stopped on the pavement and she stopped, too. Death, and the shadow of other deaths, lingered in the weird shapes cast by the streetlight and it occurred to Jude, as he stood there beside her, how close she must have come to being washed down with the fierce and unpredictable current, how Karen's misery had almost spread misery even more widely around her. Caught in the twilight zone between duty and the flood of feeling that rushed within him, he leaned forwards, touched his lips to hers, and they consumed one another in a long and life-affirming kiss.

22

At about half past five in the morning Doddsy, deputed by Jude to take on the long and unscheduled night's work of overseeing the search for Karen, had managed to snatch two minutes to sit by himself in his car by the roadside at Langwathby bridge. With one hand curled around tepid coffee in the plastic lid of his thermos flask and the other dangling a cigarette out of the car window, he shivered in the damp. November was the most brutal month of them all.

They hadn't had a cat's chance in hell of finding Karen alive from the moment she'd eluded Chris and Ashleigh's attempts to save her and given her unhappy soul up to the river's deadly grip, and in his view it was a waste of effort and resources running around looking for her before it was light. The chances were the water had already swept her down to the sea, or else it had lodged her body under some overhanging tree out of sight, and wouldn't release her until the water level dropped.

When his phone rang he dropped the cigarette and snatched at it, recognising the number of the operations centre. 'Inspector Dodd.'

'Doddsy. Where are you right now?'

'The bridge at Langwathby.' Looking at the sludge-coloured coffee in the cup he sighed, recognising he wasn't going to finish drinking it. 'Any news?'

'Yes. We've located a woman's body down at Little Salkeld.'

A grim night had just got grimmer. Doddsy allowed himself the briefest of prayers before the practicalities. 'Whereabouts?'

'Washed up on the west bank of the river, at the end of the village. How quickly can you get there?'

'Give me ten minutes.' Tipping the remnants of his coffee out of the car with regret, he set off for the short drive to Little Salkeld. It was dairy country, and there was already plenty of activity, lights on in milking parlours, traffic on the road. In the centre of the village a uniformed policewoman in a high-visibility jacket was waiting for him, directing him down a rutted farm track through dank fog towards the river's edge. He pulled in at the side of the road where she indicated, got out and plodded his way across wet grass and cowpats towards the swaying torches. There were still two hours until daybreak.

'Where is she?' he asked the policewoman.

'Along here, sir.' She gestured to an open field gate through which the roar of the river, deceptive in its calmness, ran as background to a scene of great activity. Behind him, more vehicles churned up the peace of the village. A dog barked.

'Who found it? The search parties?'

'Some poor dog walker got the fright of their life.'

'At five in the morning?'

'They're country folk. They get up early.'

When he was retired, Doddsy promised himself, he wouldn't have a dog. Dog owners were too often the ones whose pets brought them the unwelcome surprise of uncovering the lost. Whether it was murder, suicide or accident made no difference. When he hung up his notebook, he'd have nothing to do with anything that might lead him towards someone else's sudden death. 'Okay. Let's see it.'

'Down here.' The group of rescue workers on the edge of the field parted as he approached. A torch beam swept across the bubbling surface of the river, sending shadows racing away from them, until it came to rest on a shrunken huddle of wet clothes where the water met the mud. Stepping forward, Doddsy took a long, disbelieving look at the corpse in front of him.

It was Monica.

In the village of Langwathby, morning broke to news of a double tragedy. Passing the *road closed* sign and crossing the police cordon flung around the bridge, Jude made his way up the hill, turned past the curious crowd of onlookers pausing respectfully at a distance from the blue and white police tape where a PCSO studiously ignored them, and stopped as close as he could to Monica Roland's cottage. Flashing his warrant card at the PCSO, he stopped just outside the blue tape and took a moment to survey the scene. Like a geologist in front of an exposed rock face, he could read the story, reconstruct a sequence of events from a scene that was a dull canvas to the casual onlooker, and what he saw raised more than an eyebrow.

Monica's small blue Peugeot was parked on the drive, its tyres red with local sandstone mud. A deep furrow in the gravel path led from the front step to the side of the detached cottage. Keeping to the pavement, he walked a few steps to see more of the scene, and was rewarded by a familiar figure in a white forensic suit stepping carefully across the grass towards him. 'Tammy!'

'You again, Chief,' she greeted him. 'Turning up like a bad penny. One day we'll have to meet somewhere a bit more cheerful.'

'I'd hoped you were going to tell me all the signs point to an accident, but I can see for myself you aren't.'

'No. It's a pretty obvious murder scene. There's no disturbance in the house and no sign of forced entry. Those grooves in the gravel go from the front round the side of the house and off across the grass.'

The lawn glistened with dew. 'Good prints?'

'Not especially. There's been heavy rain overnight. Someone – let's just say it was Monica, until we know any different – was dragged around the side of the house and tipped through the hedge and down the bank into the river.'

Jude's mind raced to fill in the blanks in the bare story. Killed or incapacitated before being disposed of, probably. The PM would tell them the order of events. 'Is there any blood?'

'I don't see any at first glance, but I'll keep looking. There may be some traces not visible to the naked eye.'

'You're doing a good job, Tammy. I'll send someone along to take charge of the door-to-door inquiries as soon as I can. We're a bit short-handed just now.'

Tammy cast a cool eye over him. 'I heard Ashleigh and

Chris had an adventure of their own last night. Don't worry about us. We've got this end covered.'

He left her to it. With a quick word to the constable standing on the street, he started the car and drove past the stares of the locals. The bridge was closed but the uniformed officer on duty, recognising him, waved him through. He slowed as he crossed, his brow creasing at the sight. It wasn't a long drop to the river and the water was never that deep, but nevertheless Chris and Ashleigh had had a narrow escape.

Immediately over the bridge, just outside the cordon, he pulled off the road. The path on this side of the river had a view of the back of the row of houses in which Monica lived. To satisfy his curiosity, and to give himself the chance of viewing the problem from a different angle — something he always thought helpful — he jumped nimbly over the stile and wandered down the path. From there, you could clearly see the break in the tall hedge that marked the riverside boundary of the garden where Monica, almost certainly not by accident, had tumbled down to the water.

From her house, she would have been able to see Eden's End, but from this secluded nook the care home was hidden. At his feet, a cluster of cigarettes in front of a stone bench — four of them, all half-smoked, discarded close together as if they'd been dropped by someone in a disturbed state of mind — attracted his attention. He frowned at them for a moment, scanning the muddy path for any clues, but any footprints had been already obscured by dog walkers and their energetic pets.

Deep in thought, he walked along the path towards Eden's End, scanning the grass by the river and the hedgerow, rising from the foundations of an old wall, which bounded it on the other side. Two disinterested swans glided upriver but their serene progress masked the speed of the current flowing beneath them. For a moment Jude thought of Ashleigh, caught in the Eden's icy grip, and shivered. Under the beauty there was always a touch of death.

About fifty yards on, where a second bench looked upstream, he found something. Broken branches in the hedge, as if someone had leaned into them. He took a longer look, snapped a few pictures on his phone, then looked closer. A shred of plastic, buried in the rotten heart of the old hedge. A mossy stone, recently dislodged. A tuft of red thread, snagged on a thorn. They were probably nothing, but Jude was a cautious man, one who dared risk nothing. He took two evidence bags out of his pocket and, without touching them, nudged the plastic and the thread into them, sealed them, and turned back to the car.

It took him a couple of minutes to drive the short distance to Eden's End, pulling in at the front of the building and leaning on the bell. At this time of the morning most of the residents would be in the dining room or their own rooms, so he had half a chance of getting in without causing any more concern.

It was Klemmie who answered the door, her face pale. That in itself gave him a flush of relief. As he'd approached the building it had occurred to him, for the first time, that they'd no real idea exactly what direction Karen's illness might have taken her, other than that it had taken her into Langwathby the night before. At least Klemmie, alive and well, was someone he didn't have to worry about. 'Chief Inspector. I was going to call. I've been hoping someone would come from the police. I'm so worried about Karen.'

'Worried?' Jude could have done with Doddsy with him right then, composing his face into his most avuncular expression in the hope it would give her some kind of comfort. He himself couldn't do friendly, and the best he ever managed to be was dispassionate, but on such a grim day even Doddsy would have found it a challenge to be kind when comfort was thin on the ground. And he couldn't help noticing that Klemmie's hand bore a series of long, scarlet scratches, the sort you might get from a thick hedgerow.

'Yes. I haven't seen her since yesterday evening. I'm so scared she's done something silly. She was in such a state.' Klemmie put her hands up to her mouth in distress.

There couldn't be many things more silly than flinging yourself off a bridge into a shallow river and putting two other people at risk to get you out. Jude pinned his lips into a thin line, knowing it wasn't Karen's fault and he should be more sympathetic. Then he thought of Violet, and of Monica, and of how close they'd come to losing two police officers, and his sympathy evaporated. 'I need to talk to her employers.'

'Has she left?' Klemmie's eyes widened. 'Just like that?'

'She's missing, at the moment. It looks as if she may have had some kind of a breakdown.' Hardly surprising, either, if she'd done what she claimed or even if she merely thought she had.

'Oh, God! I was so worried about her I got the key to her flat – there's a spare one in the office. And I went to see if she was all right and she wasn't there, and I didn't know where she was. And I found—' She ground to a halt.

'Found what, Miss Marcowics?'

'I found a letter. On the table in the kitchen.'

'What did it say?'

Klemmie stared at him, with wide eyes. Then she thrust her hand under the plastic apron and deep into the pocket of her jeans, and pulled out a crumpled piece of paper.

23

'All right.' The clock had nudged three, the day had fled and the sun was already accelerating towards the western horizon. Jude cast a quick look around the incident room as Ashleigh pushed open the door, peeling off her coat with a sigh and dropping it over the back of her chair. She'd turned up sharp for work that morning and Chris had made it in by lunchtime, and though he knew he should have sent them both straight home he needed them too much.

'We've got time for a quick catch-up.' More than that – it was time to roll through all the information they had, see if it made any sense and put it together again. And catch a killer, if the killer was still out there to be caught, before anyone else died. 'I don't think we'll get to a solution tonight, by any stretch of the imagination. There are too many unanswered questions. But I want to talk things through and see if we can make any sense of it.'

He pulled up his usual chair, at the table in front of the whiteboard. The board had exploded in the past couple of days, sprouting diagrams and photographs and notes in Chris's excitable, near-illegible handwriting. Normally Jude found it a help but today its blossoming of information confused him. It had acquired photos of Monica, alive at some school reunion and dead upon the river shore, snapshots of her cottage and garden from every angle, a photocopy of the note Klemmie had passed to them. He needed a clear head, some way to see the wood from the trees. 'Someone start me off. Doddsy, I'm glad to see you managed to get some sleep. We've got a positive ID of your body, now. It's confirmed it was Monica.' As if they'd needed it.

Doddsy stifled a justified yawn. 'Do we have a cause of death?'

'Drowning. The PM was carried out this afternoon, and the results are just in. There's fracturing to the skull consistent with being struck on the head by a blunt instrument before entry into the water.'

'I take it we've no idea what that instrument was?'

'There's no sign of anything at the crime scene. It may turn up in the bushes at the back of the house, or in the river. It may never turn up at all.' He looked down at his notes. 'The time of death is estimated as being some time yesterday evening, probably between four and seven o'clock. When she was found, Monica was wearing a skirt and a jumper but no coat, no jacket and no shoes. A slipper that may have been hers was caught in the bushes on the way down to the river from the garden. It looks as if she'd answered the door and was surprised by whoever was out there.'

'In full sight of the village?' Chris shook his head. 'That took nerve. Or desperation.'

'Not necessarily. If the time of death is accurate, it was probably dark. It could be the action of someone who just didn't care if they were seen or not. It doesn't really matter – there's a hedge that runs across the left-hand side of the garden. You can only see the front door from part of the village green, and a small part at that. The hedge is positioned exactly for that reason, I'd guess – because whoever planted it didn't want their comings and goings to be seen.'

It had proved the perfect cover for a killer. Jude drew a quick sketch of the scene, memorising it from the one pinned to the board behind him. 'Once she'd been knocked out, she was dragged around the back of the house, unconscious. The PM found mud and gravel in her hair and scalp, and grazes on her arms, back and neck consistent with her having been dragged while alive. That's the only blood, though there are traces on the gravel consistent with that action. We're waiting for analysis to see whose blood this might be.'

'Footmarks?'

'There's nothing obvious. The doorbell had been wiped clean.' He paused for a moment, in thought. It had been a day when information came in a flood as strong as that which rode down the river to the sea. 'Twenty minutes ago, we heard a second body has been found, further downstream. We're awaiting positive identification, but I'm in no doubt it's Karen.'

Ashleigh had been silent, doodling away on her pad, but at this she looked up. 'She's your main suspect, of course.'

Fielding the look, Jude took it as reproach, as if she held him responsible for Karen's misery. Doddsy had been right, and his detective sergeant allowed herself to become far too deeply and easily involved with witnesses, and possibly with criminals. 'I think so. Ashleigh, Chris, you were there when she jumped. What's your view?'

'I say Karen's an unreliable witness.' Ashleigh put down her pen.

'She confessed.' Chris shivered very slightly, as if he recalled the cold assault of the water as he and Ashleigh had plunged into the river. 'To Violet's murder. In so many words. She never mentioned Monica, but when we first saw her she was coming down the hill from Langwathby.'

'Yes. She'd been in the village shop earlier, and there was an empty bottle of vodka and a whole load of cigarette ends by the bench near the bridge. We'll know soon if they were hers.'

Ashleigh nodded at him. 'It's certainly conceivable she could have killed Violet. Just because no-one saw her down the stairs doesn't mean she wasn't there. She certainly could have killed Monica. She has the physical strength. She could have dragged her around the back of the building. I bet we'll find that although she managed Eden's End, rather than working directly with the residents, she'll have been trained to help move people who can't move themselves.'

'But?' asked Jude, with a sigh. The woman drove him mad in many ways and this time he was going to have to argue with her. Her sympathy with Karen was about to turn into a stubborn refusal to admit to the possibility of her guilt.

'But I don't know if I believed her. Even when she was blaming herself for everything she didn't mention Monica, and as far as I know she had no reason to kill either her or Violet.'

'Then why confess?' Chris shook his head. 'Anyway, if you're unbalanced, you don't need a reason.'

'But she did have the motive, in Monica's case.' Doddsy

tweaked a photocopy of the note Klemmie had given Jude, like a man poking a wasps' nest to see if it was empty. 'It's here. Monica threatened her.'

'Are you sure about that? There's something about this note that doesn't sit right. Look at the wording.' Ashleigh had been passive long enough. She tugged at the end of her ponytail and glared at Doddsy. 'Read it. Read it out.'

He lifted an eyebrow in surprise, but he read. '*I am sorry to contact you like this and I hope you will treat my letter with appropriate discretion. Thanks to you, among others, I have been cheated out of what is rightfully mine. I'm not a greedy woman and I don't seek to ruin anyone. But I do feel that you owe me some effort, at least, to repay what I've lost. Perhaps we could meet, sooner rather than later, and with a little luck I won't have to tell what I know to keep you out of jail.*' Then he laid it down again. 'Sorry, Ashleigh, but it looks clear enough to me. Monica's threatening her and demanding money in return for her silence.'

'But Karen had no money. Don't you see? That's why she was stealing from the home, and she wasn't even stealing very much. But Klemmie had money, and it was money Monica had expected to come to her. Maybe not as much as she'd hoped, but ten thousand pounds would be a lot of money to both of them.' Ashleigh sat back. 'Here's my theory. This note wasn't meant for Karen at all. It was meant for Klemmie. But if Monica didn't know which door was which in the staff living quarters – and why would she? – surely it has to be possible she put it under the wrong one. It isn't addressed. In her state of mind, Karen would have read it and immediately assumed the worst. Catastrophism is a characteristic of anxiety. And then she'd have panicked.'

Less sure of Karen's innocence in Violet's death, Jude knew from experience that once the first murder was committed, the second became easier. 'Karen was in the right place at the right time. For both murders.'

'Yes. I agree with that. And however misplaced, she had the motive, too. But I struggle to believe she did it.'

'Don't get too sorry for her,' he said, too sharply. 'We've got two women dead, here, and you and Chris could easily have come to grief. We can't afford to be soft.'

'I think I can afford to feel sorry for some poor woman who's dead, Jude.'

'It isn't looking good, even without her confession.'

'Her confession wouldn't have held up in court if she'd lived, and you know it. She was telling us what she thought we wanted to hear. That's another symptom. It's a form of self-harm.'

'That doesn't mean she didn't do it.'

'And it isn't proof she did.'

'Okay.' Jude kept his temper, though only just. Not many people challenged him outright like that, and the fact it was Ashleigh just upped the emotional stakes. He didn't need that when the solution in front of them depended on keeping a cool, dispassionate head. 'We'll dig deeper. Right now I find it hard to see beyond her, but that's no reason not to keep looking. I know we've had a lot of information coming in this morning, and I know we haven't had a chance to process it all. Can we run through anything we might have heard, Chris? I know you've had other things on your mind, but have you come up with anything?'

'I've got a mailbox full of emails I haven't even opened yet,' the constable said, cheerfully enough. 'Give me a minute and I'll filter by the most sensational heading.'

'Start with Aditi, if she's been in touch. Does she have anything else on Violet?'

Chris squinted at the screen while Jude, waiting, sipped a cold cup of coffee. 'No. That trail looks to have gone cold. But this is interesting.' He sat back. 'Violet's file at the National Archives. Two other people have accessed it since it was made public, both within weeks of the files being released. One of them was Stefan Kava. The other was Monica.'

Jude's brain went into overdrive. 'Wait. That means they both lied to us when they said they didn't know Violet's history. I should have guessed. But even that doesn't necessarily mean either of them killed her. Stefan was in the States and maybe Monica lied because she didn't want to draw any attention to the fact Violet had a child, and was hoping he wouldn't turn up to claim the money.'

Ashleigh tapped her pen on the desk. 'But then he did turn up, and he knew the whole story. Monica must have been hoping her aunt shuffled off before he came back, or before she changed her will in his favour. Supposing Violet threatened to cut Monica off and Monica took action before she did? But she wouldn't know Violet had already done just that.'

It was all falling into place. Doddsy, for all his exhaustion, was just as enthused. 'And so Monica must have killed Violet, as we guessed, by hiding just outside the back door and then rushing back to Langwathby just in time for

Karen to phone her. Then when she realises she isn't going to inherit, she writes a note to Klemmie, threatening her, and puts it under the wrong door. Karen picks it up. She's already unbalanced. She's already terrified she may have killed Violet and can't remember doing it.'

'Yes. And the note tips her over the edge.' Ashleigh laid both hands flat on her desk. 'Poor Karen. She cracks. All she can think of is that she's going to prison. She heads up to Langwathby and she hits Monica over the head with something, dumps her in the river, and then filled with remorse, throws herself off the bridge. How awful.'

'That's a wonderful theory.' Jude picked up his coffee cup, stone cold and almost empty, and sipped at the dregs. 'But we need to start working on the evidence. We need to prove Monica was there. We need to prove Karen actually killed her. Chris. Any thoughts?'

Usually a keen participant in these discussions, Chris had been uncharacteristically silent, flicking through his emails, scanning them and moving on. 'Jesus. I wish I'd been in this morning. I've seen the reply from the US authorities. I contacted them to check up on Stefan's story.'

'And?'

'As with Klemmie, the story he gave us tallies in almost every respect with the information on file about him. He was brought up by his father's wife and her second husband, moved to America, settled there, made money, returned to Poland after the end of the Cold War. Everything is as he told us. Except for one thing.'

'Which is?'

Chris gave the smallest shrug. 'I don't know who the man is who's staying at the George, but he isn't who he says he is. Stefan Kava died of cancer eighteen months ago.' He looked around the table. 'I should have looked at those emails earlier. Sorry, Jude.'

'For God's sake. Don't go there. You shouldn't even have been in the office today.' And he and Ashleigh shouldn't have gone hurling themselves into the river, and then Jude himself wouldn't have wasted half the morning filling in health and safety forms and they might – just – have got to this stage a little sooner. 'Doddsy. Take Chris down to the George and bring Stefan in for questioning, if he's there. Ashleigh, you and I are going down to Eden's End. Because I'm thinking you might be right. Klemmie may not be Violet's granddaughter, but I think she must have some connection with the man who claims to be Stefan. And I want to know what that is.' And, to be on the safe side, Jude reached into his desk drawer for a pair of handcuffs and slipped them into his pocket.

Klemmie wasn't there. Not only was she not there, she'd disappeared without telling anyone where she was going or why, leaving Eden's End even more stretched for staff than before. Ashleigh, her own sense of disquiet growing with every minute, saw Jude's brow darken as he grilled the new, reluctant manager on her whereabouts.

'All I know is she isn't where she should be and she hasn't had the courtesy to let me know why not.' The man, old enough to be retired and giving all the indications of being someone sent from head office until an agency could find a suitable candidate to replace Karen, scowled. 'This place is in chaos.'

Ashleigh had no sympathy for him. You reaped what you sowed and whatever obligation Klemmie was under, she owed no loyalty to Eden's End.

'I'd like the keys to her flat, if that's all right.' Jude, she could tell, was in a hurry. 'I'll sign for them, obviously.'

'Take them. I don't need your signature. I don't have time for all the bloody protocols you people put us through. I'd rather you caught criminals quietly and in your own time. No questions asked.' The man brought out the keys and was turning back to deal with the next matter almost before they were safely in Jude's hand. 'Okay, Mr Parsons. You really shouldn't be wandering about in reception. Let me take you back to your room.'

'I came to look for me lunch.' Colin Parsons, Violet's former neighbour, tapped his walking stick on the floor. 'I may be old, but I haven't lost it yet. It's four o'clock. I should have had me lunch by now, and I'm hungry.'

'I'm sorry about that, Mr Parsons. Let me just finish dealing with these police officers and I—'

'Oh. That's the police looking for whoever killed Violet.' The old man smiled at Ashleigh. 'It's the detective who looks like my Caroline. So who killed the old girl, Caroline? Are you going to tell us?'

She flung Jude a helpless look. 'I can't tell you anything, Mr Parsons. I wish I could.'

'I can't work out why I never heard anything. You'd think I'd have heard the shot. The gun wasn't silenced.'

Jude stopped and stared at him. 'The gun? You saw a gun?'

'Dr Ross wasn't shot.' Ashleigh closed in on Colin Parsons, aware of the manager's gaze on her, aware of Jude's narrowing eyes. She knew he hated gossip and mistruths, but something told her this was neither. She laid a hand on Colin's shrivelled arm, inviting his confidence as she had with Karen. 'Why do you think she was?'

'Of course she was. She must have been. If you keep guns lying around, someone's going to shoot you. I had one of those Webleys meself, when I was in the army. Nice little beast. I had to give mine back. Me daughter wanted to keep it. Said it would be nice to have something to remember me by!' He chuckled. 'God knows how Violet managed to keep hold of hers. Or why they gave it to a woman.'

'Are you quite sure you saw a gun, Mr Parsons? When was that?'

'I can't say for certain. Few months back. I must have got confused, wandered into the wrong room. I was looking for me glasses in the chest of drawers. Well, that made me think for a while. Thought I was back in the war. Then I realised they weren't my clothes.' He chuckled. 'Just as well Violet didn't find me. She'd have taken that gun to me all right, poking round in her unmentionables. She didn't stand for no nonsense.'

'There's nothing to worry about, Mr Parsons. There's no gun. I can tell you for certain that Violet wasn't shot.' Ashleigh backed away from him, leaving him to the tender mercies of the manager, who was already steering him away down the corridor, and ran after Jude, who was halfway out of the room. 'Wow.'

'Yes. So now we know where the gun went. Violet had it all the time, though I've no idea why, but I want to know where it is now. Someone has it. Maybe it'll turn up at Monica's but I doubt it. She wouldn't have mentioned it to us in the first place if that was the case. So that leaves me thinking it's either Karen, which is unlikely, or Klemmie, who was the one who had the best opportunity to lift it. And who Monica has already accused of stealing a brooch.'

'It could be Stefan.'

'Whoever he is. But if he was going to steal it, it would have had to have been when he was here last year. And why steal an old woman's gun if you aren't going to use it to kill someone?'

Ashleigh followed in his swift footsteps, along the carpeted hallway and up a narrow flight of stairs. 'If that's her door,' he said, over his shoulder, leaving the question of the gun momentarily unresolved, 'I can easily see why Monica got the wrong one. They're right next to each other.'

A curious sense, part foreboding, part revelation, dawned on Ashleigh. Maybe Monica hadn't got the wrong one. 'Let's go in.'

Jude lifted a hand to the door and knocked but the sound echoed into emptiness. His mouth took on a grim expression. 'Let's hope Klemmie's okay.'

A sick feeling formed in the pit of Ashleigh's stomach. Violet, Monica, Karen. Three innocent women were already dead. Were they about to find the body of a fourth? 'Open the door.'

He fitted the key to the lock, turned it, switching the light on to illuminate Klemmie's cramped living space. 'She's not here.' He crossed the room, peered into the tiny bathroom. A pair of pyjama bottoms, hems and knees dark with dried mud, lay draped over the side of the laundry basket. He said: 'Shall I tell you what I think happened? At some point

Klemmie hid something in a hedge by the river. She'd have had to kneel in the mud to do it.'

'The gun?'

'Who knows? Whatever it is, it's gone now. She could have brought it here. I'll get the place searched.' He shrugged, stood still, frowning. 'I can't make sense of it. Who Stefan really is and how the gun fits into it.'

Turning through three hundred and sixty degrees, Ashleigh reviewed the sparse evidence on view in Klemmie's bedsit. 'That gun. The brooch, too. Why would you want them? I can only think of one reason, and that's if they were the only things that belonged to your parents.'

'Wonderful deduction, Holmes. But it was Stefan's parents they belonged to. Stefan's dead.'

Ashleigh took a deep breath. 'You forget. Zoltan Franc had two sons.'

Jude stared at her.

'They were brought up together. Supposing – just supposing – Zoltan's other son – Tomasz, the son he had with his wife, the one who was brought up with Stefan – only recently found out about what happened to his father? That Violet killed him? And supposing, once he found out, he decided he wanted to get revenge on the woman who murdered his father?'

'That's ridiculous.'

'Do you think so? When Stefan died – he had dual US and Polish citizenship – all he had to do was pick up Stefan's Polish documentation. I bet he's travelling on a Polish passport, not an American one. And if you look at it closely, I bet you'll find that passport photo will have been altered.'

'And the brooch?'

'It could have belonged to his mother, and Zoltan took it and gave it to his mistress. Violet.'

'There's a problem. That's the one thing we're certain of. Whoever Stefan really is, he couldn't possibly have killed Violet.'

'No. But he could have paid – or coerced – someone else into doing it for him.'

Jude took a second longer to look around him, then turned towards the door, phone in hand. 'We need to find Klemmie.' And he was already dialling as he spoke.

24

Langwathby bridge was open again. Running through the list of her appointments and finding just the final visit, to see Marjorie Hodgson, before she went back to Penrith to check in at the office, Becca sighed. She wasn't working in the morning and that day she had no evening commitments, so it wouldn't be long until she could put her feet up for a well-deserved rest. The rest of the day held nothing more traumatic than a hot bath and a large glass or two of wine.

She drove down through Eden Straits, where a PCSO stood outside Monica's cottage, the last reminder of the buzz of activity that had so recently surrounded it. Driving slowly behind a tractor, Becca had a second to take a look. No-one quite seemed sure what it had been all about though every one of her patients and their families had had an opinion on it, and on the wickedness of the world. The prevailing theory, that the woman from Eden's End had gone mad and could easily have killed any one of them in their beds, was at best a disservice to Karen's memory. Jude had always been tight-lipped about his work – he had to be, just as Becca herself did – but his lack of patience with misinformation meant at least he'd correct the more eye-wateringly ghoulish interpretations of the facts. *Trust me*, he used to say to her, with a sigh. *It's always much more complicated than it looks.*

She took a second, as she sometimes did, to think about the might-have-beens. Society needed people like Jude, high-minded seekers after justice. It was a pity they were so hard for ordinary people to live with. She sighed, trying to remember exactly what had made her let him go and finding the reasons unconvincing. Had she really left him because he worked hard? And then she remembered – a man who could send his erstwhile best friend to prison was someone who couldn't be trusted to put a lover first.

The tractor turned off at the village green, and she dropped down the hill towards the lights that controlled the bridge, a trace of irritation tainting memories that hadn't faded. There were things you couldn't unlearn and she knew Jude Satterthwaite's mind, inside out and intimately. The way he looked at his elegant blonde sergeant betrayed him as surely as the way the woman tried her hardest not to look at him and failed. When Jude used to look at Becca with that latent smile lurking in his eyes, he'd had one thing on his mind.

He didn't look at her that way now. It was quite clear he'd moved on, and she would have to do the same.

The lights changed to red. Running later than she'd hoped, she sighed and tapped her fingers on the wheel, watching as the remnants of the blue tape fluttered in the breeze at the spot from which Karen had fallen. A lorry, too big for the bridge, squeezed its cautious way over it. Glancing in her rear-view mirror to see whether she could reverse and give it an extra yard, Becca saw Klemmie, carrying a backpack, appear from nowhere and jump into the passenger side of the car behind her.

It's Jude who made me so suspicious, Becca told herself, hating him for it, but she took a moment to stare in the mirror and check it really was Klemmie, and to get a proper look at the driver, a good-looking man with a thatch of silver hair. The two of them seemed unaware they were being watched. He looked tense as he twisted the steering wheel sharply as if anxious to be off and Klemmie, clipping the seatbelt around her, bore the look of someone setting off on the most unwelcome of adventures.

The lights changed to green. Becca drove sedately over the bridge and along towards Eden's End, keeping an eye on the car behind her. Perhaps they were heading to Eden's End, too, or perhaps they were making for Penrith and the motorway. But just as she approached the left turn up to the nursing home, the car took a sharp right and headed off into a track in the woods.

'You should never have got involved with a policeman,' Becca admonished herself, too late. Turning into the drive, she pulled off at the side of the road, turned off the engine and reached for her phone. 'He probably won't answer. Too busy.' At work, or with Ashleigh O'Halloran. It made no difference to her.

She was right, and his phone rang out. 'Jude. I expect you're busy. Perhaps you'll give me a ring. I've just seen Klemmie getting into a car with a man. She had a bag with her.'

He'd been screening his calls, as he always did, but this

time she'd got through the guard and the phone rang back before she'd begun to think about starting the car. 'Hi, Becca. Thanks for the call. Where are you?'

'Just down at the bottom of the drive up to Eden's End.'

'What did you see?'

'It was only Klemmie. It's probably nothing. It might be her day off, and she can have a man friend if she wants.'

'Nobody's disputing that. Firstly. Are you sure it was her?'

'Yes, definite.'

'And what was the man like?'

'Tallish. Thick silver hair. From the little I could see, he was very smartly dressed. They were in the car behind me.'

'Where are they now?'

'Turned off up a track into the woods. The one before the bridge on the main road. I don't know if it goes anywhere. I don't think it does.'

'Not if it's the one I think it is. Thanks, Becca. That's great. We'll get down there and have a look.' He'd covered the phone, because his voice was muffled, but she heard him clearly enough. 'Ashleigh, call up a couple of uniformed guys, would you, and get them down here as soon as you can? Yes. It's Klemmie.' Then he was back on the phone, putting on his public voice of reassurance. 'Where are you off to now?'

'Just coming up to Eden's End to see Marjorie.'

'Okay. Carry on as normal, then. Thanks for letting me know.' And he rang off.

She waited for a moment as a flock of starlings rose up from the woods where the car with Klemmie in it had turned off, shaping and reshaping into a dark, fluid cloud against the fading sun. When they'd ducked and weaved and dipped their breathtaking way over the brow of the hill and out of sight, she restarted the car and drove up the lane to the car park. Jude's Mercedes was parked in front of it, and as she pulled up on the gravel he and Ashleigh O'Halloran came flying out of the front door as if they were auditioning for *The Sweeney*, and jumped into it. The car took off like a dirt track racer, with a spin of the wheels and a spray of gravel. Neither of its occupants acknowledged her as they passed.

Becca waited for a moment, thinking of Jude, a peculiar feeling in the pit of her stomach. Then she got out of the car, locked it, and headed into the nursing home.

'Where are we going?'

'Never you mind.'

When Stefan turned the car off the road and into the trees, Klemmie's faint hopes of a clean getaway faded. She'd expected as much. It was the way her life always seemed to go. Events threw her on the mercy of others and she trusted them because she had no choice, but what had looked like an opportunity to get away from the mess she'd got into now looked distinctly less promising.

But that's my fault, she realised, too late. *I've always been a pushover. It's written all over my face.*

The car slowed as he bumped it up the track. She guessed that whatever he intended wasn't something he wanted anyone else to see. That meant as long as they could be seen through November's leafless trees, nothing was going to happen to her.

'Turn the car round and take me to the station.' There was nothing to lose from being assertive. 'As you promised.'

He ignored her. The track turned away from the road and bumped up the hill, round the shoulder of it. Bare trees or not, the car was now invisible to any passing vehicle.

That was as far as they were going to go. Stefan slammed on the brake. 'Out of the car.'

Klemmie was too timid, too obliging. She always had been. It was the need to please others that always got her into that mess, sacrificing her own desires to theirs so that by the time her mother died and there was no-one left to need her, she'd lost the ability to take control. The tone in Stefan's voice warned her she had to find it now, or she'd never make it out of the wood alive. 'Turn the car round and take me back. If you won't take me to the station then you can take me back to Eden's End. I can make my own way from there.'

'There'll be a warm welcome for you there. They'll have worked out what you did by now, and called the police. Get out.'

Still she didn't move. The survival instinct kicked in. In her mind there was no question she deserved to die, with not just Violet on her conscience, but Karen. Killing the old lady was something she should never have allowed herself to agree to, and having agreed to it she should never have done it, but needling Karen, nudging her over the edge of insanity and into the river was different – a calculated action she'd taken to protect herself, and one she'd have on her conscience for the rest of her life. 'Why?'

'Never mind. Do as you're told.'

People who threatened you and bullied you did it because

they were scared. Stefan couldn't be scared of what she could do to him because she was powerless, so he could only be afraid of what she knew. She swallowed hard, trying to think. The worst thing she could possibly do was what he wanted. 'No.'

He opened the boot of the car, got something out, came round to the passenger side. A coil of rope was slung over his shoulder. As he reached for the door handle, Klemmie moved to flick it locked, but she was too slow. He wrenched it open and clenched his hand on her wrist. 'Out.'

'I'll scream.'

'Scream all you like. No-one will hear.' He yanked at her arm but she hadn't unfastened her seatbelt, so he leaned across and snapped it free. His aftershave, heavy with musk and testosterone, almost suffocated her. 'Now get out.'

She opened her mouth to fulfil her threat, but the scream died, deep in her throat. Stefan's other hand held Violet's service revolver and it was pointing at her. She was going to die and the last thing she'd see on this earth was the stark shape of the leafless trees, the last thing she'd feel before the pain of death would be the chill wind from the east. 'Oh, I see. So much for being sentimental. So much for wanting your father's gun because it was all that's left of him.'

'As you've stolen the brooch my father gave to the mistress who murdered him, it's all I have. He was a good man. He didn't do what they said, what she killed him for. I like the idea of it coming in useful. Between us, Klemmie, you and I have avenged him.'

People. How did they get so intense, so mad? What was this obsession with someone else's injustice? Did it matter that a man had been murdered by his lover seventy years before when the alternative had been being blasted out of the sky in a shooting star of scarlet flame? What mattered wasn't someone else's life, which was either redeemed or beyond redemption, but her own, which could still be saved.

'You used me.' She bit back tears that would cost her her life if she allowed them to blind her. 'That's okay, up to a point. But now you're going to kill me. Do you think that'll help? Because if the police are on to me, do you think they aren't looking at you?'

'That's exactly what I think. Because I wasn't in the country. I didn't kill the old woman. You did.'

'You killed Monica.'

'They think the manager did that. But when they pull you in and ask questions… I'd hate for you to tell tales on me, Klemmie.'

'I should never have had anything to do with you.' It had been the worst decision of her life. In the end, she'd become fond of Violet.

'If you'd had the courage to do it a bit sooner, maybe we could have had all this done and dusted before. You should have done it as soon as I asked you, Klemmie, not kept putting it off. And been a lot more careful about it, so no-one suspected.'

'I was unlucky.' Or else it was karma. Someone, somewhere, must have been looking out for poor Violet but no-one on the earth was doing it for her.

'It was your stupidity. Now get out of the car.'

The gun was too close to her throat for comfort. Shaking, Klemmie slid her legs round towards the door, setting her feet on the soft forest floor, sizing up her chance of escape. 'If you kill me they'll know. They'll come looking for you.'

'Not if remorse gets the better of you and you're found hanging in the woods.'

She drew a long deep breath. 'They know I wouldn't hang myself. I'm a survivor. I'll just find another way to get by. I don't give in.'

'Do you think that matters, if no-one knows about it? And anyway, you're lying, Klemmie. You won't be able to live with what you did to an innocent old lady and a poor, unhappy woman. The best thing you can do is die.'

If she went along with him, she'd be left hanging from a tree, the only villain, and the world would believe she'd died by her own hand. She looked around her again. The trees – larch, she thought – were slender, their limbs spindly and the lowest of them twenty feet above her head. Stefan was right, and she deserved to die, but if she did, then she wasn't the only one. 'You can't hang me. Where would you hang me from?' A laugh split the wet air, her own laugh. Surprised, Klemmie witnessed her own hysteria, as if from a distance. 'You can't hang me. It's the wrong sort of tree. Didn't you think of that? Why would I try and hang myself from these? I wouldn't be able to reach!'

She took a brave step towards him, laughter still echoing in her head, in the empty woods, but a trace of her rational self clung to the edges of her mind. If she made him shoot her she'd increase his chances of being caught. If she killed him, she could hardly be any more damned.

I am not brave, Klemmie said to herself, but I won't die easily.

She launched herself forwards, taking him by surprise, twisted the gun from his fingers, pressed it against the cashmere of his jacket and pulled the trigger.

The sound bewildered her, the slightest, most sluggish, most reluctant of clicks, so soft she didn't so much hear it as sense it beneath his laughter. 'Klemmie. It's seventy years old and it's never been looked after. If I wanted a weapon, do you think I couldn't get hold of one that worked? I told you. I wanted it because it was my father's. He was an honest man, unjustly treated. And so am I.'

Sensing her last chance disappearing like a rat down a drain, Klemmie ducked underneath his arm and ran.

Too late. 'Stop right there! You're both under arrest!'

The detectives, the dark man and the blonde woman, broke through the trees, one to her left and one to the right. The man must have seen the gun because he surged past her, clearly seeing her as no threat. With a rising blast of hope Klemmie accelerated, stumbling on a treacherous root. The woman, hesitating, stuck out a foot and precipitated her fall. Behind her, a shout of anger. The chief inspector. 'Drop the gun!'

Then the woman: 'It's okay. It's okay, Klemmie. We've got him.'

Not even lifting her head, Klemmie knelt on all fours in the sodden leaf mould underneath the trees and allowed the drama to play to its end around her.

'Tomasz Kava. You're under arrest. For the murder of Monica Roland. For conspiracy to murder Violet Ross.' Behind her, Jude Satterthwaite was reciting a series of words that couldn't connect with her brain. There were sirens on the main road, now, and blue lights flashing off the bare skeletons of the trees. That was why the two had run past her. They'd known she couldn't get away.

She flattened herself like an animal, trapped and in pain,

with no fight left, forehead pressed against the ground, arms curled around her head, and eventually soft steps came close to her, then the hand of the law closed on her shoulder and Ashleigh O'Halloran read out the accusation of murder.

But at least it was over, and no-one else was going to die.

'Of course,' Klemmie said, folding her hands in front of her on the table in the interview room. 'I'll tell you everything. And then you'll judge me. Because that's what people like you do.'

Ashleigh shivered, and shot a sidelong look at Jude, whose face was stern with irritation. On the other side of the table the duty solicitor assigned to Klemmie was staring at them with icy neutrality.

'I don't judge anybody,' he said, with the slightest shrug, but it was clear he did, as Ashleigh herself did. Sometimes people deserved to be judged and Klemmie was surely one of them. 'I'm only interested in facts. Tell me what happened.'

'I think you know it already.' She turned her stony expression on him, the two of them scowling across the table, each trying to stare the other out.

Was she really so heartless, Ashleigh wondered, or just so composed she seemed devoid of emotion?

'I think I do. Let's go through it. When did it start? Last year, when the man claiming to be Stefan Kava came to Eden's End?'

Klemmie dipped her head in assent. Jude had won their battle of wills and so she turned away from him towards Ashleigh. 'You'll understand. I'd been working at Eden's

End for a few months. He came and asked for Violet and I took him to her room. Maybe it was my accent, but he asked me where I was from, and we talked about Poland.'

'Did she say if she knew who he was?'

'Yes. Afterwards she told me he was her son. As far as I'm concerned, that's who he is. The story convinced me.' She reached out for a glass of water and sipped.

'And they'd fallen out?'

'I know they didn't get on. She told me he shouted at her and she'd told him to go. About a month later, he contacted me and I met him in town.'

Jude's sigh was obvious. 'Didn't you think that was odd?'

'I knew you wouldn't know what it's like.' She turned back to Ashleigh, placed a chapped hand on the table almost as an appeal for help. 'I was lonely and I was homesick. I thought I'd made a mistake leaving home, but I didn't want to go back. We had coffee, and he asked me to do something for him.' She shook her head.

So that was how it had unfolded. Stefan had taken swift advantage of her vulnerability. Ashleigh was about to reach out and take her hand but Jude cleared his throat in a loud and obvious warning so she turned the gesture into one of business, picked up her pen, put it down again. 'He tells a good story. He told me his father had been a war hero, and Violet had been his mistress and had murdered him. She was never punished for it, though he didn't tell me why. His father was accused of spying but he was innocent. He realised time was running out, that Violet would die before she had the chance to ask his forgiveness.'

'But he didn't forgive her?'

She shrugged. 'He said she wasn't sorry. He'd given her

the chance to put things right and she didn't take it. So he asked me to do something for him.'

'To kill her?'

'Not at first. To start with, he wanted me to get two things he said had belonged to his father. One was the brooch. The other was the gun.'

'Then he knew about them.'

'You didn't know Violet. Sometimes, if she didn't like people, she could be cruel to them. He said he'd asked for something to remember his father by and she'd shown him the two things and then told him he couldn't have them. I knew what Violet was like. I felt sorry for him.'

She lifted dull eyes and her gaze met Ashleigh's. 'Don't look at me like that. I had no choice.'

'I was wondering.' Ashleigh leaned forward, human interest breaking through where Jude's professional curiosity failed. She could imagine the scene – two bitter people, arguing over someone long dead, an act of spite that had led to three deaths. 'I understand the brooch and the gun. But why would you agree to kill her?'

'Is it bad to say I liked him? Not seriously, in a romantic way. But I was all alone and he was kind to me. I felt I owed him something. And he said he'd make sure I had money so I could be comfortable if I went home. And he said I could keep anything I could get from Violet, although I never asked her for anything.'

Surely Klemmie's soul wasn't so easily bought. 'And you agreed?'

'No. I said I'd get the brooch and the gun, but he started threatening me. He'd tell them I was a thief. He'd tell them I was trying to take advantage of the old people. I couldn't afford that. And I thought Violet would die anyway. I knew she'd hate to fade away, and become confused. I knew she'd rather die before it all went wrong.'

'And yet you waited so long to kill her?'

A tear squeezed its way out of Klemmie's eye. 'I liked her. She was happy and she was healthy, and we got on. Having her around was the only thing that made my life tolerable. We talked about home and we chatted in Polish and she told me stories. We made each other laugh. I couldn't do it.'

'Did you tell him that?' Jude asked.

Klemmie gave him the standard-issue scowl and looked back at Ashleigh. 'He kept on at me. I told him just to let her die, but he wanted her life cut short, like his father's. But I couldn't kill her. I just couldn't. I hoped she'd die quietly, naturally, and I could tell him I'd done it, but she hung on. Eventually he told me if I didn't hurry up and kill her, he'd come back and do it himself.' She got out her hanky and rubbed her eyes. 'I waited. I wasn't going to do it. But then I thought if she had to die, I would do it and she would die in her sleep. Because if he did it, he'd have made sure she knew. I did it to spare her. It was a mercy killing.'

Jude's presence, fierce and brooding on the other side of the table, showed exactly what he thought of that kind of spin. 'When did you steal the gun?'

'I didn't steal it. I took it after she died.' She looked up with a spark of defiance. 'It was mine. She left everything to me.'

'And then?' Jude leaned forward. 'You passed it on to Stefan. How?'

'I put it in the hedge by the river, under a stone. He was

supposed to go and get it, but he couldn't find it so I had to go and get it for him. That was when he gave me the note Monica had written to him. I don't know how she knew. Maybe she didn't. Maybe it was a guess.'

'And did you pass the note on to Karen?'

'Yes. It just seemed so obvious. The note wasn't clear. It could have applied to me as well as to Stefan. It wasn't addressed by name. It just leapt out at me, because Karen had told me she couldn't remember what she'd done, and I knew she'd be worried she might have killed Violet. She was unhappy, but I didn't think she'd kill herself. I thought she'd get locked up for it and I thought someone would help her, in prison. No-one was helping her when she was outside. Sometimes,' said Klemmie, with a long and bitter sigh, 'I think I'm the one who's mad.'

It was almost eight when Ashleigh got home, her head whirling with crime and punishment, with weakness and revenge and with the brutal cynicism with which Klemmie, still protesting her own victimhood, had driven Karen to her death. She parked the car in Norfolk Road and let herself into the house. 'Here's the fish and chips. I hope you're hungry.'

'Hungry? My stomach thinks my throat's been cut. I'm just glad I haven't been hanging by the neck waiting, or I'd be dead by now.' Lisa came bouncing out of the living room. She was just back from a rare trip to the gym, encased in Lycra, her thin limbs like those of a giant stick insect. 'Come on in. I've been itching for you to get back. Someone's sent you the most gorgeous flowers, and I'm just desperate to know who your secret admirer is.'

Ashleigh carried the fish and chips into the living room where Lisa, in expectation of a lazy evening, had set out plates and glasses on the side tables. The coffee table in the middle of the room was dominated by an arrangement of flowers – pink roses, white freesia, a mist of gypsophila. She drew in a sharp breath and put the paper-wrapped packet of fish and chips down.

'Well?' Lisa was jumping around as if it was Christmas. 'Aren't you going to look at the card? Don't you want to know who they're from? Because if you don't look, I will.'

'I already know.'

'It'll be your boss, then. It must be. Don't think I didn't see that full-on snog on the doorstep last night. Just because you weren't ready to tell me about it doesn't mean I don't know.'

Ashleigh moved across to the flowers and slipped probing fingers down between the stems to find the card that had come with them. 'They're from Scott.'

'Oh!' Lisa's eyes grew wide. 'How do you know?'

'How often do you see freesias and roses together in an arrangement? The freesias are my favourite. Jude doesn't know that.'

'How do you know? He's a policeman. He probably knows all sorts of things about you you don't know he knows.'

'There's an in-joke between Scott and me. I'm not romantic. I always used to say to him I'd leave him if he ever sent me a dozen red roses. So he always sent me thirteen pink ones.' She counted them up, and yes, there were the baker's dozen, an attempt to implicate her once more in a dead romance.

'I thought you'd given him his marching orders.'

'I have. Several times. But it's okay.' She slid a finger under the flap of the envelope and slipped out the card. *Sorry, sweetheart. xx.* 'I think the message has finally got through to him. This is a peace offering.' Because if it wasn't he'd have been on the doorstep trying to bully her into submission. She'd always known patience would pay, in the end.

'Well, that's good news, isn't it? You can add him to your long list of old friends and move on to find the next man.'

Unable to suppress a smile, Ashleigh picked up the card and slid it back into the envelope. Later she'd tuck it away in the jewellery box with her wedding ring. A weight lifted from her soul. Scott was flawed and she'd had to end their toxic marriage, but the last thing she wanted was to cut him out of her life completely. 'I don't think I'll mention it to Jude. And if you bump into him, I'd rather you didn't mention it, either.'

Lisa was looking at her. 'Seriously?'

'Yes.'

'I'm not going to lie, Ash. You haven't even got into bed with the guy yet, and you're keeping secrets from him already. That isn't exactly the recipe for a happy relationship, is it?'

'Who said anything about a relationship?' Irritated, Ashleigh plucked one of the roses out of the arrangement, just to defuse the joke, to make a nonsense of that reminder Scott had sent her that they had secrets, that there were things between them that no-one understood. He wouldn't know, but that didn't matter. She'd done it, and had consigned him to the status of a friend.

'A kiss on the doorstep looks like a relationship to me.'

'It's what it looks like to me that matters.' And Ashleigh broke the stem of the thirteenth pink rose with a satisfying snap.

25

'They always make mistakes, don't they?' Chris stretched himself in the corner of the pub, beaming at the assembled company, secure in the knowledge the job was complete, the guilty off the streets and on their way to justice. 'I'll get another round.'

'Not always.' Jude lifted his glass to his lips and drained it. 'The ones we catch do.' He had no illusions. There would be no shortage of criminals who made no mistakes and never got caught. 'And Klemmie came within a whisker of getting away with murder.'

'Yes, but she didn't. And so did Stefan. Tomasz, as I suppose we should call him.'

Ashleigh was sitting next to Jude, and the bar was pleasantly crowded, so much so he was reckless enough to chance his luck, sliding along the bench so his thigh pressed up against hers. She teased and tempted him, a diamond pendant pointing like an arrow to her cleavage. As Chris got up to head to the bar, Jude took the opportunity of turning to her, picking up the half-smile that read like an open invitation and accepting its offer to move even closer.

'Yes. They didn't think it through. Fair play, our man was

smart enough not to go after the money. He'd have known the pretence at being Stefan would only get him so far, so he couldn't afford to draw too much attention to himself. And coming to Eden's End after Violet had died was a gamble. I don't know why he did it.'

'He may have thought it would put him in the clear.'

'Possibly.' When interviewed, Tomasz hadn't bothered explaining his reasoning. 'Or to put the fear of God into Monica, if he thought she was onto him.'

'He certainly did that. She certainly thought he killed her aunt.' He'd admitted he'd been to the archives to look at Violet's file.

'Or he couldn't stay away from the scene of the crime.' It never ceased to amaze Jude how often criminals gave themselves away by their fatal inability to keep away. If Tomasz had sat tight in New York and Klemmie had kept silent, the law wouldn't have touched him.

Doddsy got to his feet, counting heads. 'I'll go and help Chris with the drinks.'

'You've not heard anything more from Scott?' Jude leaned in to whisper in Ashleigh's ear, though it wasn't really necessary in the noisy pub.

'No.' The blue eyes looked back at him, wide with innocence. 'I told you he'd come round in the end.'

'Do I get to meet him socially at your Christmas drinks?'

She almost giggled. 'We'll need to see what the situation is at Christmas. I told you. It's only for my exes.'

He chuckled. Things were going as well as he'd hoped. 'I'll take that.' He sat back, ready to be sociable now he'd satisfactorily established the connection with Ashleigh. They'd acquired a few hangers-on from the office on the way to the pub, two of them Tammy and her son, a new recruit to the police. Tyrone was Mikey's age, but the two could hardly have been more different. Jude allowed himself a wry smile, because he hadn't heard from his brother in weeks.

'The thing that sticks in my throat,' said Doddsy, blithely interfering in the conversation as he unshipped a tray full of glasses on the table and resumed his seat, 'is how badly Klemmie behaved towards Karen.'

'It was appalling. That poor woman was on the edge of a breakdown. That's the cruellest thing.' Ashleigh's voice was full of compassion. 'She needed some help, and all Klemmie did was push her further towards the edge. How miserable she must have been, so lonely. So guilty about something she didn't do. I'll never forgive myself for not being able to save her.'

Jude squeezed her hand, out of Doddsy's sight. Genuine affection, something he hadn't felt for a woman in years, surprised him by mingling with raw desire and fermenting a potent brew. If he wasn't careful, he'd lose his head. The kiss they'd shared on her doorstep lingered between them, unfinished business. 'You did everything you could.'

Doddsy took a look across the bar. There was a roaring fire in the grate and beyond it, on the other side of the pub, a group of people had arrived, shrugging off coats, dropping them over the backs of chairs. 'Funny, the way we've Becca's sharp eyes to thank for setting this whole thing running.'

Jude turned his back on the newcomers, recognising too many of them as people he'd rather not see. His enjoyment of the evening ebbed. In a twist of misfortune they'd managed to gatecrash Adam Fleetwood's homecoming, unwelcome witnesses to the local hero's first night out. Becca, who had always been friendly with that crowd, was there with them, sitting in the corner as if she didn't want anyone to see her. Too late. He stared, got the satisfaction of seeing her fail to meet his gaze and then, content with the moral victory, looked away. 'You'll understand if I don't go over there to thank her.'

Chris came back from the bar with the last of the drinks and half a dozen packets of crisps. 'It's suddenly got busy in here. They're a rowdy bunch. And they seem quite interested in us.' He stared back, with open interest.

'Yes.' Jude turned to give the group his coolest gaze. 'They are. That's an old friend of mine. Adam Fleetwood. He's just out of jail.'

'Did you put him there?'

'He put himself there.' Adam was gathering his friends around him, drinks lined up on the table. Jude could never quite understand the romantic appeal of the criminal, but it was there before his eyes. Maybe, in the final reckoning, being popular and charismatic – which Adam unquestionably was – was stronger than the fundamentals of fairness and morality. He continued to stare, until Becca looked up and looked away again, and then Adam, too, looked in his direction and met his gaze.

For a moment Jude was tempted to take on the challenge, to defend what he'd done in the past, but that would be a quick way to an unwise confrontation. His friends and colleagues would back him up and the result would be a fracas none of them could afford. He lowered his eyes and looked away. That single glance had been enough, the way Adam had placed his hand on Becca's arm as he'd looked across the bar. His charm masked a thirst for revenge and Jude didn't for a second think everything was done and dusted just because the prison gates had opened, but that was irrelevant. When he looked across the bar towards his ex-lover, all he could see was her smile, all he could think of was the brown eyes and the soft curls of the children they'd never have. If Adam had but known it, he already had his revenge in the smile Becca deployed for one man, the frown with which she scorned the other.

'You okay, Jude?' Doddsy was looking at him as if he knew what was going on in his mind.

'Fine. Why wouldn't I be?'

'I was wondering if we should maybe finish our drinks and go elsewhere.'

'Why? Adam Fleetwood wants me out of the pub, and I'm not going.' And if that wasn't enough of an incentive to self-destruct there was Ashleigh, her blue eyes on him even as he spoke. The temptation to stay and see where the evening ended was well worth the risk of attracting Adam's attention.

'No. He wants you out of your job, and the longer you stay here, the greater the chance of him provoking you. There are times to stand up for your principles and this isn't one of them.'

He was right. 'Then you lot stay. I'll go. You'll have a good enough time without me.' Jude stood up, his fingers brushing Ashleigh's as he did so, pulled his coat on, leaving his second drink untouched and turned to look back at them, surprised at how easily Doddsy had accepted that and was already turning with a smile to talk to Tammy's boy, Tyrone. Chris was talking fell-running with one of the constables and Tammy was laughing at some joke Jude hadn't heard.

He hesitated. Only Ashleigh was paying him any attention, drumming her fingers on the table. 'I definitely think you should go, Jude.'

Come with me, he wanted to say, but somehow he didn't, turning his back on them instead and heading towards the door. Let Adam fashion a moral victory from it, if he could. 'I'll see you guys on Monday, then.'

He passed within six feet of Becca, under Adam's interested gaze and emerged into the broad street. Out in the lamplight he paused, waiting for the something that he knew had to happen, for good or ill. Behind him the pub door opened and closed and a long shadow stretched out towards him.

Adam would come after him one day. He knew that. He turned round to see whether the night held good or ill for him, and it wasn't the lean, mean shadow of a wronged man who approached him but Ashleigh, her breath blowing out like smoke on the night air.

His lips curled into a smile. 'Aren't you staying for drinks?'

'Not if you aren't. Did you seriously think I'd let you go on your own?'

He hadn't thought that, but nor had he dared to hope. The pendant sparkled at her cleavage, the drift of her perfume went straight to his head. 'But you didn't want to be seen leaving with me, eh?'

She tucked her scarf around her neck, eclipsing the flash of the diamond. 'I just thought you might not want to make it too obvious. But I'm here. If you want me.'

If he wanted her? He held out his hand and their cold fingers entwined. 'Let's go back to my place.'

That kiss, that unfinished business, was about to be resolved.

Acknowledgements

There are many people to thank for their help. First up, like so many authors I've benefited hugely from the support of the online community in terms of advice, answers to research questions and general moral support. Perhaps bizarrely, I have to thank the Romantic Novelists' Association, from whose members I learned a lot about writing in general, and about persistence in particular. Thanks also to the CWA and other Facebook groups for sage advice.

If I listed everyone who's helped me I'd have an acknowledgements section as long as the book itself, but as usual special thanks go to (in alphabetical order) Kate Beeden, Sally Calder, Sara Claridge, Frances Evesham, Lorraine M, Pauline Morgan, Amanda Robinson, Kate Scholefield, Julie Stock and Liz Taylorson. Without their constant encouragement, virtual hugs and constructive criticism I would have given up long ago. And may I apologise to anyone who may have stumbled over my browsing history…

Once my book had reached the "completed" stage I couldn't have progressed without the help I got from my agent, Anne Williams, and from the team at Aria Fiction. (Shoutout to Hannah Smith and her colleagues!)

Lastly, of course, I have to thank my family, who put up with a lot.

About the Author

Jo Allen was born in Wolverhampton and is a graduate of Edinburgh, Strathclyde and the Open University. After a career in economic consultancy she took up writing, and was first published under the name Jennifer Young in genres of short stories, romance and romantic suspense. In 2017 she took the plunge and began writing the genre she most likes to read – crime. Now living in Edinburgh, she spends as much time as possible in the English Lakes. In common with all her favourite characters, she loves football (she's a season ticket holder with her beloved Wolverhampton Wanderers) and cats.

Hello from Aria

We hope you enjoyed this book! If you did let us know, we'd love to hear from you.

We are Aria, a dynamic digital-first fiction imprint from award-winning independent publishers Head of Zeus. At heart, we're committed to publishing fantastic commercial fiction – from romance and sagas to crime, thrillers and historical fiction. Visit us online and discover a community of like-minded fiction fans!

We're also on the look out for tomorrow's superstar authors. So, if you're a budding writer looking for a publisher, we'd love to hear from you. You can submit your book online at ariafiction.com/we-want-read-your-book

You can find us at:
Email: aria@headofzeus.com
Website: www.ariafiction.com
Submissions: www.ariafiction.com/we-want-read-your-book

- @ariafiction
- @Aria_Fiction
- @ariafiction

Printed and bound by CPI Group (UK) Ltd, Croydon, CR0 4YY

20/03/2026

02075568-0002